Books by Alina

The Frost Brothers
    Eating Her Christmas Cookies
    Tasting Her Christmas Cookies
    Frosting Her Christmas Cookies
    Licking Her Christmas Cookies
    Resting Grinch Face

Maplewood Falls
    It's Mother-Pucking Christmas!

The Wynter Brothers
    Good Elf Gone Wrong
    Elf Against the Wall
    Elf on the Edge

The Richmond Brothers
    The Art of Awkward Affection
    The Art of Marrying Your Enemy

Check my website for the latest news:
http://alinajacobs.com/books.html

PUCK ME
It's
CHRISTMAS!

A Holiday Romantic Comedy

PUCK ME

It's

CHRISTMAS!

ALINA JACOBS

Summary: When a blacklisted preschool teacher accidentally lands a job coaching the worst team in the NHL, Christmas hits rock bottom. Between her mom's midnight snuggles, her boozy granny drooling over hockey butts, and twenty-two overgrown toddlers on skates, Ellie's barely holding it together. Then there's Captain Fletcher Sullivan—six-foot-four of muscle, ego, and trouble. She's determined to whip his losing team into shape with juice boxes and Goldfish crackers... and definitely not fall for her infuriating, smirking captain. A chaotic, laugh-out-loud holiday rom-com where the real miracle might just be love on ice.

To my cousin who said, "It's just one family dinner, what's the worst that could happen?"

Oh, I won't ask for much this
Christmas
I won't even wish for snow
—Mariah Carey

Chapter 1

ELLIE

"**D**id you just ask me what my favorite sex position is?"

"No!" I shriek at the huge hockey player cornered in front of me. "That's not even close to what I asked you." I wave my phone that's recording in his face. "I asked, 'If you were a Christmas cookie, what type would you be?'"

"What kind of stupid question is that? No one on the internet wants to watch a video of brain-dead idiots answering questions posed by another brain-dead nepo baby idiot."

"I'm not a nepo baby." I glower up at him.

"Candy Cane, your father works for the NHL, and this is an NHL team, so, you know, nepotism." He smirks. "Or you're sleeping with someone." He hefts his stick and brushes past me, his massive six-four frame magnified by the pads and heavy hockey skates.

One of the forwards sees me with my phone out, and his eyes widen. He curses and practically sprints for the rink, almost crashes into the plexiglass divider, and then he's gone, racing away over the ice.

"Why doesn't anyone want to participate in my PR videos?" I demand.

The rest of the players have already bailed for the ice, starting their morning workout.

"It's part of your contract!" I yell at them as Fletcher Sullivan walks by, thin blades of his skates thudding on the rubber flooring, then silently glides out onto the ice.

He spins on his outside edge to toss one more acidic comment at me. "You should just take videos of the players naked in the locker room. Know your audience, Candy Cane," he shouts to me, effortlessly skating backward. "See? I can do your job and mine."

"You're called up from the minors, buddy. You don't have an NHL contract. They can and will send you back down any day now, especially if the team keeps losing games," I shout back.

He gives me the finger.

"Loser." I plunk down on the bleachers of the Rhode Islanders' brand-new stadium to get some footage of the guys on the ice.

I only have one player who actually answered the question, and the guy spoke excitedly in Finnish the entire time while gesturing to a picture of a raccoon on his phone. The rest of them ran, gave me deer-in-the-headlights looks, rolled their eyes, mumbled "I dunno" around their mouthguards, or like Fletcher, complained—loudly and bitterly.

I cannot afford to lose this job. Fletcher is right. The only reason I have it is because of my dad. I should be at the Sunshine House Daycare leading story time right now, prepping organic snacks, or ushering my tiny young charges on a fun educational field trip.

Thanks to the Apache helicopter moms of Maplewood Falls, I lost my job, was blacklisted from all the preschools in the town, and now I have to chase after man-babies to try to drum up some sort of interest for hockey's newest and worst-performing team in the history of the NHL.

"It's not my fault," I whisper as I videotape the guys on the ice.

The Rhode Island Hockey Club has only been an NHL team since October. And here it is—the Thanksgiving turkey carcass is still warm—they have not won a single game. Zero. Zilch.

And it hasn't even been close.

I coach U6 girls, and honestly, these guys need to get back to basics. I think my little girls could give them a run for their money.

Their coach should be on them. Instead, he's sitting in his folding lawn chair in the middle of the ice rink, half asleep, snoozing off a hangover.

I decorated the ice rink for the holidays, with garland on top of the plexiglass dividers and snowflakes on the glass. But the Rhode Islanders are anything but festive.

Surly, no sense of camaraderie, no holiday-inspired kindness—they're all off in their own little worlds. They are just toddlers—gigantic six-foot-plus toddlers who are two hundred and fifty pounds of muscle—but still toddlers.

Look at them squabble over who gets which of the identical pucks.

The assistant coach has zero control. He reeked of weed when I ran into him earlier. He also tried to get me to lend him money.

"Keep your head up!" I finally yell as Ziggy, a D-man, sends the laziest pass in the history of the sport to Cookie.

Cookie spooks, misses it, starts crying, then the GM—who looks like he's one dose of blood thinner away from a massive heart attack—screams at him.

My video is ruined now. No one wants to see the rookie crying.

I stare at the empty stadium. If these were the Direwolves in Manhattan, it would be packed with fans wanting to see their favorite players and kids looking for an autographed puck. I've placed a few inflatable elves around the stadium to make it look less desolate. But the elves just look creepy.

The door to the lobby squeaks open then slams against the wall.

"Hey, people!" I call. Maybe I can do a video of the fans. They may very well be the only Rhode Islanders fans to exist.

Despite my best efforts—including giveaways, dress-like-your-favorite-player contests, and even free food—I can't move the needle on attendance. We have five, literally five, season ticket holders, and one of them is a guy who bought tickets drunk and has been trying to return them ever since he found out. The people that do show up are on their phones. They come to the game late and leave early. Rhode Islanders colors have never outnumbered the away team's fans.

"Things can only go up from here," I remind myself. Look at all these excited new fans. Sure, they're not dressed in team colors, but I have extra jerseys to give out.

"Hey! Hello! Hi, fellow fans! Merry Christmas! Do you want free swag? You don't even have to wait till Christmas Eve to open it."

The fans don't seem excited to trade their all-black attire for burgundy and gray—probably because it's going to clash with the bright-yellow FBI letters on their shirts...

"Shiiitttt."

I almost trip down the stadium steps on my way to the ice as the FBI and a SWAT team swarm the Rhode Islanders' practice.

Fletcher looks freaked out for a second and turns like he's about to bolt until the agents and the SWAT team jump the GM.

"I didn't do it!" he screams as they tackle him to the floor and handcuff him.

The coach snorts awake as an FBI agent sticks a badge in his face. "Joseph Demarcus, you're under arrest for collusion in gambling, drug trafficking, and exotic animal trading—"

"I thought this was America," he says through wet coughs. "Man can't buy a gorilla?"

"Embezzlement, tax fraud..." the FBI agent continues to list.

"You'll never take me alive!" the GM screams, red-faced and sweating.

Yeah, that might be coming sooner than you think...

"Fuck this shit," one of the assistant coaches is cursing as he's forced down on the ground. "I told you that you were going to get caught. I have all the information. I can testify! I don't want to go to jail," he begs the FBI agent who's dragging him off the ice. "It's Christmas! You can't make me spend the holidays in jail. My mother is going to kill me. You don't understand..."

The FBI head past me down the tunnels that lead to the team's windowless offices, swarming and carting away boxes of electronics and paperwork.

"Oh my gosh, this is terrible. I need to call Dana Holbrook." I run around in a panic. "You can't take him away," I beg the agents as they drag Joe Demarcus to the exit in handcuffs. "That's our coach. We're already doing badly. What are we supposed to do without a coach? We have to play the Direwolves tomorrow night. You'll let him out on bail, right?"

The FBI agent snorts. "Coach or no coach, y'all were gonna lose that match."

The hockey players watch in horror.

I'm in bad shape, but they're worse off. They gave their whole lives to play in the NHL, and now with no coach, no GM? And they have to play the Direwolves in two days? They're hosed. This horrible season will be a black mark on their records forever. Once their contracts run out? They're never playing in the National Hockey League again.

It's deathly silent when the FBI clears out, the door slamming on the GM's screams.

I point my phone camera to the nonarrested skills coach who's whispering with the equipment manager. "So, how about some words of wisdom from the Rhode Islanders' new coach?"

"New coach?" He scoffs at me. "Fuck that. You tell Dana Holbrook I quit. My cousin works in Toronto, and he's giving me a job. This team sucks. You all suck!" he screams to the players. "I'm out." He tosses his clipboard on the ice.

I point the camera at the equipment manager. "New coach?"

"I haven't been paid in weeks." He spits, tosses the bundle of hockey sticks he was carrying on the ice, and follows the now ex–skills coach.

Fletcher skates over to me, blades a deadly whisper on the ice.

I glance around, trying not to panic. The ice needs cleaning. Did the Zamboni driver quit too?

"So," he asks me, "are you going to make your grand exit, Candy Cane? That's the only thing that would end this day on a somewhat positive note."

"I-I-I…" My mouth gapes, and I put the camera down and stare up into the wintery-gray eyes. "I think I need to go talk to Dana."

One of the guys raises his hand. "What are we supposed to do?"

"Um…" I look out at the sea of RIHC players—well, most of them. Some of them didn't even bother to show up to practice.

"Don't ask her," Fletcher sneers. "She's not the coach."

Fists on hips, I glare up at him. "Yeah, put that on your Christmas list. You're lucky I'm not your coach, because I'd make you lazy bums work. Hell, you might actually win a game for once."

Chapter 2

FLETCHER

"Just when you think this team can't get any worse." I pace around in the warehouse. "And then they do."

My cousins are watching me spin the puck around on my stick as I rant. "All the coaches quit or were arrested. Even the assistant coaches. We don't have anyone. Not that it matters, because the coaches we did have sucked balls." I haul back and smash the puck against Talbot's chair.

"Geez, dude." He jumps up, almost a half second too slow. "Give a guy a little warning before you bash his brain in, cuz."

"My one shot to live out my NHL dreams, and they're ruining it. And that obnoxious little PR girl was just running around squawking about ticket sales and mad that they took her coffee-cup warmer out of her junkyard of an office. Like, excuse me, but there are real men with real problems here."

I toss the puck in the air and hit it like a baseball to bury it in the pocked drywall. "We're never going to win."

"You're always a winner to us." Lawrence makes a heart shape with his hands.

"Let us know when the PR girl is giving out free tickets to fill stands." Anderson snickers.

"They're not giving away free tickets to the Direwolves game. They sent out an email about it. They need all the ticket sales they can get." I blow out a breath.

"I'm going just because I like carnage," Elsa says with a smirk.

"I have a lot of money bet that you'll win." Anderson claps me on the shoulder.

"Dummy, they're going to get cremated." Lawrence kicks his chair.

"You think Coach was making us bad just so he could make money off of bets?" I muse.

"You all already sucked. That entire team is an embarrassment to the great sport of hockey." Hudson Wynter appears like death in the shadows.

"Fletch doesn't suck!" Talbot comes to my defense. "I put down fifty bucks that Fletch gets his first NHL goal this game. *The Hockey Guys* podcast is real excited about him. They say he's good."

I preen.

"If he gets a real-deal NHL contract, they think he should get traded to Toronto," Talbot adds.

"Toronto, eh? I'll have to brush up on my Canadian."

"Soooorry."

"Double-double."

My cousins cackle.

"I think I'd look good in blue and white." I run a hand through my hair.

Hudson wrenches the hockey stick out of my hand and slams it on the wall next to my head, making my teeth jerk. "You"—his voice drops to a growl—"are not a professional hockey player. You're not signing an NHL contract. You are not moving to Toronto. You're not the star of a last-place NHL team. You're in the show because you owe me money. *I* had you signed to the AHL. *I* had you called up to the NHL team. None of that happened because you're the next Zayne Murphy. And you're going to pay back your debt by finding enough dirt on Dana Holbrook to bury the Rhode Island Hockey Club." He shakes me. "*Do you understand?*"

I nod then chance it. "Maybe Dana Holbrook isn't actually money laundering through the RIHC? Maybe the team sucks because of the GM and the coach and the embezzling…" I trail off. My much-older cousin doesn't say anything, but the temperature in the windowless warehouse definitely drops.

His breath is icy when he finally says, "Is that your final answer? And think carefully, because if it is and you can't produce the evidence, then I'm taking my debt repayment in flesh and blood."

I lean back, forcing myself not to take that step away from him. "I'm sure there's something there, boss. I'll get you your evidence."

He gives me one more long, icy glare then turns away. "And Gracie wants to know if you're coming for Christmas this year."

"I guess if I'm not playing—"

"You're not going to be playing." He's terse. "The client wants Dana Holbrook's head on a platter by Christmas Eve."

"The Svenssons want this info as a Christmas present," Lawrence says as he spins around in his chair.

"Once you deliver, you're a free man." He looks at me. He's waiting for a response.

"Yeah, I'll get it."

"I don't know how," I mutter to myself as I pull on my cap and trudge through the snow.

I don't mind the cold—love it, even. Cold feels like hockey, feels like freedom, even though it's been years since I've been stuck in my mom's house with her shitty parade of boyfriends.

I never should have stuck my neck out for her.

But then I wouldn't have gotten this chance, my only chance ever to play in the NHL. My dream come true.

My nightmare, really.

My team is bad. They could easily get beat by a minor-league team. Shoot, they could probably get beaten by a U18 rec-league team or something.

"We'll get a better coach," I tell myself, because even though Hudson says I'm outta there by Christmas, a guy can dream, right?

Maybe they'll hire a real coach. It will be like the movies—a grizzled veteran whips up a ragtag group. Like that old '80s movie *Rocky* or something. We'll win the Stanley Cup, and I'll kiss the girl at the end of the movie.

As if.

I don't have anything to offer a girl.

Not that I want love—or would want what Hudson has with Gracie.

I tried to date after I got back from the military. Couldn't seem to make myself care about the girls complaining about their office jobs or their friends. Even when I played in the minors briefly, all the girls wanted to do was go party. They chased after hockey players but could barely hold a conversation about the game, let alone play it.

In fact, the only girl I've met who gives a shit about hockey since Hudson kicked me through the back door into the NHL is Ellie. And I'd rather keep losing hockey games than even entertain any sort of interest in the PR princess.

My phone beeps. I have it set to notify me anytime there's hockey news breaking, big or small.

New coach announced for the Rhode Island Hockey Club.

I take a steadying breath, then I open the announcement.

I peer at the photo. I can't believe it.

A fucking *girl*?

Wait.

That fucking girl?

Chapter 3

ELLIE

The Holbrook Enterprises Tower looms like a fortress against the snowy sky.

I feel very out of place against the dark-gray marble floor and walls as I walk in wearing my pilling leggings and my scruffy overcoat, my Rhode Island Hockey Club tote bag slung over one shoulder.

The lobby is decorated for Christmas, though somehow the fifteen-foot-tall Christmas tree with its bloodred ornaments doesn't inspire warm, fuzzy holiday feelings. The choral holiday carols that filter faintly over the sound system sound like a funeral dirge.

"I, um—" My voice cracks, and I clear my throat.

The receptionist, an older lady, peers over the side of the desk. She slides her glasses down her nose then back up.

"I'm here for a meeting with Dana Holbrook. She asked for me to come see her immediately."

She nods to one of the security guards. Wordlessly, he buzzes me onto the elevator.

I bite my nails as I ride up. In the mirrored walls, I look like a little girl. Not a cute one. Like an inept one who wanders into traffic on a whim.

On the train on the way to Manhattan, I tried and failed to come up with a PR plan. In the fancy elevator, the plan looks even more anemic in my beat-up RIHC notebook than it did an hour ago.

I'm not a marketing major. I'm not even a girlboss business major. I majored in early childhood development. I can draw a happy cloud that shows you how to use the potty. I can read *Max the Great* over and over and over again and still make it entertaining. I know all the *Paw Patrol* characters. I can teach a child how to tie their shoes and put on their own mittens in five minutes with nothing but two stickers and an interpretive dance.

I do not know how to create a PR plan to manage the disaster of your failed NHL team's GM, head coach, and assistant coach all getting arrested and indicted on federal charges.

Where do you even start?

I should have just moved away once it was clear I was blacklisted in the daycare circuit in Maplewood Falls. My dad said one of his old NHL buddies' wives was opening a daycare in Colorado and wanted me on. But that's so far away from home and all my siblings and cousins.

My dream was to fall in love with a local boy—someone kind who loves hockey and has a real job, who wants a big family and can at the very least tolerate my overly large, very codependent family. Someone the opposite of Fletcher, who won't protest when we buy a house down the street from my parents.

Sucks for me that all the guys I dated thought I was a cool girl because I liked hockey. They didn't think it was so cool that I know more about the game than them, and they definitely didn't like that I could play better than them.

I don't consider myself that good at hockey, but to make one of the Maplewood Falls rec-level players happy, I'd have to give it up. My other option is to date a guy who's a pro hockey player, neither of which is going to happen.

I'm still young, I remind myself. Twenty-three is young.

I gulp.

The other offices in the hall are empty as I creep along, feet sinking into the plush carpet. It's December. Most people are probably out soaking up the festive holiday season.

Too soon, I'm standing in front of Dana Holbrook's office.

There's a faint clicking noise.

I peer around the doorframe that's been draped in garland.

Dana is sitting at her oversized mahogany desk, a single lamplight casting her perfect skin, perfect hair, perfectly sculpted cheekbones in sharp relief.

Click. Her nail taps on the wood desk.

Click.

I swallow.

"What are you waiting for?" The words slither out.

Shoulders hunched, I scurry into the office, dump all my stuff on the floor next to the chair in front of her desk, sit down, then stand up. "Hi, Mrs. Holbrook."

Her lip curls. "I told you to call me Dana, Ellie."

"Right." I salute.

"Sit down."

I almost stand up again.

"We need to talk about—"

"The disaster today? Yes, and I am on it. I have a whole PR plan prepared."

"Do you? Good. Did you email it to me?" She's scrolling through her email.

"Er, no." I set my notebook on the desk. "Just worked it up on the train."

Dana looks down her nose that must have cost a fortune because it's perfect yet not fake looking. There are three lines on my little notepad. "A press conference," she reads upside down.

I hurry to turn the notebook to face her. "With snacks." I point. "And a volunteer event with the players to help inform people why gambling is wrong."

"The Rhode Island Hockey Club makes eighty percent of our advertising revenue off of online gambling ads." Dana doesn't blink.

"So…"

"So?" She looks down pointedly.

"Right." I scratch it out. "Well, there's the Puppies on Ice Day."

"What does that have to do with the crisis?"

"Uh, I mean, who doesn't like hot guys and puppies?" My sweater is soaked in sweat. My sports bra is drenched. I am wearing too many layers. "It's, uh, warm in here, isn't it?"

"I will handle the crisis PR response," Dana says. "Never complain, never explain. Besides, once we announce our new coach, no one is going to care that the old one is currently being strip-searched in prison."

"Oh, we have a new coach?" I perk up. "Is it Jared Trotz from Toronto? I heard his name getting thrown around and—"

"I'm a businesswoman, Ellie," Dana sneers. "I'm not paying some overbloated whale carcass with bad feet millions of dollars to shout at the players and lose games. I can find someone to do that for much cheaper. And I have. You start tomorrow."

"Start? Start what tomorrow?" My eye is twitching.

"You are the new coach of the Rhode Island Hockey Club."

"Ha! Hahaha! Ahahaha! Funny. Sooo funny."

Dana's not laughing.

"I mean—" I start to panic. "I'm just a girl. I'm a child, a mere babe. I can't coach a team. I live at home. I don't have my shit together. Like, at all."

Dana doesn't care. Dana is bored of listening to me.

The perfectly manicured nails are tapping on the blotter again. "You are the only staff member left aside from Stacey in HR and Harlowe, who books the hotel rooms and food. We've had a wave of resignations."

"Thanks for giving me a heads-up," I mutter.

"You know hockey." It's not a question. "You played D1 at Boston University."

"Yeah, on the female team." I feel sick.

"You were on the USA Hockey team," Dana continues. "Went to world championships. Earned an Olympic silver medal."

"The girls' team. *Girls*," I repeat. "And I wasn't that good. I'm a little on the short side."

Dana stands up. She is not on the short side. And she's wearing So Kates, so that's like an extra five inches on me. "And you coach currently, and ref, do you not?"

"Yeah, again—girls. Little ones." I mime with my hands. "Tiny. Children."

"This team needs a coach." Dana takes a step toward me.

"I'm sure I could find one. There has to be someone out there—a man who wants to prove his mettle." My neck is craning all the way back.

Dana peers down at me. Imperious. A queen. "You'll do." She holds out a set of keys. "I've already had IT switch your email over."

The keys are heavy in my hand. "What about my PR duties?"

"This is in addition to your normal job. I'm not running a charity. I didn't become a billionaire by coddling people. And don't," she warns, "ask me for a pay raise."

Chapter 4
FLETCHER

"**A** girl? We have to get coached by a *girl*?"

"Not just any girl—the PR girl?" Eddie is pacing around the empty house.

The only piece of furniture in the living room is an oversized couch where Zayne Murphy—hockey legend, five-time Stanley Cup champ, two-time Olympic gold medalist, once and future captain of USA Hockey, and my all-time hero—is currently trying to cross off his one and only daily to-do list item of drowning himself in whiskey.

On the TV, the sports-news talking heads are squawking about the girl coach and how this is the beginning of the end for not just the Rhode Island Hockey Club but the NHL in general.

"I mean, might be nice to see some titties other than yours," Bramms jokes to Ziggy.

"It's a gimmick," I say flatly.

"Does that mean we get free stuff?" Jovi asks me as he chows down on a sandwich made from the last of the Thanksgiving leftovers Zayne catered last week.

"Is there more turkey left?" Ziggy sighs. "I should eat some protein in these trying times."

"Yeah, Zayne ordered enough for two hundred people, like we were going to have a big happy-hockey-family Christmas." Eddie snorts. "The Rhode Islanders are not that kind of a team."

"At least he paid." I jump to Zayne's defense.

"He better." Carlsson glowers.

We aren't getting paid a lot of money, because Zayne Murphy is getting paid over half of the Rhode Islanders' salary cap.

"All that money, and he hasn't played a game sober since Dana Holbrook squirted this team out into the world." Carlsson shakes his head.

"She should have strangled us in the cradle," Jonesy states.

"What do you care? At least you're getting paid," Bramms grumbles.

"Two mill a year," Jonesy brags.

"Not as much as—"

I glare at Eddie before he can say what we're all thinking.

Not that Zayne noticed. Murphy's Law scratches his belly, belches, and his head lolls to the side.

He lifts up his glass. "'S good you guys are here. House's empty otherwise. 'S empty."

He did let us crash in his enormous mansion in the nice part of Maplewood Falls, so at least I don't have to spend my meager paycheck on rent since Hudson didn't deign to give me a per diem for my sacrifice.

"You want to talk about people getting more than their fair share?" Ziggy mutters and nods.

Cookie is huddled under a blanket in front of the TV. He was destined to be the next Zayne Murphy. A generational talent. They gave him a huge contract with a big signing bonus right after his eighteenth birthday. He made his NHL debut as the most hyped rookie in the league. He then scored an own goal at minute 1:37 of the first period of his first-ever NHL game, and coach Joe DeMarcus screamed at him so badly he made Cookie cry on national television. Cookie's been so traumatized he hasn't played in a game since.

The Finnish giant made him some nasty-looking soup, and he's sitting there in a T-shirt, slurping it while Sportsnet shows video clips from the PR princess's social media.

There she is in a tutu.

There she is in a giant inflatable unicorn costume gliding around on the ice.

There she is baking cookies that look like hockey sticks and jerseys.

"Yep, she looks super qualified," Ziggy says bitterly.

"I just need her to be qualified in riding my dick," Eddie jokes.

"Watch your fucking mouth," I snarl at him, not sure why I'm defending her. I grab the back of his hoodie and shake him roughly.

"All right, all right." The stocky D-man waves his hands at me. "Shit, man, can't take a joke."

"He's jealous because she's going to want to go after me before either of you," Jonesy brags.

"No woman wants a man with a face prettier than hers," I joke to him.

The Finnish giant, the raccoon T-shirt he's wearing doing nothing to make him look less intimidating, looks up at the screen then back at our little group lounging around the ottomans. He says something I don't understand. It sounds vaguely threatening.

I sit up in case he's about to fight. Even though I kept up with some of my military training with Hudson and the rest of my cousins, I don't like my chances against Heikkiläinen.

We're all quiet as he stalks out of the cavernous living room then relax when heavy footsteps go up the stairs.

"Honestly," Jovi says with a sigh while stretching his hamstring on the floor, "I don't care if she has tentacles. If she can actually win games, I'll wear a pink jock."

On the screen, Sportsnet is showing footage of last night's Direwolves game. Their captain, Ryder O'Connell, cuts through four guys like they're peewee players, fakes out the goalie, slides on one knee, and the puck goes flying into the net. The goaltender doesn't even see it.

They show him scoring five more equally impressive goals. Then it cuts to commercial break, and we watch him tell everyone to drink Gatorade Limited-Edition Neon Yellow for the Direwolves.

"How much you think he gets paid for that? Like, do they write him a half-million-dollar check every time his mug appears on TV?" Bramms stretches his wrists.

"Check under your cap for free tickets," Ryder reminds us from the screen, holding up the bottle.

"Shit, we can give people free tickets, and they don't even have to buy a bottle of that stuff." Jonesy's mouth turns down.

"Not for the next game," Eddie says sullenly. "It's all sold out. They all want to see Ryder."

"He's a hockey terminator." Carlsson sighs.

"Aw, I didn't win," Cookie says, looking under his sports-drink cap.

"Probably because he refuses to play," Carlsson mutters under his breath.

Now ESPN has cut to the betting markets. "If you bet that Rhode Island beats the Direwolves—even just one thousand dollars—you could be a multimillionaire with these odds," the analyst jokes.

"I bet on us," Zayne slurs from the couch.

"Dude, no. Goddamn it, we just had the coach arrested for gambling. Players are not allowed to bet on games." I curse.

"I mean," Eddie mutters, "might be better if he's gone. We could actually hire some decent players."

I can't betray my childhood self and let my hero be dragged off in disgrace. I fish his phone out of the pocket of his stained sweatpants, grab his thumb to unlock it, and cancel the bet.

"Tens of millions of dollars… No one in their right mind would take that bet." The reporters are chuckling to each other.

"Especially not if they have a female coach. With that news, the odds that the RIHC loses just went sky-high," the analyst adds.

"We are so fucked." Jonesy sags.

"I thought this was going to be the party house," Bramms complains. "It's like the sad and depressing house."

"Eat some turkey," I sigh. "We need to bulk up for the games."

Chapter 5

ELLIE

"**S**nickerdoodle! You're home!" My mom sweeps me up into her arms and kisses my face. "Ooh, I'm so happy to have my little girl here with me. What time do you get off work tomorrow? You're not going to work as late as you did today, are you? We need to get the Christmas decorations up. Your brothers are going to be in town tomorrow! I'm trying to convince them to stay here. They can bring all of their friends. I can make wolves in a blanket."

"Wolves in a what?"

"It's just pigs in a blanket with some spicy dipping sauce and yellow food coloring and everything-bagel seasoning." My mom beams at me.

"You made those for my bingo night." Granny Murray stomps by, copy of *Sports Betting Weekly* under her arm. "They look like uncircumcised penises with an STD. You can't be serving those to people. Certainly not millionaire hockey players, especially not if you're trying to marry your daughters off to one of them. Kathy practically had an orgasm then a heart attack when she saw one. Slapped the dementia right out of Candice too." Gran flicks on a sausage.

"No one's marrying any NHL players," I say desperately.

And definitely not coaching them, right? I think hysterically.

I feel sick. I must have dreamed it, right? Right. I'm not going to coach a bunch of NHL players. I can't. I won't. I shan't.

"I'm just going to go wash my face, then I'll help you with dinner," I tell my mom.

And scream into a pillow and seriously contemplate my life choices.

Too bad in the Clarke household you are never, ever alone.

"You sleep with one of them yet?" Granny Murray whispers as she follows me upstairs. It's the same question every time I come home from work.

"I'm not sleeping with them—they're... coworkers..." *Technically my employees now...*

I need a pretzel with beer cheese and a Benadryl and some wine.

"Your cousin Dakota is engaged to that Ryder fellow. You come from these same loins." Gran slaps her thigh. "You got the right stuff, girlie! Get you a hot NHL player with a big dick. You're better looking than any of those puck bunnies that hang around the practices. And your tits and ass are real."

"I don't have time for dating, Granny Murray. I need to save money, probably get a second job."

Oh god, how am I going to coach the men's and my girls' team? *We're not going to be an NHL coach.*

My eye is twitching. I press my finger on it.

"You ought to get that looked at." Granny Murray follows me down the hall past my siblings' bedrooms.

My mom has kept each one like a shrine for my siblings when they come home to visit. My dad's big NHL-goalie payday afforded them a very nice house. Me and each of my five siblings got to have our own room, and there's still space for a guest room. Where you'd think Granny Murray would be living, right? In her time of need?

Wrong.

We are roommates.

Sometimes bedmates if she comes home drunk from the bingo hall and crawls into bed with me.

"You're twenty-three. You have to live." Granny Murray pulls up my pants, which are sliding down. It's hard to shop for clothes when you have a hockey butt. Also, yes, my extended family is enmeshed and codependent. Thank you for noticing. "Enjoy life. You're only young once."

"I can't wait to be middle-aged. I'm going to sit under a mound of quilts and read books and drink fancy tea blends."

"Boo, boring!" She blows a raspberry. "We need to go to the horse tracks."

I scrub at my face with a makeup remover pad, watching in the mirror as Granny Murray shows off all the clothes she and Aunt Babs found for me when they went shopping today.

"I can't wear that to work, Gran." I snatch the skimpy Mrs. Claus teddy out of her hands and shove it in the linen closet.

"This is for under your clothes. You get one of those guys," she says, "when they're all 'roided up and horny after a big win, show him a little of this, and you'll have a ring on your finger by summer."

"I'm not sleeping with a player, and certainly not after a win, because the Rhode Islanders are the worst team in the league. They will never win a game."

"Not with that attitude." Granny Murray snorts. She pulls up my pants again.

I'm starting to see why my cousin Gracie finally evicted her out of her house.

"I need to help Mom with dinner."

The gravy is bubbling away on the stove.

Mom gives me another big hug and a smooch. "My baby's back in the nest. Never leave home again, snickerdoodle. I made your favorite: garlic-cheddar mashed potatoes."

"Yes! I need carbs and dairy today."

"You need to get a man. You baby that girl, Trina," Gran rails. "She should be out on the town, roaming the streets." Granny Murray thrusts a mug at me. "Eggnog. Your Aunt Stacy made it. She doesn't put enough rum in it."

Golden liquid is sloshed into my mug.

I take a big, burning swallow.

"Oh, Ellie." My mom licks her thumb and tries to clean off my face.

"Ooh! Eggnog!" My older sisters clamber into the kitchen.

"You're here! All my girls!" My mom wraps us into a big hug.

Angie steals my mug and drinks it, while Maxie goes right for the rum bottle.

"There's red wine in the gravy, girls."

"You better make sure it gets cooked off," my dad's voice booms. "Jace and Adam have a big game tomorrow. We need them to pass a drug test."

My mom screams.

I catch the spatula and keep the pan of gravy from flying off the stove as she sprints to my brothers—somehow even bigger than the last time I saw them in their black-and-yellow Direwolves jerseys—and hugs them like they just returned from war or something.

"My boys! My little boys! Oh! My children are all here for dinner! I didn't know you were coming in."

"We thought we'd surprise you." Adam grins as my mom squeezes him, then she goes for my other brother.

My dad's face is lit up with pride and joy as he gazes over my younger twin brothers. Big-time NHL hockey players, both on the Direwolves. An NHL draft-day miracle.

"Don't worry, Ellie," Adam says as he and Jace rush to me and both wrap their arms around me, squishing me. "We'll go easy on the Rhode Islanders tomorrow."

"Yeah," Angie says as she steals a spoonful of mashed potatoes. "Try not to beat them by like twenty points, m'kay?"

Adam laughs. "Ryder already said that once the point count gets to ten to nothing, he's going to switch to all us rookies and let us play."

"Yeah, I bet I score a goal this game!" Jace whoops.

"Your first NHL goal!" My mom hugs him.

"It hasn't happened yet," my dad teases softly. "You'll jinx it, Trina."

My mom mimes zipping her lip. "Your grandmother and I have been making custom Direwolves jerseys for everyone to wear."

"No help from that husband of yours, of course," Gran says drunkenly.

Maxie silently offers Dad the rum bottle.

"Did you make a Rhode Islanders one for Ellie?" Jace teases and starts trying to peel the foil back on the roast beef.

"Oh, surely you can sit with the family just this one game, snickerdoodle?"

"She'll get fired, Mom, if she does that," Angie says.

"Yeah, again," Maxie adds.

"Oh, you remember Leo Niedersachen? He just retired from Boston," my dad tells me as my mom shoos us to ferry the piping-hot dishes to the dining room. "His wife just had their third child, and their nanny moved back to France. I told them that you were great in childcare, Ellie, and were looking to get back in the field."

"Wonderful!" Mom claps her hands. "You can be a nanny and sit with us at the game."

"Yeah, thanks, Dad. I'll send him an email tonight." And not show up to work tomorrow.

It still seems like a bad dream—Dana handing me the keys to the hockey castle. They're still hidden at the bottom of my tote.

We sit down for dinner. I load up on the cheddar potatoes, making a little well and drowning my potatoes in gravy.

"You want some potatoes with that gravy?" My dad delivers the standard joke, pretending to offer me more potatoes as all at once, everyone's phones go off with the Google News alert sound.

My siblings and dad all reach for their phones in unison.

"No electronics at the table," Mom scolds.

"But it could be big hockey news!" Jace cries.

"Yeah, that's my hockey news notification," Adam protests.

"They need to know what's going on in the industry, Trina," my dad, Nate, says.

Yeah, I'm sweating. I have a bad feeling about this. "No phones at the table, guys." I try to wrestle them out of my siblings' hands. "I never see you guys. It will be nice to have dinner with normal people, not just Mom and Dad."

"Oh my fucking god!" Angie yells, her voice rising on the last word.

"Language, girls."

"You cunt!" Maxie's got a huge grin on her face.

"So cunty," Angie drawls.

"Cu—C-wordy," Jace self-corrects as he and Adam scroll through their phones. "This is, like, a big-dick, fucking ballsy move."

"Maxine!" Mom swats her with a towel. "Look what you started."

My dad is looking at me like he's angry, hurt, betrayed.

"Where's that bottle of rum?" I ask desperately.

"Got you, girlie." Granny Murray scoots her chair back.

"You're an NHL coach," Nate finally spits out.

I wrench the bottle from Gran. "The food's getting cold." I chug rum into my glass and sit down, banging my knee on the table.

"How are you a coach, Ellie?" My dad glares at me.

"This is great news, dear." Mom rubs his back. "She got a promotion. It's a pay raise."

"Woo! We're moving up in the world," Granny Murray exclaims. "You and me, let's start looking for real estate. These digs are cramping my style. I'll be your wingwoman."

"Er… it actually does not come with a pay raise." I can't swallow. "It's just a temporary thing, Dad. You know, because of the arrest, yadda yadda. Dana Holbrook is a cheapskate."

Angie and Maxie are horrified.

"You take that back!" one yells.

"She is queen of the cunts!" the other fires back.

"Icon!"

"Legend."

"Her hair."

"Her nails!"

"Her car!"

"Her vibe!"

"Her attitude!"

"Her shoes!"

"Her attitude!"

"Her everything!" they say in unison.

"Yeah, I mean, you don't say no to Dana Holbrook," Maxie says.

"Yeah, Dad," my sister echoes, turning to Nate. "You do not say no to Dana Holbrook."

"Wow, an NHL coach." Dad pokes at his meat.

"You always wanted to be a coach after you retired, didn't you, Dad?" my brother asks innocently. No one ever said hockey players were smart.

I try a distraction tactic. "Wow, this roast beef is perfectly cooked, Mom."

My dad slowly sits down at the head of the table.

My mom loads up his plate then gives my brothers more meat, who attack their food like starving dogs.

"A new job for Ellie!"

"Why don't we talk about literally anything else?" I say as I shovel cheesy potatoes in my mouth.

"Be proud! You're the first female coach!" Mom hugs me.

"There's that assistant coach in Winnipeg," Angie says.

I nod. "See, not the first. Not a trailblazer."

"Yeah, she's an assistant. You're the head-honcho coach. You call all the shots," Gran boasts.

"You're the head coach." My dad sounds like he's going to keel over into his pot roast.

"More potatoes?"

"Stop trying to feed that man carbs and dairy. He needs alcohol, Trina," Granny Murray says then turns to me. "You're gonna do great, kiddo. Shit, I already placed a bet on your game tomorrow."

"You did?" My brothers are howling in laughter.

"Yep, my whole Social Security check."

"Your entire…" Nate holds a finger to his eye that is visibly twitching. "Trina," he hisses to Mom, "we agreed your mother was going to stay here while she saved up to move into another retirement home."

"Yes, Nathan," Granny Murray slurs. "My entire Social Security check, because I believe in Ellie. I raise girls' girls. Women support other women because the men in their lives won't." She waves her mug of scotch at my dad. "You're gonna do great, kid. I'm gonna be there cheering you on. And don't forget: the best motivation for men is sex. Sometimes you gotta suck a few dicks to win a hockey game."

My siblings sit there, shocked. Unlike me, they do not live at home and thus seem to have forgotten what Granny Murray is like when she starts drinking on a weeknight.

Jace raises his hand. "How many dicks do you think I'd have to suck to get a Stanley Cup?"

Our dad shoots daggers at him. "Don't you dare engage in any sex acts with anyone!"

"So, we're hosting a holiday party," I say in an attempt to change the subject.

"When are we not hosting a holiday party?" Angie interjects then turns back to hockey. "So, what's your strategy for the game tomorrow?"

"Forget that—what are you going to wear?" Maxie leans over.

"You have to wear white," my other sister says.

"No, pink."

"Her strategy is gonna be to loooose." My brothers cackle.

"No offense, sis!" Adam steals the slice of meat off my plate and stuffs the whole thing in his mouth. "I do support you, but we're still going to kick your ass."

"They're going to crucify you," my dad says. He's staring blankly at the china cabinet. "I'm going to talk to the NHL tomorrow. My daughter can't be an NHL coach. You're basically a child. You still live here. At home. With me. It's not happening. It can't happen."

"A woman can be an NHL coach, Dad," Maxie argues.

Nate turns on me. "You can't control these men. These are the best of the best."

"Uhhh…" Adam makes a face. "The Rhode Islanders team isn't *that* good, Dad."

"She'll probably be better than that coach they had," Jace adds. "It doesn't matter who they hire, the Direwolves are going to destroy you guys."

"It's just a temporary position until they get a real coach," I promise my dad.

"Maybe you can help her find a coach, Nate," my mom suggests.

My dad gives a sharp nod. "Right." He looks down at his food and slices his meat aggressively. "I'll do that. You're not going to be an NHL coach. You can't." He dishes up more salad for me and my siblings. "That's final."

Chapter 6

ELLIE

I wake up early to Granny Murray and my dad yelling downstairs.

"*My house…*" my dad is saying, "*…under my roof…*"

"*Misogynistic asshole!*"

"*…trying to protect her… don't understand what they're like…*"

"*I know very well. Trina's father was a hockey-playing piece of shit.*"

In the kitchen, my mom is listening to Christmas carols while she bakes.

"Look, I have muffins!" My mom parades me through the kitchen to look at the basket of baked goods she's made. She turns up the music to drown out my dad and Granny yelling at each other. "I made Rhode Islanders in a blanket. The dipping sauce has sriracha in it to make it the team colors."

"Looks amazing, Mom." My mom has given each wiener sesame-seed eyes and a little hat made out of celery. "We need to adopt you a kitten or something."

"Or a grandchild." My mom grins at me.

"Don't look at me. I'm grumpy."

"You said you always wanted to be a mom. You're so good with children." She cups my face. "I saw you when you took the babies out when you worked at the Sunshine House. You were so good with them. You were born to be a mom."

"Well, maybe my dream man will crawl up the side of the house into the bedroom. Oh wait, that already happened, and it was some guy Granny Murray invited over." I wipe at my greasy forehead. "Can she not stay in one of the other bedrooms?"

"Then where would your siblings stay when they come over? I want them to feel welcome. And the guest room is for guests."

"Right." I sigh. I pick up one of the pigs in a blanket.

Mom slaps it out of my hand. "Those are for the players."

"You're going to let the Direwolves players eat Rhode Islanders in a blanket? Sounds morbid." My sister stumbles in, yawning. "Are you all always up this early?" Maxie adds.

"Granny Murray is up at five," I tell her.

"Yikes, glad I moved out."

"Yeah, it's nice to have a job relevant to your degree…"

"No, these are for your players." Mom smiles as I lower the hors d'oeuvre away from my mouth.

"Mom—"

"It's your first day, sweetie." Mom kisses me noisily on the top of my head. "Everyone likes the girl who brings snacks."

"Trina!" My dad pushes his way past my brothers, shirtless, their hair a mess.

Adam opens the fridge and grabs the jug of milk and proceeds to down the whole thing.

"Hey! He's drinking all of it," Jace complains.

"There's more milk in the other fridge."

"Mom, can you make them wear a shirt?" Angie complains.

"Trina, Ellie can't bring snacks to NHL practice," Nate argues.

Jace punches Adam in the stomach, and milk sprays all over the fridge.

"Go outside!" my mother screams. "Out!"

They groan. "It's freezing cold!"

"Out!"

"Ellie." My dad shoves my brothers out the door and grabs a wet rag. "This is a serious deal. I've been on the phone all night." Granny Murray mocks him with her hand as my dad rails. "Everyone in the NHL office is appalled that Dana Holbrook even put you in this position. I've been on the phone with the chairman of the NHL, and we have a game plan. There's going to be a press conference, and you're going to tell them—"

"You're going to tell them that you don't need a dick to play hockey!" Granny Murray hollers.

Outside, my brothers are meowing at the kitchen window.

"You got this!" Granny Murray bangs her chest. "Don't let the boys get you down."

"Men!" Dad yells. "They are grown men. Violent. Uneducated. Crass!"

"I really wouldn't say that, Mr. Clarke," Harlowe says as she opens the kitchen door and stomps the snow off her boots. "They're more lazy and useless. Practice is a joke."

"Don't let them inside," my mom warns as my brothers rush back into the kitchen.

"Cold, cold, cold!"

"I think you're making this about you a little bit, dear," my mom says gently to Dad. "We talked about this with the boys when they were drafted to the Direwolves. It's their career. You already had your NHL career."

"Career," Harlowe snorts. "Girl, they are throwing you off a glass cliff."

"I don't want everyone to blame me when we get creamed." I sink in my chair.

My dad kneels in front of me and grabs my hand. "Exactly! So do the press conference, say you have another job offer, and this will all be over."

"No wonder they kept trading your ass around when you were a goalie!" Granny Murray makes a rude noise. "You're a quitter and a narc."

Angie comes in with my phone that's ringing and ringing.

I don't recognize the number, though it's a Maplewood Falls area code.

"It's the press." Angie waves the phone at me. "Tell them you won't do interviews unless they pay you."

"Ooh! Yeah, then we can go shopping," Maxine squeals.

"Aunt Babs already bought you clothes, sweetie." Mom smooths my hair down.

"Don't talk to the press," my dad begs.

"Nate," my mom tells him, "let me make you some herbal tea."

"Food!" my little brothers wail.

"For God's sake," my dad curses.

I answer the phone.

"Speaker," Maxie whispers. "Put it on speaker."

"Hello?" My voice is hesitant.

A loud, irritated male sigh echoes around the kitchen as everyone watches breathlessly. "Candy Cane?" I can practically hear Fletcher roll his eyes. "I mean, *Coach* Candy Cane."

I grimace. "About that…"

"You better not be flaking out," the deep voice warns. "You have the keys. We're freezing our nuts off out here."

Chapter 7

FLETCHER

"**S**orry, sorry, sorry!" Our new coach slips and slides up to the stadium. She's got a huge ring of keys with her. "The equipment guys didn't open this up?" she chatters. Her cheeks are pink. She's not wearing any makeup, and I'm pretty sure that's a pajama top under her half-zipped coat. She looks frazzled. Inexperienced. Incompetent.

"I downgrade our loss tonight from ten to nothing to fifteen to nothing," I grumble.

"Better make it an even twenty." Bramms nudges me and jerks his head.

Murphy's Law is puking his guts out into a skeletal bush on which someone has hung green and red ornaments. It's a metaphor for something... this team, my life.

Coach Candy Cane still can't find the key to get the stadium open.

I grab them from her, pick one at random.

"I already tried that one," she protests.

"Well, I'm trying it again."

The SUV that brought her does a J-turn, knocks over a trash can, and parks halfway on the sidewalk.

Ellie's friend Harlowe, the girl who helped me get situated with a place to live and bought the train ticket when I first got called up from the minor league, starts unloading boxes.

"Yum." Jovi sniffs the air. "Something smells good."

"I told you," Ellie is saying, jumping up and down as I fiddle with the keys.

"This is the right key." I shove my shoulder to the door and turn the key. "See. I was right. You were wrong. I'll take that apology now."

"For someone on a probationary contract, he sure is cocky." She sniffs.

An elderly woman and Harlowe carry a stack of boxes to the door.

The guys just watch.

I wait a beat. "Get those boxes," I finally snap at them.

Ziggy and Bramms jump into action and gather the boxes from the women.

"Those snacks are for after practice," Ellie warns as we stomp into the stadium.

"Harlowe," Ellie whispers as we gaze out over the ice. The rough, chopped-up ice. "Where is the Zamboni driver? Why didn't anyone clean this?"

"Equipment guys all quit. Heinze took the whole crew with him," I call over my shoulder as I head to the locker room. "Zamboni key is this one." I toss it back to her.

Ellie sighs.

"I just have to say"—I turn toward her fully and spread my arms—"and I know it's not my place—a lowly minor league player—but this NHL team is very poorly run."

"Well, you could step up and help."

"They don't pay me enough to help." I turn on my heel and head to the locker room.

Well, pretend to. The FBI raided the offices yesterday, but there has to be something left there I can get to Hudson, right? I've been on this team for a week, and I have nothing to show for myself. I have to clear that debt off. I have to.

Pressing myself flat against the wall down the windowless corridor, I sneak to the offices. The doors are busted from the FBI, and it's nothing to slip inside.

But there's nothing in there that will point to the team being used for money laundering. *Like it would be that easy.* I stew as I head back to the ice.

Heavy metal music blares over the speaker as I exit the corridor.

"What the—" I pause, watching as the gates open and the giant Zamboni machine rolls onto the ice.

"Granny Murray, be careful!" Ellie is calling to her grandmother.

"I'm old, not made of glass!"

"She's worried about the Zamboni—it's finicky," Harlowe calls.

"You girls are worse than your fathers. You think I don't know how to ride a finicky machine? I was married to your grandfather for decades." The Zamboni belches steam.

"Is that the new equipment manager?" I whisper to Ellie, who's shuffling through papers.

She jumps, and the papers scatter. "My grandmother?" she yelps. "God, no! I mean, I hope not. Dana said I couldn't hire anyone." She's chewing on her lip.

My eyes narrow.

She tugs at the collar of her shirt as I stare at her.

This girl has direct access to Dana Holbrook. Dana Holbrook who hasn't even gone to a single game and stays locked up in Holbrook Enterprises tower.

It's not a lead, but it's a concept of a lead.

"Aren't you gonna—I mean—" She clears her throat. "Go get changed and get on the ice. Stop creeping around."

"I was just waiting to see if you were going to come watch. You're the coach. You're allowed to be in the locker room whenever you want." I wink at her.

Her face is tomato red. "That's your safe space," she croaks, "so I will be out here. Where everyone is fully clothed."

"Missing out, Candy Cane."

Ellie's obviously not going to make it. She'll be gone in a couple days, tops. For one, the NHL isn't going to let some girl coach one of their teams, even if it's the worst team in the league.

I just have to goad her enough to get Dana Holbrook to come to Maplewood Falls. I'll steal the billionaire's laptop or phone or tablet or whatever and then hand over the data to Hudson. Then I'm in the clear.

And the passkey—you need the passkey.

Okay, sure, yeah, but miracles can happen, right?

Yeah, and we could win the Stanley Cup.

It's a bad plan.

A bad plan is better than no plan.

Well… except if Ellie is the plan to turn the Rhode Islanders into a real NHL team. That's a terrible plan.

Somehow, the locker room feels even more like a funeral parlor than normal. The captain sets the tone, and Zayne Murphy is slumped over on the bench. Someone has shoved a trash can between his legs.

"He smells bad," Ziggy complains.

Zayne is not dressed.

"Get your gear on," I tell him. "We have practice."

"I thought you were out there making her quit." Eddie is on his phone.

The only person dressed for practice is the Finnish giant. He makes an angry noise.

I turn on the group. "Practice is already thirty minutes behind schedule. Why the fuck are you fuckers not dressed?"

"But the ice—"

"There's not—"

"The ice is not your problem," I roar.

"It is if I break something," Eddie snaps.

"Man the fuck up."

"Who died and made you captain?" the D-man sneers.

I buck up to Eddie. I have thirty pounds and three inches on him.

Hudson's right—I am not here to play hockey. I'm here to clear my debt. I'm not playing around with Eddie.

Before I can escalate things, Zayne throws up in his trash can.

Cookie makes a face.

Zayne hauls himself upright.

Bramms hands him a bottle of scotch.

"Just a whiff," Bramms protests when I snarl at him. "Just to take the edge off."

"Get dressed," Zayne Murphy rasps. "Coach is waiting."

"See?" Ellie's Granny Murray dusts off her hands as we look at the gleaming, freshly cleaned ice. "Told ya! I gotchu, girl."

The players—already huge men—are even more massive when balanced precariously on the blades of their skates, rolling their shoulders under the pads as they join her out on the ice.

"Changing out of your PJs," I whisper to her as I pass, "is not gonna be enough to make the guys respect you." I put my back to her. "Where are the goalies?"

"Traded," Carlsson says, showing me on his phone. "We'll have to call up guys from the minors."

"Does the coach know that's how it works?" Ziggy smirks.

"I bet we show up on game day and there's no goalie," Jovi snickers.

"No phones on the ice," Ellie orders.

We ignore her. My teammates chirp at each other on the ice, skating around, shoving each other, making raunchy jokes.

"Listen up!" Ellie raises her voice.

The men ignore her.

"If we can all just pay attention and—"

One of the rookies shrieks as his friend shoves him on the ice. They scuffle, wrestling each other, slipping and sliding.

If this was a real NHL team, the captain would never have let that behavior go on. Shoot, one of the alternate captains would have stepped in ten minutes ago.

Zayne Murphy is half passed out, leaning heavily on his stick, his head lolling down.

It's so early in the season no alternate captains have been named, and well, Ellie's the only coach in the room.

I wink at her. She looks pissed.

"Man." Jovi is ADHD-caffeinated on a slushie of energy drinks and Five-hour Energy shots, and buzzing. "You think Ryder O'Connell will sign my puck tonight?"

"You can't get a player on the opposing team to sign your puck, idiot." Ziggy gives him a hard shove.

"Why do we even have to practice before that game?" Bramms sighs.

"We should go pray." Carlsson is solemn.

"My parents are coming in," Jovi says, talking a mile a minute. "My sister wants to go to the Christmas market, and so does my aunt. My aunt likes to shop. My dad thinks she has a shopping addiction, but I don't think so. And so I want to leave early today. You think Coach will let us leave early?"

"I think you can probably just walk outta here whenever the hell you want," Eddie jokes.

A few yards away, Ellie is steaming. "I need you all to pay attention—"

I smirk behind my glove, chewing on my mouthguard as I slowly spin around.

"They have reindeer at the Christmas market—real reindeer," Jovi chatters, "and you can pet them and feed them and—oh!" Suddenly, he freezes. "I know this game. I know this game!" He slaps a glove over his mouth and holds up his hand.

I peer behind me. Ellie is standing there on center ice, calmly, quietly, one finger over her lips, the other hand raised, index finger up.

"What the fuck?"

Cookie claps his glove over his mouth, and his hand goes up.

She puts two fingers up.

The Finnish giant mimics the motion.

Bramms follows, then Ziggy, then more of the team does it, too, especially once Zayne snorts awake and puts his hand up.

"What are we, in kindergarten?" I cross my arms. "The groupthink is strong with you all." My voice sounds weird and awkward in the silence of the ice rink. I cringe like I've done something very wrong.

At that point, even Eddie unwillingly covers his mouth and puts his hand up.

I'm the last one standing.

The guys all give me ugly looks.

I hate being human, I decide, as I, too, finally cover my own mouth and put my hand up.

Ellie holds up the fifth finger. "My class," she says calmly but weirdly authoritatively. "We have a game tonight, so we're all going to pull together and—"

"I need to speak to the manager of this establishment!" a woman yells from across the ice.

Chapter 8

ELLIE

"**D**o one-touch drills," I instruct the players, shooting a quick pass to Fletcher.

I keep my attention partially on them as I skate over to head off the irate woman. From my time in early childhood education, I have eyes in the back of my head, and I am not turning my focus off the players while I address the angry mom in front of me.

"I'm Coach Clarke. How can I help you?"

Behind me, Bramms puts Cookie in a loose headlock. Cookie starts crying.

"We keep our hands to ourselves!" I bellow.

Bramms gives me a wide-eyed look and jumps back. "You saw that?"

"Yes, just like I saw you miss the net."

The guys snicker.

"I need to know what your safety protocols are," the mom is telling me.

"Ma'am, I think you might be in the wrong location. This is the Rhode Islanders team practice, not hockey camp. That's over at the community center and starts after school lets out…"

The pimple-faced boy next to her pulls down his scarf.

"Ah, our backup goalie is here. Welcome!"

"Braxton is a child," his mother snips.

"He's nineteen, Mrs. Beavers."

"A child!" she rails. "I need assurances that he's going to be looked after… never mind," she says, grabbing her son. "I can see that this team is mismanaged. I will not allow my baby to participate in this tomfoolery."

"Mrs. Beavers." I plaster on my best customer service face. "We need Braxton to play. He has to play. We need a second goalie."

"Of course he's playing," she harrumphs. "I'm going into the locker room with him to make sure he isn't kidnapped. Obviously, I'm going to have to be at every practice. I clearly can't trust you with my only son. He's so young."

The kid is six foot six and looks like he weighs a hundred pounds.

He's the backup—just the backup goalie, I internally chant. *My real goalie will be here soon.* I hope.

"Ma'am, you cannot go into the locker rooms with the players." I race after her.

"Then he won't play."

"Mom," the kid whines.

"I am your mother!" she thunders to Braxton.

I will be losing this battle.

"Fine, just put a sign up or something when you're in there." I sigh.

"How come she gets to go all Peeping Tom on the players," Granny Murray complains to me, "and I don't?"

"Gran, why are you still here?"

"I'm your equipment manager." She slaps her chest.

"No, you're not. I mean, just let me handle it." My eye is twitching again.

On the ice, the men have stopped doing the drill and are trying to stuff pucks down each other's pants.

"Saint Nick, give me strength."

Separate out the troublemakers. This would be easier if the captain wasn't hungover. "Jovi," I call to him. "Come here, please." I grab a bucket of pucks. "The rest of you— two-touch drills."

Jovi follows me like a puppy to the other side of the rink and watches excitedly as I scatter pucks around all over the ice.

"I'm timing you," I tell him. "All these pucks need to be in the net. Ready, set, go!"

I call Dana as I skate back over to the rest of the group.

"I thought there were no phones on the ice?" Fletcher is snarky.

"Go help the rookies with their backhand passes."

Dana is annoyed when she answers. "What?"

"Ready for the game?"

"I don't go to the games."

Fletcher is watching me. I point to the rookies. He ignores me.

"Well, we have one tonight, and we don't have an equipment manager or anything like that."

Silence from Dana.

"And I know you said hiring freeze, but someone has to manage sticks and sharpen skates and—"

"He ripped my jersey!" One forward skates over to me, fabric in hand. I peer at it while I talk to Dana. There's a hole in the collar of his jersey.

Dana sighs over the phone. "You can hire someone for minimum wage."

"Well, actually, the going rate for this position is—"

Dana hangs up.

"Trouble on Mount Olympus?" Fletcher drawls. The forwards snicker.

The guys obviously respond to Fletcher. He's setting the tone. And it's a tone of dismissive disregard for me.

"Done!" Jovi is panting. "I did it!"

"Okay, gather up the pucks. Our new backup goalie should be getting onto the ice soon."

"My jersey," the other forward begs, hopping on his skates.

I wave over Granny Murray. "You're getting a promotion."

"Hell yeah! And your dad thinks old people shouldn't work."

"In his defense, I think he just meant *you* shouldn't work since you got arrested for stealing at Trader Joe's."

"They were just throwing all that food away. It was still good!"

"Team! Meet our new equipment manager."

"Whoo! You studs are gonna have skates sharp enough to slice off the Direwolves' balls!" Granny Murray whoops.

"Hell yeah!" Several of the guys pump their fists.

"First order of business," I tell her. "Fletcher is our new associate captain. Let's get an *A* on his shirt."

"I—what?" Fletcher growls. "Candy Cane, I'm not taking any responsibility for any of these morons."

"Excuse me. He's allergic to nuts." Braxton's mother is slipping and sliding toward me on the ice.

"Ma'am, you cannot be on the ice."

"I birthed him for nineteen hours. You don't get to tell me where I can and can't be with my own son."

"We're about to do shooting drills."

Braxton settles in his crease. He looks the part, at least.

Zayne Murphy hacks up a lung, taps a puck with his stick, hauls back, and shoots the puck.

For a man that has been day drinking, still probably drunk from last night, he's surprisingly steady as he follows through on the slap shot.

"That's why he's Murphy's Law." The players are impressed as the shot rockets down the ice and flies right into the corner of the net.

In a delayed reaction, Braxton shrieks and jumps. "It almost hit me."

"It almost hit him! It almost hit my baby!" his mom yells, batting me with her handbag. "My husband is on the NHL board, and the chairman will hear about this."

"It's hockey," I say desperately. "Someone might get hurt."

Jovi one-touches Zayne another puck, and he buries it in the net. Which yields more yelping from Braxton.

"You have to try to catch it." I mime the motion. "Use your blocker."

Behind me, Fletcher is cursing. "We are so fucked tonight. So fucked."

Chapter 9
FLETCHER

"**G**reat practice, everyone. I'm seeing a lot of improvement," Ellie announces.

It's so obvious Ellie is lying. Her eye is twitching.

It was a terrible practice.

Harlowe is waiting by the tunnel, the good-smelling boxes by her side. "You get one corn muffin and one pig in a blanket," she announces. "One!" She slaps at Cookie.

"He shouldn't get any," Eddie complains as he accepts his snack. "He won't even play."

"You don't want to play?" Ellie coos to Cookie.

"I can't." The words are barely a whisper.

"I wish I could get paid a million dollars to sit on a bench," I announce loudly.

Cookie shrinks into himself. I almost feel bad.

Ellie gives me a disappointed look, which shouldn't bother me, but it does.

The Finnish giant brushes past me, gives Harlowe a brilliantly white smile—must be all the fermented fish bones they eat over there—says something that sounds like "eel guts" to her, and waggles his eyebrows suggestively.

Ellie's friend giggles and hands him two of the pigs in a blanket.

There's more unintelligible, garbled language from the Finn, then he's happily strutting to the locker rooms with more than his fair share of the snacks.

"This is so good," Jovi groans as I accept my snack from Harlowe.

"Aren't captains supposed to eat last?" Bramms smirks at me as he accepts his food on a napkin.

I glare down at the *A* that's sprouted up on my jersey then glare even more intensely when I bite into the sausage roll and it's somehow the best thing I've eaten all year.

As I take another bite, Ellie's up on me like a little Yorkie—like the one my mom used to have—barking at me. "You need to be nicer to Cookie. He's having a rough time."

"I'm not his mom."

"He looks up to you."

"He will be firmly disabused of that notion."

"You know, you could be a great NHL captain one day."

For a second, I believe her, like my childhood dreams of being the next Zayne Murphy could come true. Too bad that dream was dashed when I beat up that star NHL player's son in juniors five years ago and, instead of getting drafted, had to go into the military to avoid jail.

You're not an NHL player. You're a hired gun, I remind myself.

"Cookie needs to learn life sucks," I tell Ellie.

"We can make it suck a little less for our teammates." Then she's off, flitting between the players, offering kind words, praising them each for something they did in practice.

She's making them soft, I think then remind myself that our team literally cannot get any worse, so who cares.

Cookie's anxiously hanging back from the group. He looks young and lost.

Not my problem.

He gives me an anxious glance as I walk up, balancing on my skates. I nudge him with my glove. "You want my muffin? I don't really eat them."

"Oh yeah, thanks!" He gives me a small, nervous smile. "Do you really think we're going to lose tonight?"

We definitely will if you don't play. I bite back the words. "Probably. But you know," I coax, "you're good. If you play, we'd have a shot."

Cookie cringes.

"You don't have to help us win—just score a few goals. Everyone will see that you're as good as they promised. Hell, kid—" I lay a hand on his shoulder. "You were this year's first-round draft pick. You could get a trade deal out of it, go to a real team, have the star NHL career every kid who ever strapped on a pair of hockey skates dreams of."

Cookie looks down at the snacks in his hand. "I don't know if other teams will give you homemade snacks."

"Probably not, but they'll give you a Stanley Cup."

Jovi rushes over to me. "There's a woman in the locker room, and not a nice one."

"Out!" a heavyset, middle-aged woman screams when we try to head to the showers. "My baby, Braxton, needs to use the shower first."

Ellie elbows through the men huddled away from the locker-room door.

"Back!" the woman swings her designer purse. "Heathens!"

The purse whacks my elbow.

"Please don't hit my players," Ellie begs.

"We've got an injury!" her grandmother bellows, rushing over to me with ice packs.

"It just got my body armor—I mean, pads." I'm not supposed to have been in the military the last four years. According to my cover, I was playing hockey in Switzerland. But no one seems to have noticed, because Mrs. Beavers has pulled out pepper spray.

"And I want you to make sure my baby has ice time!" She berates Ellie.

"Mom, I don't wanna play! I told you I want to be a video game streamer." Braxton throws himself down on the bench.

Fucked. We are fucked, Bramms is mouthing while I try to keep Ellie between me and the large can of pepper spray.

"So we're not going to have a goalie?" Jonesy is freaking out.

"I was supposed to be the backup goalie. You said I didn't have to play," Braxton whines.

"Fletcher!" Ellie's using her teacher voice. "I need you to get dressed. You're coming with me, Mr. Associate Captain. We are going to bail our starter goalie out of jail."

I gesture helplessly to the woman. "Can the guys shower first, then Braxton can shower?"

"We have homeschooling co-op!" Her nostrils flare.

I strip off my gear in the hallway and leave it for the new equipment manager.

The old woman looks me up and down in my skintight underlayer and whistles appreciatively. "Nice work."

"Thanks." I wink at her.

"Granny!" Ellie hisses.

"Hey, I read a management book once that said compliments go a long way to getting people on your side," the old woman says.

"I won't file a sexual harassment lawsuit against you if you tell me what a nice ass I have." I smirk at Ellie.

"Your ass is going to be benched if you don't behave," Ellie warns.

"Yikes, Coach. Straight to the nuclear button, huh?" I pull on my sweatpants and shove my feet into my boots. "If you think a goalie with a criminal record is the thing to save this team, you're an even worse coach than I thought."

I hold on for dear life as Ellie whips the SUV around a corner, narrowly missing a stop sign.

"I think you were supposed to stop there."

"You're not from Maplewood Falls, are you?" she says as she floors the gas and runs through a yellow light right as it turns red.

Someone wearing an inflatable reindeer costume yells at her and gives her the finger. Ellie rolls down the passenger-side window to scream at the guy and almost runs into a car decorated to look like Santa's sleigh.

The cold air blasts in my face. "At least if I die, I won't have to play the Direwolves."

I roll up the window, or try to. Ellie rolls it back down. "I just think you could have showered before getting in my car."

"You don't like the smell of hot male?"

"Hockey players smell atrocious."

"You didn't need to bring me along. Are you scared of the big bad goalie?"

She gives me a blank look. "No."

"Of course you are."

She then gives me a patronizing look. "I see that you have never worked as a camp counselor or in any sort of early-childhood development. Staff are never alone with a child."

"So we are going to have two child-bride goalies? We're not just going to lose—we're going to be utterly humiliated. Are you part of the gambling ring?" I demand.

"You're my other adult in the room. You're the alternate captain."

The other adult.

I'm not an adult. I mean, Hudson's the adult. I'm just… I'm the guy who fucks up, who's too stupid to accept that his mom is a lowlife and puts his neck out for her over and over until he almost gets his head cut off.

I do owe Hudson, though, I think vaguely as I follow Ellie to the squatty cinderblock prison. I could be here right now, rotting away behind bars instead of playing for the NHL.

The police officer in the front office looks bored when we enter.

"Merry Christmas!" Ellie chirps. "I'm here to bail out a prisoner—Stonewall Renwick, goes by Ren?"

The guard grunts and types something on her computer.

"Um…" Ellie's fumbling to get her wallet out. "Do you take credit card?"

"Two-point-five percent fee for credit card transactions." The guard snaps her gum.

There's a loud buzzing noise, then a metal gate opens, and two heavyset police officers are dragging out a barefoot, shirtless man covered in tattoos—yes, on his face, too—and missing a few teeth. "And I'll take a piss on your mother's grave as soon as I get out of these handcuffs!" he hollers.

The cop unlocks the cuffs. Ellie's eye is twitching.

"Uh, the ankle bracelet..." Ellie points to the chunky bracelet. "We won't be able to get his hockey boots on, let alone any of the goalie pads."

"Where are my flip-flops?" Ren demands. "I have a constitutional right to have my things returned to me."

"Not me." The officer shakes his head. "You gotta talk to his parole officer."

"Great. Well, we'll talk to the equipment manager." Ellie sighs.

"Your grandmother, who I'm pretty sure I saw doing shots with Murphy's Law—that equipment manager?"

"It's a team effort," Ellie tells me through a gritted smile. "We're all trying to make sure that we win."

"Well, goddamn," the goalie drawls in a thick Southern accent and looks Ellie up and down. "The rumors are true. I heard the guard gossipin', but I ain't believe a word I heard."

"Watch your mouth," I snarl at him.

"The boyfriend?" He raises one eyebrow, causing the tattoos crawling all over his forehead to wrinkle.

"Alternate captain."

"Damn Yankee." He spits on the ground. "And a shitty hockey player too."

Fuck this guy.

"Guess this weather is a little different from Mississippi," Ellie says as Ren makes a big show of getting the door for her and letting it slam in my face.

"Aw, shucks, ma'am, my birth daddy's actually a damn Yankee. Piece of shit from upstate NYC." Ren walks barefoot through the snow next to Ellie. "He played for Boston back in the day. That's the only reason I took this goalie job. Free plane ticket up to New England, all so's I can take a shit on his front lawn. Got arrested for public indecency, public intoxication—oh, and I stole a police car."

Ellie giggles. Why the hell do women find men like him charming?

"Back seat, Yankee Doodle," he barks at me when I reach for the door.

"Fuck you." I shove him away from the front passenger door.

He shoves me back. Harder. "I'm important. You're just some shithead call-up from the minors."

"Fletcher, get in the back seat, please." Ellie gives me a stern look.

I hate that goalie.

Ellie beams at Ren as I crawl in the back of the SUV. "We brought you a snack!"

"Thanks, darlin'."

"The hell—don't talk to our coach like that."

The goalie turns in his seat, peers at me, then, quick as a snake, his arm darts out and snipes the sunglasses off my face. Strangling a curse, I scuttle back on the seat.

"Ooh!" Ellie squeals and giggles. "You're fast."

"You're fast," I mock.

"It's all the tattoos," Ren says in that molasses accent, slipping my shades on his face.

"I have tattoos too," I say before I can stop myself.

Ren turns, snaps off part of the snack Ellie brought with the side of his mouth that still has teeth, and looks at me over my sunglasses.

"You gonna do a show-and-tell, Yankee?"

I bare my teeth at him.

"Very intimidatin', cap-ee-tan."

"I can't wait to see what you do," Ellie gushes as she peels out of the parking lot, tires screeching as she skids on an ice patch. "We have a game tonight. You don't have to play if you're not up to it, of course, after your ordeal."

Ren stretches his leg out. "Just a little rusty. Been sitting in jail for two weeks, ain't been practicing. But I'll do it for you, darling."

"Good. We need you." Ellie blows out a breath.

"I heard we're up against the Direwolves. Fixing to get slaughtered, you reckon?"

"I have faith." She must, because she blows through another yellow light.

"Fuck faith. We need a goddamn Christmas miracle."

Chapter 10

ELLIE

"The snacks were a hit, at least," Harlowe says as we head into Costco. It's decorated for the holidays, and inflatable elves dressed in hockey gear hang from the rafters, slowly rotating.

Even our local Costco can't support the Rhode Islanders. The elves are dressed in the Direwolves' black and yellow.

"Costco. My happy place." I sigh happily.

"There's something about being able to buy two years' worth of cheese puffs that really reminds you of your place on this earth." Harlowe scans the offerings.

"Your mom says she needs more butter." Granny Murray grabs a cart. "She said not to tell your father that's what she puts in the mashed potatoes. No offense—I know you love him—but he's an idiot if he thinks mashed potatoes taste that good because of oat milk."

"Hockey players aren't known to be the brightest. Present company excluded." Harlowe nudges me.

I load several cases of Lunchables into the cart. "No offense taken. I'm not a hockey player."

"You kidding me? You looked great out there in practice. My ass never looked as good in leggings." Harlowe adds five gallons of milk to the buggy.

"It's not hard to look halfway decent when the guys are just phoning it in. I mean, it's like they've already given up."

"They are facing the Direwolves. It's not as bad as facing Seattle, but, like, they are going to get slaughtered. You have, like, three and a half decent forwards, one okay D-man, and a felon for a goalie."

"I really need that ankle bracelet off of him." I chew on my lip.

"Your equipment manager's got you." Granny Murray salutes.

"Legally, Gran. We have to do it legally," I beg as she heads off to the tool aisle.

Harlowe stacks two boxes of protein bars on the bottom of the cart.

"I think my dad is right. We're going to lose. Badly," I fret. "Geez, I mean, the guys weren't even paying attention when I was reviewing the plays. I don't think anyone's read the game notes, and I tried to get Ren to come to the rink for a quick goalie practice, but he just blew me a kiss and said he needed to nap and jerk off. I mean, God knows what he's been eating in prison, and he hasn't touched a puck in what, two weeks? I really shouldn't play him, but it's him or Braxton."

"And Braxton's mom."

I groan. "It's like being back at the daycare."

"That bitch never should have fired you."

"Her sorority sister complained about me. Of course she's going to side with her rich friend over me."

"Her little brat deserved to get punched in the face." Harlowe is emphatic. "He pulled that little girl's pants down. If it were me, I'd have taken his eye out with a crayon."

"I give it three days before Braxton's mom is trying to get me fired," I say with a sigh as I contemplate the oil drums of whey powder.

"So you are going to stay on as coach?" My cousin gives me a knowing smirk. "Your mom does want grandkids."

"Ugh, not you too. Hockey social media gossip accounts are all acting like I'm sleeping with the players."

"They're jealous. I mean, anyone would want to sleep with one of those guys."

"Some of them are children."

"Fletcher's not." Harlowe giggles.

I'm not thinking about Fletcher and the way my car still seems to smell like him. *There is something wrong with you if you think an unshowered hockey player smells nice.*

Not nice. Intriguing.

"We'll see how this game goes. I'll probably get run out of town after the historically bad loss." I toss a marked-down advent calendar in my basket.

"Don't you already have an advent calendar?"

"It's on sale, and sometimes I can't wait for the next day to get a treat. I need days' worth of surprise chocolate at once."

"The Rhode Islanders haven't been losing as bad since they called up Fletcher," Harlowe reminds me as we make our way to checkout.

"He's played two games, and they lost by five points, but the Rhode Islanders haven't gone against the Direwolves."

I wince when the cashier rings up my purchases. Not that I was making that much money at the daycare, but at least we got reimbursed for snacks and treats and whatnot for the kids.

"Oof," Harlowe says as I swipe my credit card. "And to think we all wanted to have big families. We do not have big-family jobs or big-family money."

"Or big-family, high-income husbands."

"Though," Harlowe says as we head to the food court, "now that you're high up in the NHL, you could get a rich hockey player."

"The highest-paid players are the Finnish guy, who doesn't speak English; Zayne Murphy, who really needs a twenty-four seven nurse; and Cookie, and I already have two little brothers—I don't need another."

"There's Fletcher." Harlowe waggles her eyebrows. "He's hot. And he smells good."

"Not good." *Intriguing.* "He's a dick. And a problem. He's making an already-impossible situation even worse. He's fighting me every step of the way." I take a bite of my hot dog. It crackles under my tongue, the mustard spicy on the roof of my mouth. I close my eyes and sink into the bliss that is cheap grilled meat.

"You oughtta be ashamed of yourself," a woman says shrilly behind me. I almost choke on my hot dog as I turn to see who is yelling at me.

I gulp down my Diet Coke as Harlowe stands up. "Ashamed?" my friend demands.

"You stole that coaching job."

"Stole from who?" I cough.

"You conned your way into that job," the woman rails at me. "You're not qualified to coach an NHL team. You slept your way to the top."

"It's the worst damn team in the NHL. If she's sleeping her way to the top, you'd think she'd be in NYC fucking her way through the Direwolves," Harlowe yells at her.

"You're just jealous, Moira," Granny Murray hollers at the woman. "You think your precious son, who lives in your basement, may I add—"

"Gran, I live at home. Maybe don't throw stones from glass houses and all that," I mumble.

"He couldn't even make it onto the junior A-team, and you think he was going to be a coach? He can't even find his own dick under his foreskin."

"You witch! He'd be better than her!"

We are drawing a crowd. I recognize several people from Mom's book club.

"Ellie!"

"Hi, Mrs. Harrison." My mouth is dry. "How's your cat doing? My mom said you had to take her to the emergency vet."

"Yes, she ate a sock, but all is well now! I'm bringing my famous peppermint bark by—let your mom know."

"That's perfect. We're having family over."

"...a bum," Granny Murray is railing. "You wiped his ass up till he was age seven then never taught him to do it himself. You were co-sleeping with him when he was a teenager."

The woman huffs. Her shopping buddies glare at me and Gran. "I know you don't belong there," she says, "and you're going to lose that game tomorrow and ruin those poor boys' futures. Then everyone else will know it too."

Chapter 11
FLETCHER

I stand half hidden in shadows on the top tier of seats in the Holbrook Enterprises Stadium, watching the Manhattan Direwolves swagger in for their pregame practice.

When I was a kid and I dreamed of being in the NHL, these guys were who I wanted to be. Specifically, someone like Ryder O'Connell. He came into the league in a roundabout way but is now considered one of the best players of his generation: Fast. Acute hockey IQ. Handsome. Sincere. Smart. Good on camera. Team player. "Leadership" is what hockey players spew out whenever they're asked to describe him. That or "aura."

The whole Direwolves team is god tier. Even the coaches. Their coaching team is basically the USA National coaching team.

I know I'm not supposed to be watching as their coach calmly but assuredly calls out drills and the guys react like they're trained military operatives or something. Everyone locked in, focused.

"Man. I remember those days. The world at your feet... when we were gods..." Zayne lets out a belch and takes a swig of vodka.

The noise ricochets around the empty stadium, and I drag him back into the shadows as the Direwolves all look up at the stands as one.

The media's already lining up. I grab Zayne's now-empty bottle and toss it into a trash can before the media can get photos of him. He's obviously drunk and gonna cost us the game, but shit, he's my childhood hero. I can't let him go out like this.

"Everyone wants to see the NHL's first female coach lose her first game," Eddie remarks when I shove Zayne into the locker room and head to the meal spread to get him something to soak up the liquor. In his prime, he would have been the terror of the Direwolves. Now? Maybe he'll be a puck sponge.

"Fuck off, Eddie."

"Yeah, fuck off, Eddie." Ren swaggers into the locker room. He's barefoot in a wifebeater and cutoff jean shorts, the ankle monitor big and bulky on his leg. He flops down next to Jonesy, props his dirty foot up on my bag, stuffs something in his mouth, and licks the grease off his fingers.

I glare down at him. "What the hell are you eating?"

"Your dick."

"Did you get McDonald's? We're already gonna lose— you can't be in a fast-food coma in the net," I bitch at him.

"I want chicken nuggets," two of the rookies complain. "That's not fair."

Ren grabs my water bottle and squirts it in his mouth. "It ain't chicken nuggets, kids, it's a bagel pizza. I guess this is what your people eat up here. Not as good as a biscuit and gravy."

"The fuck—"

"Pizza!"

I stalk into the kitchen after the rookies.

"Are we ready for a snack?" A pleasant-looking woman beams at me. She looks unsettlingly familiar.

"My daughter told me that you all are supposed to eat before a game." Ellie's mom. *Trina* is the name embroidered on the apron. "These are what I always make my boys. I took some to the Direwolves too. They have fancy nutritionists, and my boys said they wouldn't eat these—can you believe it? But you look like you want some." She holds up the pan.

My stomach grumbles. "It's not in the meal plan. Did the nutritionist okay this?" I know it sounds sour and ungrateful, but geez, she might as well serve us beer and pretzels.

Ellie rushes in, red-faced. "The nutritionist quit." The door slams behind her, cutting off yells from the media. "Mom, healthy—I said healthy!"

"It's got protein, and that's real tomato sauce—home-made, not ketchup like Hilda puts on her pizzas. And she wonders why her children never come home to see her." Trina is offended.

"Mom," Ellie complains as her mom tries to scrub at her face.

"You have to go on camera. I want you to look your best, snickerdoodle."

"So you have your whole family working here, Coach Candy Cane—or should I say, Coach Snickerdoodle?"

Ellie glares at me.

"I'm a volunteer," Trina says happily. "I'm so excited to be a team mom again."

"It's temporary, Mom, temporary until Dana removes the hiring freeze."

"Paid nutritionists won't make team snacks with love." Ellie's mom loads up a plate with steaming bagel halves oozing cheese and pepperoni grease.

Jovi and Bramms come in drooling, followed by Cookie, who is immediately babied by Ellie's mom, a napkin quickly tucked around his neck.

"Is she hand-feeding him?" I whisper to Ellie.

She grimaces. "You don't have to eat that. I have protein bars."

"Do I want a bitter-tasting, freeze-dried protein bar?" I muse. "Nah. Screw it. I'm about to be slaughtered by the Direwolves in front of a crowd of twenty thousand plus the millions and millions of people watching to see if a girl can, in fact, coach in the NHL."

Ellie claps a hand to her mouth. "I think I'm gonna be sick."

I take a bite of the bagel as she races off to find a bathroom. "All the bathrooms are male only," I call after her. "You might need to pee in a—goddamn, that's fucking good." After years of military meals then whatever protein-rich slop the nutritionists prepared for us, it has been a while since I've had a good meal.

Ellie's mom beams as the team stuffs our faces.

"Cheese," Ziggy groans. "I need more women in my life."

"Can we have pot roast for the next meal?" Carlsson begs.

"With mashed potatoes," Jonesy begs.

I should protest, should insist on chickpea pasta with a sauce made out of bean-and-chicken paste. Instead, I stuff another bagel in my mouth, the hot cheese singeing the roof of my mouth.

"You know what?" Bramms says around the bread and cheese. "I have a really good feeling about this game. It might be the grease-and-sodium high, but I think we're gonna win this one."

"Yeah, we fucking got this." Jonesy downs more pizza.

"I made a Milky Way bar cake for dessert," Ellie's mom calls.

"Chocolate!" the rookies cheer.

"No." Ellie rushes back into the room, her hairline damp like she's splashed water on her face. "No cake. Brush your teeth then go get dressed. We have a game."

Ellie's mom sneaks us slices of cake while Ellie and Harlowe try to manhandle Zayne into his uniform. Ellie's also trying to stuff food down his throat without choking him.

Her grandmother pulls up a chair in front of Ren and pulls out a hacksaw and an electric drill and starts going to town on the ankle monitor.

"Gran, delicately, delicately—we can't—" The thing starts beeping angrily.

The elderly woman takes out a mallet and smashes it to pieces on the floor. "Fuck the government."

"No, no, no!" Ellie tries to piece the ankle monitor back together. "My goalie cannot go back to prison. We need him."

"She needs me." Ren waggles his eyebrows at me, one of which looks like it was split open and superglued back together crooked.

"We haven't actually seen him play," I say snidely. Ren pulls out what looks like a prison shank.

Ziggy yanks me away. "We can't lose you, man. He's good, he's all good," Ziggy says to Ren.

Granny Murray dusts off her hands. "I have a gun in my purse. The feds show up, I'll hold them off."

Ellie's mother appears in the doorway with more slices of cake. "Your dad's cousin Beater is on the parole board, Ellie. I'll bake him a Victoria sponge cake and get that sorted right out." She beams at us. "Oh, I'm so happy to be involved with a hockey team again!"

Bramms helpfully takes the tray of cake slices she's carrying so she can wrap Ellie into a big hug.

"Mom, Mom, *Mooom!*"

I take another piece. If I'm going to die in humiliation, at least it will be hyped up on sugar.

"I can't play," Braxton whines in his oversized goalie gear. "I'm allergic to dairy. I didn't get a snack. Didn't my mom tell you I have a dairy allergy?"

"I pulled your file—you don't have a dairy allergy. But," Ellie adds, "that's okay. You can sit on the bench with Cookie and cheer on your team."

The Finnish giant eats his cake in two massive bites, says something in Scandinavian, then slams his helmet on his head.

It's the chocolate or the sugar or the carbs, but I'm feeling pumped as Ellie tells us to gather around.

"Story time," she sings. Cookie and the other rookies flop down on the floor at her feet. She holds up a book.

"Wait, we're actually having story time?" I scoff.

"We're actually looking at the plays. I've been watching tapes of the Direwolves' games, and here's how we're going to win."

It's so matter-of-fact. She has this soothing but authoritative way of talking—it lulls me back to elementary school, when school was the escape from home and my teacher Mrs. Smith would let you select a prize if you answered a question correctly.

The plays are good. Not overly complicated. Thoughtful. And well drawn. All my other coaches—not just the one in jail—would just scribble wildly on a board while yelling angry and conflicting information at us then wonder why we didn't know what we were doing on the ice.

I perk up when Ellie starts giving the line assignments of which players are going to be on the ice together. I'm on a line with Zayne Murphy and the Finn. My childhood self is freaking out right now.

"Captain," she says to Zayne after we all have our line assignments. "How about a speech?"

Zayne hauls himself up then immediately doubles over and pukes.

"Bad omen. Bad, bad, bad," Jonesy mutters and clutches his lucky bobblehead.

Ellie's eye is twitching as her grandmother pulls out a mop bucket.

"I'll make him some mint tea." Her mother bustles off.

Granny Murray tips Zayne over, practically holding him up. She's surprisingly strong for an old woman.

"Oof." Jovi makes a face when the old woman sticks her finger down Zayne's throat. I curse as he pukes the rest of his dinner into the bucket.

Zayne shakes his head. "Pucks in net, boys," he slurs. "We got this. Watch out for Jagr—he favors his right leg. Keep him on the boards, and we'll get shot after shot when his line is on the ice." He sucks down the water Ellie hands him then splashes some on his face.

"Jagr hasn't played for the Direwolves in five years," Bramms hisses at me as Ellie shoos us down the tunnel to the ice.

Ellie is excited, practically jumping up and down next to me as I stand there watching Jovi try to coax Cookie onto the ice. "It's your first NHL game as an alternate captain!" she says. Perched on the blades of my skates, I look down at her. I can't tell if she's being condescending, but she looks genuinely excited and happy for me. "Enjoy it! Have fun! You're a pro hockey player."

She grabs my wrist. I can barely feel her fingers through the padded wrist guard and the heavy fabric of the jersey, but they're there.

I'm an alternate captain on an NHL team. Exhilaration, spurred on by the sugar and caffeine and carbs, surges through me as I step out onto the ice with Zayne and the Finn and the two D-men.

Ren strides by in the bulky goalie gear. He bangs his stick on my ass as he passes. "Keep those fuckers away from my net, Yankee Doodle, or I'm gutting you like a hog."

The chocolate high wears off as the crowd cheers while we do our warm-ups. The ref's waiting with Ryder O'Connell, captain of the Direwolves. Zayne is barely with it. Probably can't even write his own name. The Finn narrows his eyes at me. I give a helpless shrug as his icy blue eyes flick to the ref and Ryder waiting.

I skate over. Ryder nods, clearing his throat.

"Sorry," I tell him. "Our captain's trying to get in the zone."

Zayne looks like he's falling asleep on his stick.

Ryder gives me an earnest smile, then his face goes serious. "I think it's admirable that you all have a female coach. I know a lot of girls are really excited to see history being made tonight." He really is a fucking Boy Scout. "Now," he adds, "I told my team that I don't want to hear any nasty comments about Coach Clarke. We don't speak that way about women on my team. And you tell me if you hear anything from any of my players, and I'll deal with them." He's nice, but there's steel in his voice.

"Sure, man—I mean…" I try to match his professionalism. "Yessir, I appreciate it."

"And I hear you're the league's newest alternate captain. Congratulations." He takes off his glove, shakes my hand and everything.

Then he proceeds to beat the ever-loving shit out of us.

Chapter 12
FLETCHER

"We're only down by three goals," Ellie says brightly as we file into the locker room after the end of a brutal first period.

Ren grabs me by the collar of my jersey and shoves me against the wall, holding up his stick to my neck. "I thought I told you to keep them pucks away from my goddamn net." Then he shoves me away, making me stumble on my skates.

"You made some amazing saves," Ellie gushes to him.

"Be nice if someone could score," Ren snarls in my direction.

Granny Murray buzzes around, replacing skate blades as we suck down water and protein bars.

I'm gassed. I didn't know it was possible to sweat that much.

Ellie's at the whiteboard. Other coaches usually have footage playing and are scribbling nonsense on the whiteboard as they ineffectively describe plays and scream at the players.

"Offense," Ellie says as she draws perfect little dashed lines to show how she wants us to pinch the D and create more offensive opportunities.

I peer at the whiteboard. "Is that a butterfly?"

"Let's raise our hands," Ellie says like it's an automatic script that she can't help.

Jovi raises his hand. "Is that a butterfly?"

"Oh," Ellie says brightly, "it does look like a butterfly. Good job, Jovi! But-ter-fly," she sounds out the word.

He beams.

What the fuck, Bramms mouths next to me.

"Ooh." Ellie looks at the clock. "It's time to play!" She claps her hands. "Line up, single file, hands to yourselves."

This chick is insane.

I cut forward in line.

"Hey, no cutting in line!" one of the D-men complains when I jump in front of him. I shoot him an ugly look, and his mouth snaps shut.

"Fletcher," Ellie begins.

I grab her arm, shifting my stick as my teammates file past me onto the ice. "I don't know what the fuck kind of hippie, gentle-parenting nuttiness is going on here, and I don't care. We are losing. Butterflies and snack time aren't gonna save us. You gotta make Cookie play," I hiss to Ellie.

She gives me a helpless gesture. "He's traumatized."

"Cookie," I snarl at the kid. He squeaks then runs to hide in the players' bench.

"Stop it," Ellie snaps at me. "He will play when he's ready. I think he needs some therapy. Zayne," she calls to my once and future idol. "Dig deep to win that face-off."

"Are you freaking kidding me?" I force through gritted teeth, mindful of the cameras hovering around us. "Zayne can't play. I saw your grandmother give him a shot of tequila."

"I can get another three minutes out of him." Ellie is stubborn.

"Whatever, Coach." Disgusted, I hop over the boards onto the ice.

Zayne reeks of alcohol next to me as we take the ice—it's leaking out of his pores. The ref raises the puck, and Zayne almost pitches into Ryder O'Connell as he leans forward for the face-off, righting himself at the last moment.

Fucked. We are fucked.

Ryder wins the face-off. Again.

We're on the defensive. Even with the tequila surging through his veins, Zayne is still one of the better players on the ice on our side, at least.

Which is truly a testament to how piss-poor the Rhode Islanders are.

Against all odds, Zayne gets the puck away from one of the Direwolves forwards. He surges forward.

He's doing it. It's like when I was a kid watching the Olympics—Zayne Murphy with the puck, racing to the net.

Except Ryder's there somehow, materializing in front of him. He does this little stutter step. Zayne's reflexes just aren't there, and he loses control of the puck.

I skate backward, trying desperately to stay up ahead of Ryder, keeping my body between him and the net as he zips up to it, cutting through our defense like they're peewee hockey players trying to poke check the puck away from him.

He's gonna fake it. He's gonna fake it, I tell myself. *I've watched him play. He's gonna fake it.*

He fakes it.

I'm ready for him, collecting his pass with my stick, trying to manage it and head for the boards. But three Direwolves are on me, banging into me, trying to knock me off-balance. I dig in, but I can't hold onto it. It's three-on-one because Ryder actually has teammates who have his back, because the Direwolves are a real team.

The puck gets passed back to Ryder. I'm not fast enough to leap across to block Ryder's shot.

It goes in the net right over Ren's shoulder.

Ren's screaming at me as the goal horn blares and lights flash, making me wince. "You should have just stayed the fuck on the other side of the blue line. You blocked my sight. This is your fucking fault!" He throws his glove at me. "Goddamn motherfucking—"

I skate away from him, breathing hard.

"You can't be in here, Mom," Ellie is saying when I hop the boards into the bench. Is she even paying attention to the game?

Her mother hands me a bottle of some sports drink with Ryder O'Connell's face on it. "I'm just trying to be helpful. You don't have any assistant coaches," Ellie's mom argues.

"You're not even wearing the right jersey."

"I have to support your brothers."

"Mom—"

I snarl at Cookie, and he scoots all the way down the bench so I can collapse and choke down the cool liquid.

I stare blankly over the ice as the Direwolves score two goals in quick succession. The numbers tick up: 0-8. And we have thirty-seven minutes to go.

"Did you just put in all forwards?" I snap at her when I see her send in the next line. "We need to be playing defense. What are you doing?"

"Offense is the best defense."

I will one of the giant inflatable Christmas decorations hanging from the roof to crash down, smother us, and put us all out of our misery.

Ryder and his team score another goal.

"I remember my first NHL game," Zayne slurs next to me as he sips from a bottle.

"Is that—did someone give him more alcohol?" I yell.

"Goddamn it, Gran, I told you," Ellie hisses as the goal horn sounds again.

"There's no mercy rule in the NHL, is there?" Jonesy chews on his mouthguard.

"No," I say, disgusted. "The whole country is going to watch as the score goes up. It's going to be twenty to nothing at this rate."

"… won that game." Zayne's head nods as he talks.

"Do you think you can play?" Ellie asks Zayne.

"Are you freaking kidding me? You know who needs to play? *Cookie*," I demand.

The rookie cries into his glove.

Ellie reshuffles the lines again and sends out the next wave of victims…

Who are not facing Ryder or any of his linemates because Ryder has pulled all their star players off the ice and is sending out the rookies. They can barely stand on their skates. They stare up at the ceiling and are out of position, and yet still, somehow, we cannot score.

"We're losing against that?" Bramms cries, throwing his helmet to the ground.

"Bramms, you and Heikkiläinen join with Carlsson's line."

"Who?" Bramms squints.

Ellie clicks her tongue. "You've been on this team for two months now. You need to know everyone's name."

"Fuck their names. Get out on the ice," I scream at them.

The Finnish giant is, I assume, cursing both my ancestors and my future descendants like I'm the problem here. Meanwhile, Zayne, the actual fucking captain, is drinking again, supplied by an elderly woman.

"Gran, stop giving him alcohol. He has a problem." Ellie tries to fight the elderly woman for her thermos.

Zayne makes a gurgling noise, pitches back, and falls backward off the bench. Ellie and I both swear and grab him, hauling him back upright.

"Why did you let him drink?" I scream at her. "Why are you letting your grandmother serve hard liquor?"

"I thought he was done for the night." The elderly woman shrugs.

"No!" I bellow at her.

"Hold onto your nipples, hot stuff. I'll get him rearing and ready." Granny Murray starts digging in her fanny pack. "I got Adderall, I got cocaine, I got—"

"Oh God," Ellie moans.

"Can I have some chocolate cake?" Cookie asks.

"No!" we both shout at him.

Third period's not much better. Actually, scratch that—third period's an epic disaster and will go down in NHL history as such.

Zayne's passed out on the floor.

"You should have just let the old woman give him cocaine," Jonesy tells me as we line up for face-off.

I don't even want to look up at the scoreboard to see how badly we're losing.

One goal. Dear Santa, all I want for Christmas—please, just one goal. One. I don't need to win. I just need a goal. Not a Christmas miracle, just a Christmas pat on the back.

The Direwolves rookie in front of me has his game face on. I lean in, set my legs for the face-off just like I used to do when I pretended to be Murphy's Law way back in Juniors.

I win the face-off. The puck shoots to Carlsson, who's ready. He backhand passes it to the Finn, who's *there* then out in front, and I'm waiting, collecting the puck effortlessly on my skate.

It's suddenly like I haven't been playing the last hour. There are rockets on my skates as I head to the goal. I can hear Ellie cheering. The crowd roars. I can taste it—my first NHL goal. I crossover, sweep the puck, and—

The goalie comes out and poke checks me, and I go sprawling, tumbling and colliding, dazed, into the net, my back slamming into the pole.

Right.

Just because the Direwolves took out their star forwards doesn't mean they're letting us win. They left their iron curtain of a Czech goalie in the net.

He yells at me in guttural Eastern European language while I try to untangle myself so I can help my team so the Direwolves won't—

"GOAL!"

"Dammit. *Fuck*." I smash my stick on the net then dance back before the goalie can go after me.

"Fletcher." Ellie's calling me back. I ignore her.

"Dude," Jovi tells me as I skate back to the red line. "You're not on my line."

"There are no lines," I snap at him, taking my spot at center ice. "She's just randomly pulling names out of a hat. She doesn't know what she's doing."

"*Fletcher Sullivan.*" She's using that teacher voice. Everything in me is screaming to obey, to go back to the box like a good little boy.

"I want my goal." Snarling, I set my legs for the face-off.

The ref seems confused then raises the puck.

"Fletcher," Ellie is yelling, "you will not be getting a sticker today."

"Ooh!" Eddie snickers to the right of me. "Fletcher's not getting his dick sucked after this."

"Your coach is sucking your dick?" the Direwolves rookie yelps, half standing up just as I turn to lay into Eddie—

Which is bad because I clip the Direwolves rookie in the face with my stick as I whip around to attack my defenseman.

The baby-faced rookie stumbles back, bleeding, red dripping onto his white uniform.

"Ah, shit, kid, I'm real—"

The wind and all my ribs are knocked out of me as a huge Direwolves D-man clears like twenty feet of ice in half a second and launches into me.

"Fight! Fight! Fight!" the crowd chants as the huge Midwesterner pummels me.

Zayne, who either can hold his liquor way better than I can or who did actually partake in that cocaine that Granny Murray was offering, leaps over the boards onto the ice. "Get him on the ropes, Fletch," he hollers, skating toward me.

The rest of the team hesitate a beat. They know that leaving the bench to fight is breaking a cardinal sin and gets you ejected from the game. But Murphy's Law is rushing into the fight, and by God, they're following their captain.

Which is good because now it's two-on-one, and I just took a glove to the nose, and there's blood in my eyes.

Zayne roars as he collides with the second D-man about to kick me in the face with a sharp skate. *Wow, he's still got it!* My inner child is oddly excited as both teams clear the bench while the crowd roars their approval.

The Finnish giant grabs up a forward who's bear-hugging Jovi and ragdolls him. The refs blow their whistles, and the linemen try to separate the crush of violent players. Eddie is swinging blindly.

I grab one of the forwards around the legs who's going after Zayne. I gotta hand it to my old hero—no one gets him on the ground. His legs are tree trunks. Zayne grabs one of the D-men pummeling me by his calf and physically picks him up then body-slams him on the ice.

Ren is in the swarm with his oversized goalie stick, slicing through the players. The Direwolves Czech monster then knocks into the fray. All the players scramble away as the two huge goalies muscle through the crush, trying to get at each other.

"Fucking communist," Ren screams as he goes after the Czech goalie.

"*Goalie fight!*" The announcers are ecstatic.

"Fight! Fight! Fight!" the crowd screams as the goalies circle each other then charge.

Ren takes a punch to the side of the head then headbutts the other goalie, who slugs him in the mouth. Teeth fly. The linemen jump in to separate the two men as they scream obscenities in their mother tongues.

It's chaos.

Ren accidentally belts a lineman in the groin, and the rest of us players use the excuse to go after each other. More refs swarm up, screaming about game misconduct penalties. The coaches sling obscenities at their players while the goalies threaten to shoot each other in the parking lot.

We're all finally herded to be crammed into the penalty box and have to sit there, bleeding and bruising, as the goalies are sent back to their nets to flip each other off while the clock counts down to the end of the game.

Jovi's pressed right up against me, and Cookie is half sitting in my lap. Bramms's crotch is near my head. The entire team's crammed into a penalty box designed to hold seven max. The crowd cheers and sings fight songs.

"It's nice to play in a full stadium," Jovi says happily.

"Shut the fuck up." I clutch my ribs and skate back to the tunnel to ecstatic cheers from the crowd when the timer runs out and the refs let us out of the penalty box.

Ellie is in the tunnel talking to the sports media scrum when we leave the ice bleeding and disgraced. She speaks rapidly over the roar of the crowd, her hands flapping.

My nose is still dripping blood, which runs over my upper lip to spatter on my uniform. I'm pretty sure I'm going to need stitches on my eye, and, oh yeah—we lost. Big fucking time.

And Ellie's what? Talking about putting pucks in net next game?

"Next game?" I scream at her. The cameras swing onto me. I wipe at my bloody face with my jersey. "I am not playing another game with you as the fucking coach. You suck. You're a terrible coach."

"Really? Because your last one is in jail," she screeches back at me.

"We never lost this badly with him."

"Maybe it's your fault. You just got called up from the minors, and you're still playing like it."

"Don't put this on me, *Coach*," I spit. "You made terrible calls. I didn't have the same line the entire night."

"I have a method." She clamps her mouth shut. "I'm not arguing with you. Go to the locker room. We can talk about this later."

That sets me off. The fury pulses in tandem with my throbbing eye.

I grab her. "You don't get to dismiss me like I'm one of your preschool children. And yeah, I did look you up, and you're not qualified to be here."

"Really? You want to have this fight here?" she snaps. "That's fine. Let's fucking go." She pulls out her clipboard.

"You missed not one, not two, but three easy shots on goal. I kept changing the lines around because I was trying to find the best player who would keep up with you because I erroneously thought that was the reason you kept sitting on the puck—because you needed a better winger. I admit I was wrong. It wasn't them. It was you. You're the problem. Word to the wise: if you're gonna be a puck hog, at least get the puck in the fucking net. My grandmother could have done better."

"Your grandmother does cocaine, so that's not surprising. Stuff me full of amphetamines, and I'll be all over this ice." I spit blood.

"Second, you ignored all of my plays."

"I'm not making the butterfly play," I say stubbornly as her lip curls.

"The Direwolves overly rely on that diamond formation. You need to push through then back pass to Ziggy, Jovi, or literally any of the other people I put on your right wing and cut away. You could have scored. You had several chances that if you had just listened to me—"

"I'm not listening to a crazy person."

"*Third*," Ellie screeches over me, "you disobeyed a direct command. I ordered you to get off the ice. Even if you hadn't started that fight, you were too spent to perform an effective play anyway and would have cost us another goal."

I don't even tell her that the fight was an accident. "I'm not your dog on a leash."

"No shit. You can't even come when you're told. Now go to the locker room."

"Uh-oh, sounds like a lovers' spat," some doughy hockey commentator who barely bag skated when he was in rec league chortles. And now he's making me feel like I have to defend her.

Fuck it. I'm itching for a fight.

"The fuck did you say?" I turn on the man.

He doesn't have the God-given sense to shut up. Chucklehead says, "There are rumors that she's sleeping with players." He yelps when I buck at him.

"*Sleeping with players*." My fists clench in my heavy gloves.

I look down at Ellie. Her face is pinched.

"Funny. I didn't get my dick sucked today."

"Yeah, because you lost the game," she snaps.

"So if I win?" I let the words hang there.

"Well, that honor should go to the captain, and I don't know if you're captain material." She looks me up and down, chin set stubbornly.

I'm going to punch someone. Probably one of the media idiots with their cameras in my face.

"No way would anyone want to be with her," I tell them. "She's argumentative. Stubborn."

"I'm stubborn? Mr. Can't Follow Simple Directions."

"You have your whole fucking family working here, princess."

"You liked my mom's cake. You had two pieces. Yes, I saw that."

"You feed your players cake?" one of the reporters asks.

"Why, you want some, fucking bag of milk?" I grab the reporter's shirt collar, lift him up in the air.

"Sullivan, now that you've suffered one of the worst losses in the history of the NHL," a reporter asks as the crowd around us, "do you think hiring a female NHL coach was a terrible idea?"

"Leading question much?" I spit. I toss the other reporter away.

"I think you're putting words in his mouth." Suddenly, Ryder O'Connell's there like a poster boy for the NHL.

No helmet hair. The golden boy is perfect.

While my face looks like I lost a fight with a garbage truck, Ryder only has a bloody scrape under one eye, looking like he's out of Central Casting for a movie or something.

"I think I can speak for the Direwolves when I say this is the most exciting game we've played all season." The crowd is still roaring around us as Ryder speaks calmly. "Usually, after a Rhode Islanders game, the anemic crowds can't wait to go home. Now they're all here, still excitedly soaking in the atmosphere. We haven't had an NHL bench clearing," Ryder says, brilliant blue eyes sparkling like glaciers in the stadium lights, "in what, a decade? And Ellie Clarke makes one happen. Watch—you'll see viewer numbers skyrocket for the next few games. This is a great opportunity to bring new fans into the sport."

He gives a brilliant smile.

"Everyone's fired up about hockey, and we have you to thank, Coach. Can't wait until our next match. See you in Manhattan." He shakes Ellie's hand. She seems a little dazed by the handsome captain.

I prod my teeth. They're all there.

My pride's not.

That's the thing about Ryder O'Connell. He smiles as he flays you alive then says sorry for the beatdown.

I stalk down the hall, slam my way into the locker room. Ellie's mom bustles around with ice and a first aid kit, trying to stem the bleeding. Granny Murray shoves a tampon up my nose.

Jovi bats the little blue string. "It's like a mouse."

I scream as Granny Murray uses the heel of her hand to push my busted nose back in place. "I bet he's glad I brought alcohol now." She waves the half-empty bottle of tequila at me.

Zayne is congratulating the rookies. "Your first NHL fight!"

I gulp tequila, letting it numb the pain as Ellie's mom tapes an ice pack in a paper towel to my head.

I breathe through my mouth as Ellie knocks on the locker room door.

"Are you decent?"

"Unfortunately not," Granny Murray calls.

Chapter 13

ELLIE

Still hyped from the fight, the rookies chatter excitedly, comparing battle scars. Granny Murray yanks the tampons out of Fletcher's nose. He bites back a curse.

I peer at him, inspecting the handsome but bruising face. He glares up at me with slate-gray eyes. Fletch looks like he's going to murder me.

"You still have all your teeth. That's something..." More glaring.

"I'm trying to figure out how to work the X-ray machine so I can see if his ribs are shot or not," Granny Murray announces.

"Do you need help with your skate?" I start to bend down to untie his shoes.

"I'm fine," Fletcher hisses out and turns away from me.

He's having big feelings. I step back to give him some space.

I open the cooler. "I just want to tell everyone what a fantastic job they did tonight. This is the most fire and passion I've seen from this team all season. You should be proud of yourselves—you left it all on the ice. And we're going to win the next game."

"Ren didn't—he still has some teeth left," Ziggy jokes.

"I got a real good dentures guy," Granny Murray tells him. "I'll hook you up."

He wordlessly fist-bumps her.

"For an after-game snack, we have Lunchables," I tell them.

The rookies cheer. The older guys smirk. I've interviewed them after losses before, and they weren't ever this amped up. There was a lot of quiet dejection. But now they're keyed up as I pass out the snacks, ripping off the plastic.

"Can we have pizza Lunchables next time?" one of the rookies begs.

"No, the nacho ones."

"Those are only for winners," Bramms drawls at them.

"We're never going to win." The rookies are sad.

"Don't bet against hockey."

Jovi piles up his Lunchables, making a megastack of crackers, the little pressed turkey rounds, and the squares of American cheese, and stuffs it all in his mouth and chews.

The Finn crushes up the container, dumps the entire contents into his mouth, and chews.

The rookies are very carefully assembling their crackers and taking pictures of each other eating them.

Fletcher slowly peels back the plastic. I itch to peel it off for him.

"He can do it himself," I whisper.

Fletcher glares at me. He doesn't eat the crackers—just the cheese and meat.

"Can I have your crackers?" The rookies crowd around him.

"No, I want them."

"That's Fletcher's food." I try to shoo them away.

Fletcher shifts. "Share it," he says gruffly, shoving the container at them.

"So you're staying on as the coach?" one of the rookies asks me.

"Of course she is," Carlsson scoffs.

"Yay!" they cheer. "Can we make pregame meal requests?" They raise their hands. "I want pancakes."

"Protein," Fletcher barks.

"Err—"

Fletcher perks up when Dana Holbrook walks in.

"Now, that was a hockey game, boys!" She acts like she's walking down a catwalk, not into a dank locker room.

"I've just gotten calls from several big advertising agencies. Seems the brawls attracted a lot of eyeballs, and that means dollar signs. Ellie"—she addresses me—"I gave them your and Harlow's emails. I know you have her helping you on the PR side. Don't sell them any advertising for less than ten million."

Fletcher is watching her like a starving man.

Of course he is. Dana is the perfect woman—tall, thin, athletic but still curvy. She could put any *Sports Illustrated* swimsuit model to shame.

Those hockey players like sex after a game. Dana's not dumb—she knows it, and she's scouting out her pick of the night like they're her tasty prize in an advent calendar.

Well, let her have it.

Her eyes go to Fletcher. Dana's gaze flicks up and down him.

One of the D-men opens his mouth, probably to make a lewd comment. Fletcher picks up the puck next to him on the bench and, without even looking, hurls it at the D-man, who yelps.

Dana smirks at Fletcher. They're doing that silent-flirting thing that really attractive people do.

I busy myself packing up the cooler.

Bet she takes him home to her fancy-pants penthouse and they have *S-E-X* all night.

What do I care? I don't want Fletcher Sullivan's dick in my mouth.

The party is in full swing at my parents' house when Granny Murray and I pull up. The house looks like a holiday postcard.

Normally, I love the holidays—love food and family and Christmas cheer. Now, with the snow and the dark, it all just feels cold and lonely. We lost. I lost. They're all going to hate me.

"Should have taken one of them home." Granny Murray fiddles with the radio.

"Who?"

"The hot men you have wandering around half naked—who do you think? Bed 'em and bag 'em."

"Home where, Gran? Home here?" We pull up in front of the house.

"It's an expression. I would have sprung for a hotel room for you. That place near the interstate lets you rent by the hour," Granny Murray says.

"With what money? We lost—that means you lost. How much money did you bet on this team?" I ask desperately.

"It's okay, girlie." Gran lays on the horn.

"Gran—"

"I took out a payday loan to bet on your next game. You're like me"—she mimes boxing—"you're a competitor."

"Gran, the next game is—oh my god, I don't even know who we're playing next." I pull out my phone as Gran keeps honking the horn.

My cousins tumble out of the house, oversized Santa Claus wineglasses in hand, sweaters pulled around them as they race across the snowy yard.

"Gran, stop it," Gracie scolds. "The neighbors are going to complain."

"That cunt from the HOA? And no, I don't mean 'cunt' in a complimentary way. Let me at her. Do you know she had the audacity to complain that Trina didn't have the right color Christmas lights up? My own daughter. You need to take me to Costco so I can buy rainbow lights just to stick it to her."

"Costco is closed. It's late." Though you wouldn't know it from the celebratory party music thumping from my parents' backyard.

"Where are the men?" Gran complains.

"Eating, drinking, scratching their balls," Dakota says as she hands Gracie the box with the electric warmers.

I'm not usually the center of attention at family gatherings, unlike Dakota and Gracie. I'm not sure I want to walk into the Direwolves' celebration party in a whole parade.

Gracie beams at me. "I just have to say, I thought your interview was hilarious. Everyone's talking about it. They can't wait to hear about your first game. And wasn't that so nice of Ryder to come to your defense?"

"He's a Boy Scout." Yep. That Ryder. Dakota's dating him, and he's here at the house to celebrate his win.

Yay.

"I actually think I left one of my notebooks at the rink. Maybe I should go…"

Too late. Ryder's coming out of the house like an eager golden retriever to help unload all of the hockey gear, coolers, and empty food trays out of the SUV.

Someone's put a little Band-Aid on his face. I wince, thinking about Fletcher's beat-up face.

Again, Ryder's part of the cool upper echelons of my massive extended family. It's, uh, very weird that we're having this interaction.

"I hope you're not too upset about the loss," he says as he picks up a heavy box like it weighs nothing and heads to the house. "We studied you guys' tapes beforehand, you know, to get up to speed, and you guys played way better than I ever saw you play. And you haven't even been coach for what—twenty-four hours?"

"The power of pussy," Granny pipes up.

"I'm not sleeping with them!" I screech.

"Of course not. Who would think that?" Ryder's brow furrows.

"Like, uh, everyone," Dakota says as Gracie gets the door.

Ryder's husky almost bowls us over. "Down, Dasher. He's not trained."

"Fletcher's not trained," Gracie snickers.

"She's drunk, and she's been watching that interview on repeat." Dakota rolls her eyes.

The living room is decorated with streamers and signs proclaiming "Congratulations on your first NHL goal, Adam and Jace" in big sparkly letters.

Someone has added with a Sharpie, "and game, Ellie."

Holiday music thumps. I keep to the wall, expecting my family to crowd around Ryder to talk hockey.

Except they ignore him and bum-rush me. Ryder's eyes crinkle as he takes the box I'm carrying. All the men in my family crowd around me and loudly and drunkenly give me their opinions on how I need to coach the team.

"You gotta trade Zayne Murphy," Adam insists. He's got a bandage on his neck from the big fight and is clutching his game-day puck.

"She can't trade him—he's family," my uncle slurs.

"He's not family." His wife swats him.

"No, no, no," my cousin Nico tells me, holding out his phone. "You see this? This is the play that won Boston the game in '06. That's the drill you need to run."

"Bag skates." A great-uncle raises his glass. "When I was in the league, they had us run bag skates from noon till dusk."

"Actually, bag skates aren't as good for cardio or strength training as—"

Another uncle cuts me off. "Now, I'm gonna give you some advice." He drapes an arm around me, beer in hand. "This is the line that you need. Okay, listen, write this down: Fletcher on center, that new rookie—what's his name—Genovia…"

"You're thinking of *Princess Diaries*."

"Whatever his name is." My uncle leans on me. "Winger. Put the Finnish boy on defense."

"He's better on forward. I'm actually thinking about building another line around him as center."

"No, no, no. I know hockey, and I'm telling you—"

"Back, back!" Granny Murray hollers. "Blowhards!"

"Here's what you need to do," Dakota says loudly as she steals food off her sister's plate. "You need to do something about Fletcher. He almost killed Ryder."

"He wasn't anywhere near Ryder," I argue with my cousin.

"You all aren't asking the right questions," Aunt Babs insists. "I want to know how big their dicks are."

"I am not looking at their private parts."

"This is why you don't have any grandchildren," Aunt Babs tells my mom. "This is why."

"You should have invited the boys to the party." My mom clucks her tongue at me.

"I'm not inviting the Rhode Islanders to a party"—I point to the yellow-and-black sign—"celebrating the people who just beat them."

"It wasn't a beating—it was a massacre." Jace smirks, tossing his puck in the air.

"Just brutal."

"Best game ever."

"And we got in a fight."

"You barely fought," Angie scoffs.

"Are you a virgin?" my cousin Violet demands.

"No, I walked in on her and Gabe from two doors down once," Maxie says, rolling her eyes as she selects a piece of turkey from the carcass on the table for her sandwich. "She's not a virgin, but she was definitely faking that orgasm."

"Then set me up with one of them," Violet begs.

"Set me up with Zayne—he has money." Her sister giggles.

That sets off the men, who begin another ill-informed argument about the salary cap and how much of it is being spent on Zayne. A noisy argument breaks out in the living room.

I finally escape to the kitchen. My dad is in front of the stove, stoically checking the temperature of a ham warming up in the oven. Gracie's fiancé, Hudson, leans against the fridge.

I don't mind Hudson. He minds his own business.

Several drooly pugs snuffle at his feet.

"You get another dog?" I joke as he moves aside so I can grab some eggnog.

He sighs loudly.

"Maybe Santa will bring you a German shepherd in your stocking this Christmas Eve," I joke.

"He's only getting coal," Gracie snickers at him.

"Maybe if you put a spiked collar on Pugnog he'd be a little more GSD-like. Hey." I pause. "You were in the military, right? I have this player, Fletcher. He's really difficult to handle." Hudson doesn't seem to like that we're having this conversation. "I just need tips on how to—control him? Motivate him."

Hudson waits a beat then shrugs. "A Taser."

"I believe he's got the potential to be the best player on the team."

"Hmm," Hudson grunts.

"Not that it's saying much," I continue to ramble. "He just doesn't believe he can do it. It's like when you have really little kids and their parents insist on dressing them and tying their shoes and feeding them. They're physically capable of doing it—they just need someone to believe in them and tell them that of course they can. Don't make a big deal about it. Just do it and let's go outside."

"I have a piece of advice for you." Hudson rolls his shoulders.

"Here we go," Gracie says, sprinkling cheese on a dish of pasta.

"Mine's actually good advice," Hudson argues. He reaches into his coat pocket and hands me a pair of handcuffs. "Lock Zayne Murphy in his hotel room before the next game, and clear out the minibar."

I take the handcuffs. "That's actually pretty good advice."

"You can ask Gracie for a handcuff key if you need it." The sexual energy just wafts off of him. You could blow up a house with him. He has eyes only for Gracie, of course.

He looks down at my dad, who's fussing with the oven. "That ham is overcooked," he states.

Nate sets it down hard on a trivet. "The oven's free, Gracie."

"Thanks, Uncle Nate."

Hudson wordlessly picks up the ham to follow Gracie into the dining room.

"So…" I wash my hands at the sink. "Crazy game. Adam and Jace got some sweet goals, didn't they?"

"I saw that interview."

"Yeah, they ambushed me a little bit." I dry my hands on the kitchen towel hand-embroidered with Rudolphs I made for my mom one year.

My dad takes a deep breath. "You need to take this seriously. Coaching at the NHL level—there are men who dedicate their entire lives to being where you are. Everyone wants to see you fail."

"I can't just quit now, Dad. We have to play"—*Gulp*— "Seattle next. I can't leave my guys out to dry."

Nate sags. "You're going to get crucified." He looks sick. He grabs my shoulders. "Just promise me," he begs me, "please don't sleep with one of the players."

"Dad!"

"Just promise me."

I think of Fletcher—of the way his hair curls over his forehead, the chiseled abs, that mouth… that mouth twisting into a sneer and spitting out a snide comment. "Don't worry. Never going to happen."

Chapter 14

FLETCHER

Dana Holbrook. This is my shot.

I see the way she's looking at me. She wants to fuck one of the hockey players she owns. I'm going to fuck her brains out, then I'm going to get that info off her phone.

And Hudson will pull you, and you won't play Seattle in a few days.

So? We're going to lose. Seattle is the current Stanley Cup champ—undefeated. They have Emil Maynard on their team, Zayne Murphy's rival since they were drafted at eighteen. And unlike Zayne, he's not playing drunk.

Hudson's right. I'm not here to play hockey. I need to get my head in the game. The real game.

I'm making a risky play here, faking Dana out like you fake out a goalie. If I flirted with her, she'd think I was coming on too strong—it would be too obvious. But not a few too-long looks. Let my eyes flick to her tits then back to her face, send the signal that I'm interested. Keep looking at her as I undress, but not fully—let her admire my ass through the skintight Under Armour bodysuit.

She's lingering. I can tell as I head to the showers, only moving to strip off the shirt when I'm just about to turn the corner so Dana only gets a glimpse.

I plot my conquest as I shower, mindful of the bruises forming all over my torso.

I think of Ellie and feel ever so slightly guilty as the water runs over my skin. Not about sleeping with her boss, because Ellie and I aren't in a relationship. I don't want to be in a relationship with her. I don't even want to sleep with her, which is weird, right? Because she's not that unattractive, and she does have a cute body. I can see it in those skintight leggings when she skates in practice.

Dana.

I shake my head, sending my nose throbbing. Turn the water to cold. Stay under the spray until the rest of my teammates have cleared out.

Dana's perched on one of the benches, legs crossed, typing with one immaculate fingernail on her phone.

I let the towel drop from my waist, use it to towel my hair. "You here to offer me a big-boy NHL contract?"

I see her eyes slide over the tattoos tracing my hips. She draws that fingernail over her perfect lip.

She stands up. "Did you have fun fighting out there on the ice, Fletcher Sullivan?"

Something about the way she says my last name sends a shiver up my spine, and not in a good way. She steps up to me. For some reason, it feels like I no longer have the upper hand. She draws her finger down the bridge of my nose.

I stifle a wince.

Then she jams a nail in the bruise on my cheek. I bite my cheek to keep from yelling.

"For all the shit you gave my coach, someone thinks his life plan is to sleep his way to the top."

"I don't—"

"And you're just half hard because you're thinking about the furry porn you're going to watch tonight in your unwashed sheets." She looks down. My dick shrivels up. "If you want to keep playing for the NHL, you better shape up, Sullivan." She turns on impossibly tall and skinny high-heeled shoes and struts like a cat, like a billionaire who literally does own the place. "Tell your idiot, brain-dead hockey pals that I don't fuck little boys. If your net worth is shorter than your credit card number, I'm not interested. Oh." She turns over her shoulder, glossy brown hair cascading down her back. "Your nose is leaking. Go to urgent care. You're not on an NHL contract, and I don't have to cover you with my insurance."

Ellie is bubbly and happy at practice the next morning when I stomp down the tunnel and glide onto the ice.

"We are still technically the worst team in the league," she says, "but the important part is that we are still a team. I'm loving the team energy!"

My teammates don't look all that upset about the loss, nor are they resigned.

"We're not that bad." Bramms grins. "I've got like five requests to be on hockey podcasts. Shit's lit!"

"Yeah, we're famous." Jovi is giddy.

"And look." Ziggy shoves his phone at Ellie. "Vegas changed our odds. Bookies think we'll only lose by one or two points against Seattle in a few days."

"Still a loss," I mutter. One of the rookies who hears me seems to wilt.

Ellie calls out the drill she wants us to do, then she skates over to me. "You need to keep a positive attitude," she scolds. "Don't bring down the group. They look up to you." Her tone has that *I'm not angry, just very disappointed in you* edge.

Screw her.

I hate the way that makes me feel like I'm a kid again and my mother and my fucking teachers are trying to tell me that I'm the problem—that if I only just applied myself, I could be someone.

"Shift your weight like this," Ellie says, demonstrating how she wants us to come into the shot. "Everyone, do it slowly. If you can't do it perfectly slow, you're not doing it perfectly fast."

As soon as she lets us line up, I send the pile of pucks in front of me ricocheting into the empty net.

The Finn whistles.

"Wow!" The rookies are impressed.

Ellie beams at me. "See? Fletch did it perfectly."

She doesn't have any right to be pleased. She didn't do anything.

My mood gets worse and worse as we run the drills and practice the plays then finally do a scrimmage.

Ren settles in the net a lot more confidently than Braxton, who seems like he'd rather be anywhere else.

I'd rather be anywhere else. I skate around in a tight circle.

"Now, Seattle is tough," Ellie says as we line up on the red line. "But I think we can beat them."

"No, you don't. No one does."

She glares at me. I match it.

The mood has shifted in the ice rink. The players are antsy from the slow control and focus of the drills. Everyone wants to play fast.

We position for face-off. Ellie drops the puck, and I slam it to Eddie and rocket forward.

"No!" Ellie yells as we ignore her, heading for the net.

She blows her whistle as Ren catches the shot.

"Go back to the center line. We're running it again. Do the butterfly pattern."

"This is how I always play," Eddie complains.

"And you've always lost."

I mutter a curse.

Ellie drops the puck, and I fight Carlsson for it. "No!" Ellie blows her whistle again, right in my ear. "I don't need you to do it perfectly, but I do need you to try. Be the butterfly." She holds out her hand. "Give me the puck. Again."

I don't hand it to her. Instead, hauling back my stick, I slam it to the glass. It cracks in a spiderweb.

"Go get the puck." Ellie sets her jaw.

"Get it yourself."

"Fletcher, I'm going to count to three. One, two... three..."

I don't move.

"That's it. Go sit in time-out."

"Time-out? We have a game. I have to practice," I scoff.

"Fifteen-minute time-out. You're having big feelings, and you need to do some deep breathing."

"I don't have to. I'm not a child," I snarl at her.

"Cookie, come play center for this drill."

I'm furious. "I played forty-seven minutes last game. Cookie didn't play shit. He can't have my spot."

"I told you to go to time-out. Can you do it yourself, or do I need to help you?" Ellie says simply.

I stare down at her, throw my stick on the ground, and cross my arms. "Go on, make me."

My teammates watch us.

The Finn looks disgusted. Fuck him—he eats rotten fish he digs up on a beach.

I hear Ren in his heavy goalie gear leave the net. "Yankee," he warns.

I sit down on the ice.

"You can take yourself off the ice, or I'm going to pick you up." Ellie hands Bramms her gloves and stick.

I smirk up at her. "More of your preschool shit?"

She rolls up her sleeves. She's going to try to push me. I dig my skate into the ice as she grabs my shoulders.

But instead of pushing or pulling, she crouches down and hooks her elbows under my arms.

She's not—there's no way. I have a foot and a hundred pounds on her. There's no fucking—

She tips me over and picks me up. My helmet pops off my head, clatters to the ice as she deadlifts me over her shoulder.

"What the fuck!" I curse.

Ren is howling with laughter like a bobcat, slapping his leg. Even Zayne snickers as Ellie slowly skates toward the door to the penalty box.

I could struggle and fight her and topple us both on the ice, but she's not wearing a helmet or padding like I am, and

I don't want to hurt her. Mainly because Ren might hurt me, not because I care about Ellie.

So I freeze as she mortifyingly slowly skates across the ice, carrying me.

"I don't tolerate misbehavior from boys. Or men," she says in that teacher voice. Jovi helpfully opens the gate for her, then she dumps me on the floor and sets her watch. "Fifteen minutes of deep breathing, then you can rejoin the team."

Stunned, I sit on the floor. How did she even—that shouldn't be physically possible.

For the first time, I look at her, really look at her as she skates back to the group. Her legs are curvy, yeah, but that's all muscle. Her legs are tree trunks. Her ass is huge, and yeah, her chest is big, but there's muscle there, not just her tits.

I throw my gloves against the wall. "Don't think about her tits." She's a girl, though. How can I not?

A girl who got the upper hand on me. I fume as Ellie tries to corral the hockey players on the ice.

We're going to lose. I'm never going to get the data I need for Hudson, and now I can't even burn off my frustration skating.

The rink gate opens. "Fifteen minutes are up."

"Practice is almost over," I complain, shoving past her. She skates after me. I snarl at Cookie, who's in my spot.

"From the top!" Ellie blows her whistle.

I don't want to sit out the rest of practice. As much as I hate it, I pass to Jovi just like a good little hockey player, slip around behind him, collect the puck from him, then pass it under my leg behind me right to Eddie's tape.

"Eddie, what the fuck!" I scream at him. He's not where he's supposed to be, and the Finn on the other team snatches it and takes off toward Braxton's net.

Ellie blows her whistle. "That's it. You all have not been following directions or listening. Therefore, you aren't getting pizza Lunchables after the game."

"But you promised!" one of the rookies whines.

"Then act like you're paid to be here," Ellie tells him icily.

"I'm not getting real pay, and I'm going to be out of here before I get a real contract."

"Yeah, who gives a shit?"

I turn on Eddie, slap my stick at him. "What the fuck were you doing?"

"Not her stupid-ass play."

"You started it, Yankee," Ren snaps as he skates past me in the oversized goalie padding.

The practice ends with Ren throwing his blocker pad at Ziggy.

"Aren't you gonna put him in time-out?" I complain.

"You can pick me up anytime, darling." Ren winks at Ellie.

I rip off my gear in the locker room while Ellie walks through the schedule for Seattle. Her grandmother whistles as I strip off the skintight Under Armour pants. I'm not wearing anything underneath.

I turn to face Ellie, fully naked.

I expect Ellie to blush or something. Maliciously, I want to have the upper hand.

She just looks down her nose at me. "I used to be a preschool teacher. I've changed many a little boy's diaper. It's nothing I haven't seen before. The plane leaves at six tomorrow morning. Please make sure you pack enough undies."

Chapter 15

ELLIE

"**P**rivate jet time!" Harlowe crows.

As the PR girl, I hadn't been allowed to go on the private flights. The team didn't want to pay for a hotel room for me. Now?

"This is that fancy NHL life, girl." Harlowe pulls out her tablet at my mom's kitchen table to show me the hotel rooms she booked. "The Soundview Hotel. Five-star service. Comes with its own billionaire."

There's a photo of Fitzgerald Svensson—hotelier, real estate mogul, owner of the Seattle Orcas. I stare. "Come to mama."

"Hmm, he's blond," my mom says.

"I don't care if he has tentacles growing out of his head. He's rich!"

"He'd be lucky to have you." Mom kisses me on the top of my head.

"Wait, you're actually sleeping with your players?" My cousin Violet comes over.

"Like, all at once?" my cousin Bella asks.

"Which one has the biggest dick?"

"I bet it's the new boy, Fletcher."

"Yummy!"

"That mouth!"

"Do it," my uncle demands. "Think of the family. I want him on our hockey team, then we can give Ryder a run for his money next family Christmas skate."

"I don't think poor Fletcher wants to go up against Ryder again when he's not even getting paid." I sigh.

"He got beat up the last time, poor thing," Aunt Stacy says.

"Did you kiss his bruises and make them better?" Cousin Belle snickers.

Yes, that's right. I can't just pack for my work trip like a normal person—my entire family is involved.

"Don't you all have to work?" My eye is twitching again.

"We had to take mandatory PTO." One of my aunts sips her wine.

"Your mom said the entire family has to come to Seattle to support you. Everyone wore Direwolves yellow and black last game, and she felt like it wasn't sufficient support, even though *she* works for the Rhode Islanders and didn't even wear the team colors when she works for the literal team," Aunt Janet hollers at my mom.

"She doesn't work for the team," I say automatically.

"I'm just a volunteer," my mom trills.

"That's not how the NHL does it," my dad mutters as he carries suitcases into the house from the garage in the back.

"There aren't unpaid volunteers. It's not rec league—it's professional hockey."

His sister flips him the bird.

Granny Murray leans in to me. "Don't listen to him. He barely played for the NHL. He's jealous."

"I played for eight years after college." My dad dumps the suitcases on the floor.

His sister drapes her arm around him. "Don't listen to him, Ellie. He's upset you're around all those big, strong, attractive men—all that naked muscle in the locker room."

Dad shoves his sister off with a disgusted noise.

My aunt continues. "You get that Swedish fellow. Make a bunch of big blue-eyed babies."

"He's Finnish."

"He'll make me finish!" My aunt giggles.

My dad turns up the Christmas carols my mom has playing.

"You youngsters don't know this, but a man who can't speak English is a big appeal," Granny Murray says matter-of-factly. "The less they talk, the better."

"Did everyone place their bets?" Dakota's brother announces to glares from his siblings. "Just small ones."

"Yeah, I bet against the Rhode Islanders." My cousin Bobby snickers.

"If Ellie wins, you can make, like, thirty times your money back." Another cousin has dollar signs in his eyes.

"Please don't bet money on me," I groan.

"You need to trust in yourself and your team."

"Is Cookie gonna play?" Uncle Teddy asks excitedly, hovering over me. "If he plays, I could win, like, five grand on this bet."

"I, uh… he's having some… well, hockey is eighty percent mental, after all."

"Dammit, you need to make him play," my uncles demand.

"Here are the therapy toys back," another second cousin announces, coming into the house with three of her children traipsing behind her. "Marco ate one of the slime balls. I told him I have four boys, so he's a spare, and if he doesn't make it through the night, them's the breaks."

"Thanks." I look down at the dirty toys.

"I'll sanitize these," Gracie offers, taking the box.

"Therapy toys? You need to threaten that boy." My dad's third cousin waves a bottle of beer around. "You're going to lose if Cookie doesn't play."

I sigh. "I know. I am trying. What am I supposed to do? They're a mess. Violet, stop filming!"

"What? I can sell this shit to Sportsnet."

I look helplessly to my dad, the only person in the family since my two brothers who's played regularly in the NHL semirecently.

"Any tips?" Nate's brother finally prods.

"I don't know. Quit." Dad shrugs.

"Boo!" His sisters throw things at him.

"I can't. I need the money. I'm trying to save up for a house."

"You want to move out?" My mom sobs. "My baby!"

"Move where?" my sister demands.

"Toronto, I don't know."

"Ooh, is one of your players getting drafted?"

"You said you weren't going to sleep with them," Nate cries.

His sisters jump him. "Her sex life isn't your business. Gross, Nate."

"You need to get in touch with your inner superwoman. You got this. I believe in you, and I've put my money where my mouth is. I have fifty thousand on you," Granny Murray declares. "Put up the good silver as collateral."

"She's never leaving," Nate murmurs to his brother.

"She will outlive us all and inherit your house." His brother ruffles his hair.

"Oh, Trina." My dad covers his mouth with his hand as my mom parades into the dining room with an eye-wateringly bright neon-pink suit.

"Look what I made you for your big game! I didn't have it done in time for your first game, but now you can go to Seattle in style." My mom beams.

"Mom, that is… wow. Are those rhinestones?"

My mom smiles proudly.

"This is some fancy tailoring."

"It is fancy tailoring. You're going to be the most visible thing in the Orcas' stadium tomorrow night." My cousin snickers.

"Try it on." My mom holds it up.

Please don't fit, I pray as I go to the bathroom to put on the suit.

Of course, it fits. My mom sewed all my siblings' and my Halloween costumes and was the volunteer for all school plays. She learned from Granny Murray, who can sew a men's three-piece suit drunk and upside down.

"You look so cute," my mom exclaims when I walk out. "Like Elle Woods and Barbie!" She claps her hands, so happy.

"Trina," my dad hisses, "I don't think Ellie can wear a pink suit to coach a *men's* NHL hockey team. She's going against the Seattle Orcas. Emil Maynard is the captain of that team. He's the best player in the history of hockey."

"Uh, Zack Murphy," one of my uncles says, clearly offended.

"Did we watch the same game yesterday?" Nate argues.

"Hey, you can't skate that well drunk," his brother retorts.

My dad turns back to me. "They are a dynasty team. They have five cups and won one last year and the year before that. The Orcas are undefeated this year. They'll laugh her off the West Coast if she wears that."

My mom looks a little hurt. "Oh, you don't have to wear it if you don't want to, snickerdoodle. I want you to feel your best. We just want you to know that we are so proud of you, and we believe in you." She sounds sad.

I take a deep breath. "I'd love to wear it, Mom. It's amazing! You're so talented and crafty."

"Oh, you are going to look amazing!" Trina squeals.

My dad crosses his arms.

"Look!" My mom walks me through the details. "It has rhinestone hockey sticks on it. And a matching headband." She slips it on my head. "You look so cute! You're going to win. I just know it."

The rookies are yawning when I herd everyone into the waiting plane early the next morning. The runway's been cleared of snow. The drifts line the runway, big and ominous in the dark.

"Yeah, this is the life." Ren settles down in a seat, stretching out his long legs.

"You have to wear a suit," I remind him. "We're going to get fined."

He opens one eye. "You're worried about a suit when we're losing, darling? Really?"

I give a helpless shrug.

Fletcher shoots me another ugly look as he passes me on his way to the back of the plane.

"You don't want to sit with the team?"

"If the plane goes down, this is the safest place to be."

"Hell, I don't care. Take us down." Ren takes out a flask from his pocket and offers it to Zack Murphy, who slumps next to him.

He hasn't shaved in days. His eyes are bloodshot.

I grab the flask from Ren, who yells, "Hey, now!" and in exchange, I unpack a thermos full of Granny Murray's hangover tonic.

"Drink all of that," I tell Zayne.

"You servin' bacon on this flight with these virgin Bloody Marys?" Ren's mouth screws up.

"Bacon," Jovi mumbles from his seat.

I pull his blanket up around his neck as Braxton's mom storms to me and huffs, "Braxton can't have bacon. It makes his tummy runny."

"I'll make sure to update that dietary restriction in his file."

"No need. I brought all of his food." She pushes through me, her enormous bag banging Jovi in the head.

"Braxton needs a window seat," she tells the Finn, who just looks at her.

"He can't speak English…"

"A *window*. *Seat*." She raises her voice, slowing the words down as if that's going to help. "You need to move." Mrs. Beavers mimes with her hands.

The Finn seems to get it and grabs his book and heads to the back of the plane to sit with Fletcher. Mrs. Beavers shoves her son in the window seat then settles down next to him.

"Um… parents don't really travel with the team…"

Braxton's mother is irate. "You will not separate me from my son. He is a child. He has never slept apart from me. I have to supervise him. There is a felon on this team."

Ren blows her a kiss. "We also have a war criminal, so…"

Fletcher's lip curls back. I sit down in my seat.

My mom sits next to me and opens a container. "Oatmeal?"

"Trina, the charter company serves food on the flight," Harlowe calls.

"Oh! I brought a breakfast casserole, though." She unzips another bag. Suddenly, all the guys are wide-awake, sniffing the air.

It does smell good. My mom makes a mean breakfast casserole.

"Butts in seats," I order the guys, "or you're not getting any."

"And I made cinnamon rolls."

"Not before a—you know what? Fuck it." I open up Ren's flask. He toasts me. "What's a few cinnamon rolls and a couple shots of liquor among losers, eh?"

Chapter 16
FLETCHER

Jovi is trying to use Google Translate to talk to the Finn, who is stoically ignoring him and reading his book on North American wildlife.

"Google, how do you say 'We're going to get slaughtered' in Swedish?" He frowns at the phone. "Google, how do you say—"

I snatch the phone from Jovi. "Stop it."

"You think there's any more breakfast casserole?"

"That's not in the diet plan."

"Does it really matter at this point? Google, how do you say—"

I throw the phone at Jovi. It misses and hits Cookie, who looks like he's about to start crying.

"I hope you're not going to shoot with that kind of accuracy," Carlsson chirps from a few rows in front of us.

Ellie bustles over to reset the therapy toys and give Cookie a bag of Goldfish crackers.

I am in hell.

Jovi raises his hand. "Coach Ellie, can I have some Play-Doh? I want some Play-Doh."

Ellie pulls down his tray for him. "Fletcher, don't let him get that over the seat." She pulls out a wet towel and wipes Cookie's face then reaches over like she's about to wipe mine.

"The hell—"

"Sorry!" Ellie's cheeks color. "Force of habit."

The Finn is smirking.

I watch the gray clouds outside the window. Try to think about anything other than the fact that we're about to lose worse than we did against the Direwolves. There's also the small matter of repaying Hudson's debt. "Maybe Emil Maynard will give us a mercy killing," I muse.

Christmas carols blare over the sound system as we file into the hotel. Christmas trees and garland festoon the lobby. One of the staff has added hockey ornaments to an oversized tree in the lobby.

The rookies snap selfies in front of the decorations as Ellie hands out room assignments. "Put your things down. We have practice in an hour. Do not miss that bus."

I'm rooming with Zayne Murphy. Kid me is currently having an aneurysm and writing his thank-you letter to Santa. Adult-ish me is wondering if he's going to be kept awake by Zayne puking up his liquid dinner.

Zayne dumps his stuff by one of the beds. "Gonna grab ice."

The door unlocks a few minutes later as I'm changing into my workout gear. "Yeah, I didn't think those fancy hotels had ice—oh shit." I stand up as one of the most beautiful women I've ever met saunters into the room.

She perches across from me on Zayne's bed and crosses her long legs.

"Hudson send you here to kill me?"

"Was in town working on a job," Skylar says, pulling up the delicate strap of her silk jumpsuit. "Seeing as it's the season of giving and everything, your cousin says you're striking out with a certain cougar." She trails her fingers up my bare arm. "Your hot body's not enough for her?"

"Does your wife know you're talking to me like that?"

Skylar laughs—it's musical, intoxicating. I shake off her spell.

She's Hudson's highest-paid employee and his secret weapon. She can get any man to give her anything she wants. Always. She never misses.

"Dana talked to me. She definitely checked me out. She's interested," I insist. "Though I'm not as pretty as you," I joke.

She preens. "So then why are you so scared?"

"I have the game," I say quickly.

"Dana's in the city." Skylar inspects her nails.

"I'm gonna try again after the game," I say in response to her unspoken question.

"Hudson's trying to make an actual profit off this job," Skylar warns. "He doesn't want to have to send in a team. Word to the wise—do you need to write this down?"

"I'll remember."

She sniffs. "Dana enjoys a challenge. She won't respect you if you give up too easily. You want to be upfront. She doesn't have time for back-and-forth. Just go up to her."

Skylar approaches me. *It's fake, it's fake, this is what she does*, my mind screams as Skylar's breath kisses my ear.

"And whisper in her ear, 'I want to know what it's like to fuck a billion dollars.'" Skylar hasn't even touched me, and I already feel like fucking like a rabbit. "She'll appreciate it." Skylar's eyes flick down my chest then up. My T-shirt feels tight. "Also, her password is 9-0-2-1-0. I know, right?"

The room's door clicks unlocked. Skylar picks up her silky jacket, throws it over one shoulder, and saunters to the doorway.

I follow her, mainly so Zayne doesn't think I'm getting laid the night before a big game. He might be a drunk, but he's still my idol, and I don't want him to think I'm not taking my NHL shot seriously.

I huff a laugh at the irony right as the door opens.

Ellie's standing there in the hallway, mouth slightly open. Skylar looks her up and down and gives me a pointed look. "Evening, doll." Skylar blows her a kiss as she saunters by.

"I, uh…" Ellie stammers.

"Trying to round up the troops. Didn't know you were, uh, busy." Her hands are doing a nervous fluttering.

I pull on my sweatshirt. "Yeah, I'm ready." I step up to her. Her brown eyes are huge in her head, her eyebrows raised. The pulse in her neck jumps as I close the distance. "You gonna let me by, or are you gonna give me a big speech about how you're disappointed and you might have to drag me to time-out again?"

"Oh, uh…" Ellie jumps about two feet in the air then over as I swing past her.

I wait for her to make some snide comment about Skylar, but she just chatters nervously next to me about the plays, about the Orcas, about the strategy.

On the fancy bus—not a school bus like my U18 team used to travel around in; this one's got Wi-Fi and AC—I snarl at one of the rookies. He jumps out of a seat near the front, and I stretch both of my legs out across the seat.

Ellie keeps chewing on her lip as the bus drives to the stadium.

She can't be jealous, right? Ellie can't stand me. She's the hardest on me of everyone, and I'm neither a drunk nor mouthy, and I actually do try in practice. Usually.

Ellie turns in her seat to fuss with the useless rookies and catches me staring at her. She startles, sending her sparkling pink mug clattering to the floor.

She seems to calm down at practice, herding us like one of those corgis my cousin's always threatening to buy as she acts out the plays with probably way more enthusiasm than is decent for an NHL coach to have.

After practice, she bounces over to me.

"I hope you're not wanting to come up to my room to burn off some game-day jitters." I wipe my face with a towel.

"God, no." She wrinkles her nose.

So she's not interested after all.

But there's that rash of red on her neck.

So maybe a little.

"I need you to do something for me."

I lean down. "This better not be another manipulation tactic from you."

"It's for the good of the team."

"The team?" On the ice, the rookies are playing around, kicking snow at each other. One of them screeches as ice is shoved down his jersey. "If you cared about the team, you'd chuck us into the river in full gear and put us out of our misery."

"I think we can win tomorrow." She's stubborn.

"No, you don't."

"We have a good team."

"We have a terrible team."

"We have Zayne Murphy."

My idol is leaning against the boards and resting his chin on his stick, watching the rookies play with a pained expression on his face. "That man never should have been on this team." I feel sick saying it, but it's true. "They gave him a pity contract."

"He's fine if he's not drunk or hungover." Ellie grabs my wrist and slaps something into my glove.

I stare down at the handcuffs gleaming against the fabric.

"You know, princess, this really feels like you're coming on to me. I might need to file a report with HR."

Ellie sighs. "HR quit. Dana refused to give her Christmas off."

"Maybe I should quit too."

"No!" Ellie yelps. "Just..." She grabs the front of my jersey, pulls me down.

"You're the alternate captain. It's your responsibility to keep Zayne Murphy sober for tomorrow's game. That's the only way we stand a chance of winning."

"You can't do it?"

"We're dividing and conquering. Or you can take the rookies. They keep talking about going to clubs. There's talk of sneaking down the laundry chute. I'm organizing a board game night. Maybe that will keep them occupied."

"I don't think half of them can read, so good luck with that."

"Please," Ellie begs. "I don't want to lose again."

"This team? That's all we do, Candy Cane."

She grabs my arm. "Please, please, please."

"Fine. Only if you make Cookie play."

Ellie makes a face as we look across the ice to Cookie, who is slowly spinning around in a circle, staring up at the ceiling.

"We are so fucked."

I can't even enjoy the perks of finally being in the NHL, because I have to babysit.

Zayne Murphy heads for the lobby bar as soon as we shuffle off the bus in front of the Soundview Hotel.

"We should go over plays for tomorrow," I say desperately, "and watch game tapes."

"Yeah," Zayne says, "yeah, I guess we should."

I round up Bramms, Carlsson, and the Finn so that it doesn't look like I'm trying to manage Zayne.

"Got anything of the good stuff?" Bramms opens up my minibar fridge.

I wince as the little glass bottles clink together. "Let's just see if they can send up some room service or something. The team is paying."

The Finn says something garbled and shoves a menu in my face, pointing at the steak tartare.

"Yeah, yeah, you want your raw egg and meat. I got it."

We eat steak, watch old Orcas games, and do a deep dive into Ellie's proposed plays.

"No, man, like this," Bramms is saying, demonstrating with his stick, pretending the desk chair is the Orcas defender.

Zayne keeps *not* looking at the fridge—like, he's looking everywhere but the fridge. *Keep him sober.* "Protein bars," I say loudly. "Protein is good. It's better cold, though." The fridge door slams open, and I grab all the bottles out of the fridge.

"I'm just going to take these to management. Ellie's got cheese I can put there instead," I say lamely so it doesn't look like I'm treating Zayne Murphy like a child who can't control himself.

I almost backpedal when I approach the front desk and Dana Holbrook is there wearing a big fur coat and those superhigh heels like she's walking on stilts.

Keep it together. Calm, confident, no bullshit. *Make her respect you.*

The iPad's in her hand.

I've got the small plug-in that will let Lawrence remote into the iPad. I keep it in my pocket—I take it everywhere, just in case I get lucky. If I can get her to bed, I'm pretty sure I can slip it in there while I'm keeping her busy.

Dana pulls off her sunglasses when she sees me. She nods to the handful of mini liquor bottles in my hands.

"Just protecting your assets." I shrug one shoulder. "You spent way too much money on Zayne Murphy."

She blinks at me. "No, I didn't."

I set the bottles on the counter then lean on it casually to look at her while the hotel clerk types the number into the computer.

"Zayne's only thirty-seven, and he has already sold more in merchandise than I'm paying him," Dana says. "He's the only thing keeping this team afloat financially."

"Huh." I level my gaze at her. "I bet you make all those self-absorbed finance bros in Manhattan cry on the regular, don't you?"

Dana just raises an eyebrow. "Apparently, I wasn't harsh enough with you a few days ago."

"You hired me to play hockey—one of the roughest sports out there. I don't just give up."

"You're cute." She takes her room key from the clerk.

"We'll have your bags taken up, Ms. Holbrook."

"Good. I need a drink."

"The private terrace is available for you, ma'am."

I make a gamble and pick up her black leather suitcase and walk ahead of her to the elevator, trying to keep my heart from hammering. I jerk my chin up to her as I hold open the doors and hit her with my smoldering smile that Skylar made me practice.

Dana seems more amused than intrigued, but better than her busting my balls.

"Can I come up and have a water with you?"

"A water?"

"Game tomorrow. No drinking." I wink.

"Hence the bottles of liquor?"

Yeah, she's definitely not attracted to me. But hey, a boredom fuck is all I need from her. I'm making progress. A few more hours, and I'm in and done. I may not even have to play that game tomorrow.

The elevator across from me dings, the antique brass doors open, and Ellie careens out. "Where is he? Oh my god, this is a—" She sees me then sees Dana.

Ellie claps a hand over her mouth then thinks better of it and clasps them behind her back. "Dana! Hiiii."

Do not yank the well-dressed billionaire into the elevator, I chant to myself. *Her shoes cost more than your salary.*

Ellie is giving me a *look*. But I don't speak nonverbal caffeinated annoying girl.

"How about that drink?" Dana purrs.

"Uh, Dana, hi, hey, can I just—" Ellie takes the suitcase from me, her fingers brushing mine, then sets it on the floor.

"I'm just gonna borrow him if that's okay. Official hockey business."

"I'm on my off hours," I growl.

"No"—she pinches my arm—"you're not." She gives Dana a big smile. Her eye is twitching. "Have a nice drink. Alcohol sounds fantastic right now."

I watch, dying inside, as my mark dismisses us silently and steps into the elevator. A bellboy rushes for her bag.

"You," Ellie hisses at me, jabbing her finger in my chest, "are on babysitting duty. That means you don't go around trying to get laid."

"I'm not," I scoff.

"Yes, you are. God, you NHL players are the worst. You know, maybe you'd be a better player if you weren't thinking with your dick all the time."

"Holy—"

"Don't," she warns.

"Shit, you're jealous, aren't you?"

"I'm not attracted to any of you. I know how you smell after a game," she sputters.

"Yeah?" I round on her. "You wish it was you I had in my hotel room earlier. Don't you?" She's backing away from me. Her back hits the wall with the elevator buttons. "Tell me, and be honest—did you take this coaching job because your love life is a disaster and you thought you'd make a rich NHL player fall in love with you?" I step up into her personal space.

"I like my men to have teeth and job security. I also like them to follow instructions, so where the hell is Zayne, whom you're supposed to be watching?"

"What? He's in my room."

"Try again. He's not there."

"Dammit. I wasn't even gone that long." Ellie races after me as I exit the elevator and head across the lobby. "What are you doing? Go up to the terrace—they have a bar up there," I snap at her.

She turns and runs back to the elevators.

Zayne's not in the fancy main hotel bar, where all the sports media are gathered to schmooze and network and talk shop about tomorrow's game. I sprint down the hall and around the corner to the little speakeasy in the back of the hotel.

In a dark corner, there's Zayne, settling in to five fingers of scotch. There's an empty glass next to him already.

"Dude, what the hell?" I blow out a breath. It's reminding me of having to take care of my mother, where I had to be the adult even though I was still having to walk in a single-file line and raise my hand to speak in elementary school.

Zayne looks down as I grab the glass.

"We have a game tomorrow." I let my frustration lace the words. I slam the glass on the bar. "Do not," I tell the bartender, "serve that man for the rest of his time here, or I'm going to get my hockey stick and smash every goddamn bottle up there."

"Fletch, I just—"

"I don't want to hear it." I drag Zayne up to our room.

He slumps on the bed. The handcuffs are still in my pocket.

I snap one cuff on his wrist then snap the other on my own and turn out the light.

Zayne breathes in the dark.

"I used to want to be you," I say into the blackness. "I used to want it more than anything in the world."

Zayne rubs his eyes. "I'm really sorry, Fletch." He sounds like he means it.

Chapter 17

ELLIE

"**W**hy am I so concerned about who Fletcher's hooking up with? He's an NHL player. They like to sleep around." I pace in front of Harlowe.

I couldn't sleep last night—I kept thinking about Fletcher and that pretty honey-blonde with the good hair, then to the game that we're going to lose and my dad being upset, and then back to Fletcher.

"Coffee." I grab my second mug. Yeah, it's that kind of day. The jet lag doesn't help.

"I thought you wanted to practice your media talking points," Harlowe reminds me.

"That girl was everything I'm not," I cry. "Same with Dana." I guzzle my coffee.

In the mirror of the stadium bathroom where Harlowe and I barricaded ourselves, I don't look like an NHL coach in charge of a team. I look like what I am—a pathetic mess. I blot my cheeks with a wet paper towel.

"He has a type, and it's not me. And I don't care." I fan myself.

"Uh, it kind of sounds like you do…"

"Sure, I always wanted a boyfriend that my aunts, cousins, and sisters would be jealous of. But Fletcher hates me, and I am his boss, technically. So it's unethical, and I'm not attracted to him, nor do I care what he's doing on his off time."

"Exactly. You're a boss." Harlowe tries to fix my hair.

The media is setting up in the crowded hallway outside of the locker room, getting B-roll for tonight's broadcast. Ignoring them, I determinedly start pinning up motivational posters in the locker room.

"The hell is that?"

"Gran!" I drop my box of pushpins.

Granny Murray starts tugging down the posters sporting sayings like ONE TEAM ONE DREAM! "These are grown-ass men. They aren't skating hard for an arts-and-crafts project." She unfurls one of the posters in the box she carried in.

"Granny, no!"

"Sex is the Lord's performance-enhancing drug."

"Oh, hell yeah!"

I squawk as the players crowd through the door.

Fletcher covers a rookie's eyes. "Don't look."

"Hey, those were expensive," Gran complains, trying to block me from tearing down the nude posters.

"There's more where these came from, boys," Granny Murray declares, "but you only get to see more titties if you win this game! I've just put down another fifty grand. Got my life savings riding on you."

"Gran," I hiss, "you didn't take out a loan for all of that, did you?"

"I believe in you, girlie. Make those Orcas players eat unwashed pussy for dinner."

Fletcher is staring at me, not the giant boobies above my head.

I start sticking Post-it notes over the most egregious sections of the poster.

Jovi is hopping around, anxious. "You're on my seat," he finally says, raising his hand.

"You're in his seat." Fletcher grabs me around the waist and sets me down on the floor.

He looks down at me. It's not in that interested, seductive way—the way he looked at Dana. Oh, no, it's the way you'd look at someone who has a bug crawling on their forehead. "What the hell are you wearing?" Fletcher flicks the collar of my neon-pink suit.

Self-consciously, I touch the rhinestone-encrusted headband.

"I think your suit looks nice," Bramms says as he starts pulling out his tape.

"He's color-blind, so he thinks it's blue."

"Circle time!" I call, frazzled. Most of the guys are still staring at the posters.

"See," Granny Murray tells me, "motivation."

The rookies all sit on the floor around me as I run through the plays. Unlike yesterday, Fletcher and several of the other older players seem to be absorbing and buying into the plays, asking questions and acting them out to the younger players.

Harlowe walks in and blinks up at the posters. "Um, whoa. Um, the press is outside, sooo…"

"Get your last looks in, boys. Seems like communism's come to the NHL." Granny Murray sighs and starts taking down the posters.

I turn to the players with a big smile. "You're in the NHL. No matter what, you're still winners."

The players head out for warm-ups. A giant inflatable orca in a Santa hat swings from the ceiling. The stadium's filling up. Mostly with the blue-and-silver Orca colors, but there's a large chunk of seats where I see Rhode Island burgundy.

My family cheers when they see the bright-pink suit. I give a weak wave. Then I head to the media scrum.

There's laughter when I stand in front of the bank of microphones; the light bounces off the rhinestones on my suit, dazzling over the media. *This isn't worse than dealing with entitled daycare parents*, I tell myself. *No one is trying to get every food known to the natural world banned from my classroom because their tarot reader thinks it's going to make their precious child an educational failure.*

I take a deep breath and smile. "Welcome to a bright and beautiful day in Seattle, everyone," I say with as much cheer as I can. "I'll take questions."

The first sports writer pipes up. "Do you have a statement about the Orcas players throwing tampons at your players?"

Chapter 18
FLETCHER

You're not supposed to cross the center line during warm-ups. Guess the league doesn't want people fighting. They apparently don't have any rules about throwing things at people, however.

The first tube hits me in the back of the neck. Any lower, and I probably wouldn't have felt it through the jersey.

"What the hell?" I turn to the rookies who are tossing pucks back and forth. "Did you hit me?"

Cookie points.

I stare at the ground then across the ice to the smirking Orcas player. "Motherfucker." I slap shot the wrapped tampon back across the ice toward them. "Are you that worried about losing to a girl?" I snap at the alternate captain of the Orcas, Alexei Vidic, a big guy with a flat face and a buzz cut.

"Just thought you might need them when we bleed you out." He gives me a lazy smile.

The other Orcas players snicker.

A wiry forward pitches a handful of more plastic tubes at the rookies; they patter onto the ice. The fans who have shown up early for warm-ups hoot and shout, jeering as the cameras zoom in on us. Several fans start throwing boxes of tampons onto the ice.

Ren, furious, sets his feet like he's about to rush across to fight.

"Dude, just ignore them," I hiss at our players and grab the back of Ren's jersey. "Fuck these guys."

"I'm gonna bash their heads in," Ren spits.

"I don't feel well," one of the rookies croaks as more tampons rain down on us while the Orcas players chirp at us from the other side of the line.

I keep waiting for Zayne to do something—he's the captain, goddamn it. He could at least cuss out Emil Maynard.

The Orcas captain, Zayne's old rival, is cold and aloof as he warms up, puck handling over the logos under the ice even better than the day he came into the league at eighteen.

"I thought he's supposed to be old," Jovi whispers to me as we watch him. He's like the Orcas' namesake—apex predator, a silent, ancient killing machine.

"He's like thirty-seven-year-old cognac, somehow even better than when he started."

Zayne sucks in a breath as we watch Emil then lets it out. "He's right. We're fucked."

"You have better hockey sense than him," I say stubbornly, like I'm back in the schoolyard playing street hockey and defending my idol. "He's a scorer. You're a craftsman."

A box bounces on Cookie's helmet and busts open, raining more tampons down his jersey.

"Are you seriously letting this happen?" I skate over to one of the refs.

He sucks on his teeth. "Let what happen?"

An Orcas fan throws a huge box onto the ice, and it explodes, sending more tampons scattering. Cookie is hurriedly trying to sweep them all off our side of the ice.

The ref finally sighs. "You gotta have a thick skin in the NHL, son."

Another box is badly thrown and bops one of the linesmen on the head. He turns and screams at one of the security guards, who scampers to berate the drunk fan.

The fan pumps a fist, and the Orcas players raise their sticks to him in a salute as he's dragged away. Their alternate captain makes a vulgar gesture to me as his team skate like pros—like NHL players, like Stanley Cup champions—back to their tunnel.

I hate the Orcas team, I decide. Hate them more than my dad, more than Ellie, more than Hudson.

The rookies look rattled as we head back to the locker rooms, nervously kicking the snow off their skates, chewing on their mouthguards.

And here's Ellie in the bright-pink suit. Her smile's strained.

Someone asks from beside me, "Why does she even have to wear that?"

I jab Eddie with my stick, sitting there as Ellie grits out her toxic positivity. "Guess you heard the good news," I say as she picks a tampon out of Cookie's jersey.

"Sticks and stones," Ellie singsongs. "They're trying to get in your head."

"And it's working," Eddie mutters.

"Just ignore them, and they'll go away."

"No, they won't. We have to play them," Ziggy complains.

I steal glances at her as I'm getting ready. She looks nervous, worried. Guilty. Sad. *Scared.*

I work my jaw.

"Zayne, you've been in the league a while. Do you have any words of wisdom and encouragement?" Ellie sounds desperate.

"Bend down and kiss your ass goodbye," Eddie mumbles.

I growl at him. He gives me an ugly look.

Zayne stands up, rocking on his skates. "You know…" Zayne scratches under his helmet. "I think we've got a great group here. And sure, the Orcas are the reigning champions, but don't bet against hockey, right? If we all work together, I think we can have a really good showing. No one expects us to win, so we can just go out there and try our best, try some new moves. Just don't give up—even when we're down. No one dies from losing. We get paid either way."

There's half-hearted clapping from Jonesy and a couple confused but enthusiastic rookies. Ren's eyes shift behind his goalie mask.

It's the opposite of inspiring. It's lackluster, demoralizing.

Jovi looks like he wants to crawl under the bench and hide.

"Why do we have to play them?" one of the rookies asks in a small voice.

"Fuck this shit." I stand up. "Ellie, get out."

"What? Why? You can't kick me out. We have to—"

I pick her up around the waist and throw her into the hallway. "Out." I slam the locker room door behind her and stare down my team. "Now, you motherfuckers, listen to me. I am not losing to these fucking self-absorbed dicks. I don't want to just—*shut up, Eddie.* I don't care if they have Emil Maynard on their team. We have Zayne fucking Murphy, the greatest hockey player who ever lived, whose name is inscribed on the cup not one, not two, not even three, but six goddamn times."

I make a knife hand at Ren. "We have the craziest fucking goalie in the league. He's not some pampered player whose parents bought him a spot, either—he's a redneck from Mississippi. You want to know how insane you have to be from Mississippi and play hockey? And Cookie—" The little forward looks like he's going to pass out. "You were the number one draft pick. They called you the next Ryan West." I get in his face. "You will man the fuck up and get on the ice tonight and score a goal."

His mouth drops open.

"I don't want to hear shit from any of you about how we suck and we're losers. I don't care if we're the worst fucking team in the league. We're sitting at a bar in hell? Fine, then we're dragging them all down with us."

"Fuck yeah, let's do this shit!" Jovi hollers as the players whoop.

Ren snorts a line of powder off his glove. "It's caffeine pills and Pixy Stix, man."

"Hell yeah, let's fucking go!"

"No one saw that," I threaten as Jovi bangs his helmet on Bramms's.

"Go to the box," I bark at Ellie as I brush past her like I'm going to war.

The Orcas aren't done fucking with us, though. I can tell something's wrong when the ice rink is washed in pink light as we step out. Then the first tinny notes echo around the stadium, followed by the "OoooOOOOHHH" of the crowd as they recognize the '90s pop song.

"Are they playing the fucking Barbie song?" Ren snaps at me. Either it's the caffeine powder or the pink light, but the goalie looks unhinged as he circles the ice.

Several drunk fans in the audience sing along. The camera pans to Ellie in the box with her pink suit as the music screeches, "I'm a Barbie giiirrrlll!"

It's not even the Nicki Minaj rap version. I'm pissed as the pink lights pulse around. It's the '90s one—all bubblegum pop and techno consumerism.

The Orcas fans screech in laughter as we skate up to the blue line for the national anthem. I seethe as the Orcas players line up across from us. Vidic, the alternate captain, stands next to Emil, smirking at me.

"Let's fuck him up, boss." Jovi's antsy next to me, like he's just waiting for me to snap the leash so he can fly.

All through the national anthem, I'm fuming.

"Good luck, Barbie," the Orcas players chirp at us.

"Let's go, Barbie!"

The rage pulses behind my eyes. I want to beat someone with my hockey stick. I settle for trying to beat them at hockey.

It's going to be an impossible task.

We lose the face-off. Well, Zayne loses the face-off to Maynard. The veteran player passes it to the alternate captain, and the Orcas are off, racing to the goal.

Bramms skates backward, keeping pace with their assistant captain, trying to throw him off his shot. The puck ricochets off Vidic's stick, and the crowd roars as the first goal is scored and it's not even five seconds... but it's not a goal.

"Hell yeah, Mississippi!" Jovi whoops as Ren holds up his glove, the small black puck dark against the white.

It's another face-off. Zayne digs in. He used to win face-offs, was the king of face-offs. Maybe still is—the way his eyes are sort of glazed, like they're seeing everything at once.

He's still got it! The kid in me whoops as he gets possession of the puck.

The puck goes straight to my stick; then I'm tear-assing down the ice like clockwork. I spin into one of the plays Ellie created, that we repeated in practice and analyzed in my hotel room last night. Bramms gets it, turns back to Zayne, over to me, to Jovi, to the Finn—into the net!

"Yes!" Jovi screams, throwing himself at me.

We jump on the Finn, hugging him, patting his head as he roars something in Scandinavian.

The Orcas are pissed. We scored against them early, too, made them look stupid, and they're going to make us pay.

I'm breathing hard when Ellie changes out the lines. Two of the rookies are out there skating with Carlsson.

"You got a goal!" Ellie's congratulating our line, patting us on the helmets. "Good job! I knew you could do it!" We bask in the praise.

Zayne's locked in, though—barely acknowledges it as he watches the game from the bench.

I look back at Ellie. She's resting her arms on the Finn's helmet, craning over our heads to see the ice. Like he's her boyfriend or something. I feel the frown crease my forehead as I see the tiniest of twitches at the corner of the Finn's mouth.

I turn around, kick Jovi to scoot over, grab Ellie by the waist, and set her in her pink shoes on the bench.

I get one pale-eyebrow raise from the Finn.

Chewing on my mouthguard so I don't punch him in the face because we actually, you know, need him to win, I face back to the ice, trying not to think about Ellie right behind me—like I could literally just turn around and grab the back of her legs and…

Fuck. The Orcas are brutal. One defender slams into Carlsson as he's cutting across the ice. My teammate goes down, sliding across the ice as the Orcas take the puck.

The ref waves his arms. "Clean hit?"

"No fucking way," I scream at the ref. "Are you gonna do your goddamn job?" The ref turns to scowl in my direction. "Yeah, I'm talking to you, you fucking ass—mhmff."

Ellie's got her arm wrapped around my neck, hand covering my mouth.

The ref skates over, hand up like he's about to give us a penalty. That's the last thing we need—to be down a man.

"We didn't say anything," she says cheerfully to the ref, leaning over to talk to him.

The fucking guy is old enough to be her dad, and he's clearly trying to pretend like he's not stealing a peek down the plunging neckline of the pink suit jacket.

I lunge, and the ref skitters back. "You fucking—"

Ellie's hand is back on my mouth; her knees dig into my back as she yanks me backward. "We're good here. Everything is fine. You're doing an awesome job! No," she scolds me, wagging a finger in my face after the ref skates away. "We cannot afford to have you thrown out of the game. If I put you back in, can you behave?"

"No." I jump over the boards onto the ice, Zayne behind me.

The Orcas chip away at us; we're on the defensive. The only reason that we're not down by five already is because of Ren.

"I hope they don't test for Pixy Stix," Jonesy jokes.

The Orcas get shot after shot on goal. Our defense hasn't completely collapsed—thank God Bramms is digging in, trying to get the puck up. The Orcas are good, though—big and fast. And they beat us back, keeping the puck longer and longer in our zone each time we lose possession, until—

"GOAL!" the horn blares through the stadium.

First period isn't great, but it also somehow doesn't completely suck. Carlsson got another goal with a sick assist from Zayne, but so did the Orcas.

Second period, though?

"If you don't keep them goddamn pucks away from my net," Ren hisses at me through his missing teeth, "I'mma skin you, boy. You hear me?"

I incline my chin to him, and he skates off, still somehow graceful despite the goalie pads.

"You see his skates?" Zayne says to me as he skates around, warming up before the period starts. "They're like ours. They're not goalie skates. That's why he's so good against the Orcas. They aren't expecting him to move like that, that fast, you know?" Zayne taps my helmet with his stick then leans over for the face-off.

The whistle blows. Zayne sends the puck straight to my tape… and that's the last good thing that happens all period.

We dig in.

I don't want to lose. It's not that I want to win—I just don't want to lose. I'm sick of fucking losing.

I break through the Orcas players, try to find Jonesy, don't find him, see the Finn. Emil cuts in front of my pass. Zayne goes after him, but he's just a hair too slow. I cut in, slam into Emil—it's like running into a brick wall—collect the puck, trying not to get rattled, trying to get it up, trying to keep it away from Ren in the net.

Ellie keeps switching the lines, trying to keep us fresh.

It's not enough. Seattle breaks through all of them, crowds around the net, slashing, attacking over and over until the puck is in the net and the goal horn is blaring and Ren's screaming at me, sounding like a crazed Baptist preacher as he condemns me to hell.

Third period. We're down by two.

"We have a goal," I remind myself. "It can be done. We can score." I hold onto that last shred of hope like a drowning man.

The Orcas look like they've all been huffing crazy Ren's Pixy dust. The Rhode Islanders? We're all tired.

Everyone except for Cookie, who hasn't fucking played.

"She gonna put him in?" Bramms hisses as we do a quick turn around the ice. "What the hell were all those therapy toys for?"

"At least they're not throwing feminine hygiene products anymore."

Jovi's got a cut under his eye that's been patched with a Hello Kitty Band-Aid from Ellie's purse.

I can't lose. I cannot lose.

We're losing, though. Seattle scores a goal then another. Ren's cursing at me with threats of the rapture as we line up for face-off.

When the Orcas winger hurtles down the ice to our collapsed defense, Ren loses it, rushing out to meet him, jamming his stick between his legs. The Orcas winger goes sprawling; Ren bats the puck to me with the huge goalie stick. Against all odds, I get it, take it up the ice, and pass to Jovi, who passes to Zayne.

The Orcas defender is on him. "He's gonna lose it, he's gonna lose it…" I mutter.

But Murphy's Law just draws in the defender, pivots, and sends me a blind backhand pass, and I send it—right into the corner of the net.

"Goal!" Jovi's screaming, jumping on me. "We're only down by two," he hoots.

I can't bask in the glory of my first NHL goal, though. Have to focus. The Orcas aren't going to let it be down by one. They send out their first line—their best players.

Zayne's locked in, but he's only one guy. And we just don't have the depth of talent the Orcas have.

We're not good enough. *I'm not good enough.*

I desperately chase down the puck, my lungs burning, ears ringing from Ren's rage-filled cursing.

What the hell is in those Pixy Stix? I wonder, thoughts almost hysterical as the Orcas get another shot, only to have the puck glance off the metal bar of the net.

"Thank you, baby." Ren kisses the net.

He turns to me. "Fuck you," he hisses.

Ellie blows her whistle and signals to the ref. TIME-OUT blazes across the screen.

"The hell?" Bramms narrows his eyes. "Who calls a time-out? No one ever uses their time-outs."

There's confused murmurs from the crowd, and over in one corner of the stadium behind the glass, I can see incredulous broadcasters making jokes about needing a bathroom break.

I gulp down water as Ellie stands on the bench next to a very well-rested Cookie to address us.

"We have seven minutes left," she says calmly. "You all can play hockey. You scored two goals. We need two more to tie the game and make it to overtime."

Might as well ask us to fly to the moon. I wipe at my face.

"Zayne, do you have a feel for the game? Got your sea legs back?" Ellie says brightly as she holds up her clipboard. "Offense," she directs. "We need full offense. Defenders, I need you guys to stay up. These are the plays we want to run. Zayne, you're the guy who's going to be on the lookout to set these up. Forget about everything that just happened. This is a brand-new seven minutes. You have all the time in the world. Don't freak out. It's hockey—it's not nuclear engineering. Don't overthink it."

"Easy to say when you don't have the Stanley Cup champions baying for your blood."

The time-out helped reset the energy in the game. But it's not quite enough. We still can't get the puck up. Still can't get it to the net, still can't keep from losing to the Orcas.

The clock ticks down as once again, I chase an Orcas player down the ice.

He bum-rushes Ren, who doesn't back down or give any ground—just screams as the Orcas player crashes into him, rolling on the goalie's head. Bramms slams into the Orcas player, punching him with that big right hook.

"Power play," Jovi says as we ready.

Except the ref doesn't call it.

Carlsson is scuffling with another Orcas defender, and the ref pushes them apart and gives my teammate a warning. Ren's shaking out his arm, rolling his neck, and hauling himself up.

"You motherfucker!" Ellie screams at the ref. "That's a penalty! That's a roughing penalty! Do not ignore me! I know you can hear me!"

She's red-faced, and her hair's messy. She pulls off her headband and throws it on the ice.

"Shit." I rush over and grab her just as she's about to jump over the boards and attack the ref.

"Put me down, Fletcher! I'm going to rip his face off!" I dump the angry girl into the box and toss her headband in after her.

Ren skates over, rubbing his shoulder to get checked out while the Orcas players skate around on the ice, laughing at the replay of Ellie trying to jump onto the ice looping over and over on the jumbotrons above.

"I'm fine." Ren waves us away.

"We need you for the game next week." Ellie sounds furious as she runs her hands all over Ren's shoulder.

He takes a swig from a bottle of what smells like kerosene that her granny gives him.

"Got some pills too," the old woman offers. "If you want to play roulette. Why not? Live a little."

He shrugs and takes two from her palm.

"We're not putting you back in." Ellie says angrily.

"Are you putting in Braxton?" I ask.

We look at the kid eating a granola bar and scrolling on his phone at the other end of the bench.

"We have four minutes, and we need two goals to make it to overtime," she says. "We're not putting a goalie in."

"So a Hail Mary." I blink.

"Pulling the goalie is a legitimate strategy."

"Four minutes, boys," Zayne says. "A lot can happen in four minutes."

The Orcas see the six of us forwards on the ice and Ren sitting on the bench. They dump in all their defenders. It's going to be a bloodbath.

"Swan Lake," Jovi says, calling one of the plays we looked at last night.

"Doesn't the chick die at the end of that movie?"

"It's a ballet."

"And yeah. Jumps off a cliff."

"Yeah, but the music is killer at the end."

On the loudspeakers, the Barbie song starts screeching. We're going out in style. I hear Jovi singing along behind me as we face off.

I dig in—we all do, to the last of our reserves.

Two goals, four minutes. Two minutes per goal. It can happen.

I have to hand it to Ellie—when her plays work, they work.

The sixth man is just enough for us to maneuver around the defenders.

And Zayne Murphy—Murphy's Law—he's got a crowd of them on his flank. He fakes right, then cuts left, snow spraying and misting around him. He sinks to his knee and threads the needle—it's a highlight-reel shot of the puck going between the legs of three defenders and lightly brushing over the goalie's shoulder to thunk in the net.

"*Murphy! Murphy!*" There are some chants from the crowd. He's been in the biz twenty years and still has fans out there.

For anyone else, it would be a career-highlight goal, but for Murphy, it's just another Thursday.

"One more," Jovi pants as we reset for face-off.

"One more."

"One more. We can do it. One more."

Emil has taken personal affront to Zayne's goal. Zayne barely touches the puck before Emil has it ricocheting to Vidic.

He cuts around us. I block one of the forwards, forcing the winger to go around right into Zayne's path.

He gets the puck and swings around the back of our net, up the ice.

Emil appears out of nowhere to crash right into him— it's a legal hit; it's just Emil is built like a truck. Zayne and Emil go sprawling on the ice. Then, in a split second, they're back on their feet, totally focused on the puck.

Emil gets it first and doesn't even need to collect it—he's that good—he just makes the shot to the empty net.

We're going to lose.

Jovi burns all engines and rushes after the puck, springs like an alley cat, and dives in front of the puck, sliding to a stop right at the red line of the net.

"Hell yeah!"

He's panting as Ellie pulls him out, swaps him with the Finn so he can collapse on the bench.

"Can't lose, can't lose, can't lose." I'm begging the hockey gods. Though I'm on the ice with two of them, and they aren't answering my prayer.

The clock ticks down. I can feel the loss settling deep in my gut, rotting me from the inside.

Loser, loser, loser, the ice chants as I make a desperate rush to the goal.

Vidic knocks me, gets the puck. I slash at him, and he loses control. The Finn gets the puck, but he doesn't have the shot; he sends it back to Zayne.

Zayne can't shoot. He's defending against the boards as the Orcas players crowd him. Looking, looking, not surrendering. He doesn't have any way out, and the Orcas are just running out the clock.

But Murphy's Law prevails—if there's even a crack in the defense, Zayne Murphy can get a puck through, and he finds me. Like magic, the puck's there on my stick.

I don't have a shot. Maybe if I were Zayne or Emil or, shit, even Cookie—if someone would just get that kid a couple tequila shooters or something—I could have made it. There are seconds left.

"Let's go out with a bang." I don't even need the split second to aim. I already know where I'm sending the puck.

It fires off my stick, flying straight and true to its target—right on the side of Alexei Vidic's ocean-blue helmet.

Crack! It sounds like a glacier breaking apart. Vidic grunts as the puck ricochets off his helmet…

And into the Orcas' net.

There's a split second of silence, and then the goal horn blares through the stadium.

"Holy shit!" My teammates are jumping all over me. "Goal! Goal! We're going to overtime! Fuck yeah!"

The Orcas' captain is arguing with the ref, who's blowing his whistle and making the goal sign.

"We made it! We made it!"

There's shocked murmuring in the stadium as we head down the tunnel to the locker room.

"One more goal," Ellie tells us. Her eyes are dancing. "You showed them! Did you see their faces?" She's giddy.

"They didn't think you could do it, and you have them on the run! Oh my god, I love hockey! Okay." She rubs her hands together. "Here's how we're going to win…"

Then she rattles through the plays as she draws with a pink marker on the board. "We just need one goal. It's sudden death. One goal. Then we win."

"Ren, are you good?" I ask him. His eyes are bloodred, and I think he's missing another tooth.

"Fuck yeah." He slams his helmet on his head. "I want these fucking West Coast bastards squealing like a stuck pig on the back of my pickup truck."

We can do this. We can beat the Orcas. Ellie thinks we can do it.

The hope, the elation, is short-lived.

The Orcas aren't giving an inch. It's like being struck by a typhoon.

We hang on. The game somehow is twice as fast as the last period. The refs can't even keep up with us as we speed across the ice. It's just like the second period, though. The Orcas get more shots on goal than us. The puck stays on our side, not theirs. Sure, Ren saves them, but they just need to get lucky once.

And I'm gassed. I'm a split second slower than the Orcas players. The puck doesn't fly quite as fast across the ice as it should. Hudson's right—I'm not a real NHLer. I didn't spend all summer honing my hockey skills. I just walked onto this team. I don't belong here.

We need a miracle.

And he's there, sitting right next to Ellie on the bench, swinging his feet.

Chapter 19

ELLIE

"Wow, overtime! Go team!" I scream as the huge men speed a hundred miles an hour across the ice. I can barely follow the puck.

The Orcas want to win. They want to win at all costs.

The Seattle coach is giving me the evil eye through the glass. He thought this was going to be an easy win, thought they were going to go home ten to one. And we had them on the ropes the whole time. Now the game's in overtime.

Fletcher screams my name as he zooms by with the puck. One of the Orcas defenders smashes him against the boards. I wince, and Cookie covers his eyes.

"Put Cookie in!" Fletcher yells as he races past the bench after the Orcas player.

The Finn has the puck and is heading to the net.

"You have to put him in!" Fletcher roars, the words fading as he flies through the neutral zone. He's tired, though.

I chew on my lip. He's played the most minutes, and he never stopped. The Orcas' roster is more balanced than ours, and while they're not well rested per se, they are slightly more rested than Fletcher, and that kind of edge is all you need in hockey to make a break.

I suck in a breath as the puck bounces off the post and Ren pounces on it, tossing it to the Finn.

"Make it happen!" Fletcher bellows.

"Cookie." I rub the eighteen-year-old's shoulder. "Cookie," I singsong to him. "Don't you want to go play with your friends? Look, everyone's having fun."

"I'm going to make us lose," he says in a small voice. "I can't play."

"Cookie, you can play. You're amazing."

Cookie covers his face with his towel.

I steady myself and prepare to keep my tone neutral but positive, trying not to look at the clock as it ticks down, down. We cannot go to a shoot-out, because we will lose. The Orcas shooters are stacked. I resist the urge to shake Cookie and scream at him. That won't help.

He's having a hard time; he's not giving you a hard time.

"I really want to see you play, Cookie." I pet his helmet. "Just try. You don't have to score, just try."

"I can't," he says in a small voice. "I messed up the last time, and everyone was mad at me. I can't do it."

"Mistakes happen. We try, try again."

"I can't." He looks like he's about to cry.

Fletcher whizzes by. I can hear him gasping for breath.

Cookie wants to play. I see it in his eyes. When he's on the ice, he loves hockey. He just needs a final push.

I dig through my proverbial bag of tricks from my time in the daycare trenches. "If you play…" I begin.

Cookie starts to perk up.

What to give him?

Fletcher whizzes by. "Put him in, fucking—oof!"

Fletcher gets creamed, goes sliding across the ice to crash into the boards as an Orcas player speed-runs the puck to the net. Ren barely keeps the puck out of the goal using his skate.

We can't lose. My whole family is here. There are twenty-five thousand people watching me, plus another what, million on TV? I'm wearing a pink suit. They played the Barbie song and threw tampons at my players.

"I'll give you… a surprise, Cookie, if you get me a goal."

"What kind of a surprise?" I've got his attention now.

"A surprise…" I roll my hands, grasping for straws as on the ice, my team collapses. "A surprise you pick from the surprise bag!"

"The surprise bag! Okay!" Cookie hops over the boards as Fletcher drags his bruised body toward us. I grab the back of his jersey, hauling him into the box before we get a penalty for having too many players on the ice.

"Holy shit." He half rests against me. His lip is split, and he's holding his side. He's sweaty and panting, but there's wonder in his eyes as Cookie flies across the ice. "Fuck." He coughs. "I can't believe you did it."

"We have thirty seconds. It's too late." Eddie points to the clock.

I'm biting my nails. But I hide my hands when I see myself on the jumbotron.

Thirty seconds is all we need. All Zayne Murphy needs, anyway.

As if he's got a sixth sense, the veteran player crashes into Emil, knocking him off the puck just enough for Zayne to send a blind backhand pass hurtling to our net.

"What the hell is he doing?" Eddie yells. "He's gonna score an own goal!"

I don't even have to hear Ren to know he's cursing as the puck hurtles towards him, the Orcas forwards too startled by Zayne's hit to react. Zayne has a knowing smirk on his face.

"Oh my god," Fletcher breathes. "He's the god of fucking hockey."

Because Zayne knows that it's not a pass to nowhere.

Cookie zips around the net and darts in front of Ren, the puck glued to his stick.

The Orcas forwards seem shocked to see him, but then he's gone, dancing across the ice like one of those cartoon mice in a Disney movie. He crosses the blue line, dodging defenders like they're skating in slow motion.

The crowd is counting down the seconds as Cookie races through the players and darts around one final defender who crashes, tripping over his feet trying to keep up with Cookie. He leaps over him with the puck, does a pirouette, pops the puck up, and passes it to himself.

"Four… three…"

The goal horn blares as Cookie flicks the puck off his stick and it slams into the net, sending the Orcas goalie's water bottle that had been resting on the net flying, spraying water everywhere.

"Cookie!" I scream, throwing up my hands as the Barbie song blares from the speakers.

"They had that cued up because they thought we were gonna lose!" Fletcher's laughing, coughing around his bruised lungs.

"I fucking love this song!" I wrap him in a hug.

"Of course you do." He stares down at me. "Of course you love this horrible song."

I cup his bruised face.

"We won. Goddamn, we won, Ellie." He looks like he wants to kiss me for a moment.

I choke on the smell of him—the sweat and the ice—then he's gone to join Cookie, who's dancing alone to the Barbie song at center ice before the players all rush him, singing the lyrics at the top of their lungs as they jump around and hug Cookie.

The pink spotlights wash the stadium in pink while lots of drunk people in the crowd sing along off-key. I join in, dancing on top of the bench.

"Shots!" Granny Murray hollers, handing me the bottle of tequila. The camera pans to me, and I'm on the jumbotron right as I take a swig from the bottle of tequila.

Whoops.

The Orcas players glower as they file into their tunnel while their coach screams obscenities and throws his clipboard at them.

"That's the power of pussy!" Granny Murray has a bottle of rum in one hand and a bottle of Jack in the other as she yells at one of the cameras focused on our box. "These guys won game seven after a brutal slog with the Direwolves, only to get their balls handed to them by a girl! Who's on her period now, motherfuckers!"

We can't even make it to the locker room with the crush of media swarming us. The players are giddy as the sports reporters pepper them with questions.

A reporter sticks a microphone in my face. "Ellie, Ellie!" The sports media are grabbing at me. "Was that a planned strategy, to save Cookie for the very end?"

"Zayne Murphy's playing better than he has in a year. How did you do it?"

"What made you call a time-out?"

"Is that your new lucky suit?"

"I'm from *Vogue*!" a young woman screams at me. "Is that suit Givenchy?"

"Uh, actually, my mom made it."

"Slay!"

"Your equipment manager made a statement that made it sound like you're sleeping with your players." One man is right up in my face.

A big hand shoves him away. "Back off." Fletcher's there behind me. I can feel the heat from the exertion during the game steaming off him in the cold air of the stadium.

"Fletcher, that tie-breaking goal—how did you feel when your shot went wide but happened to hit Alexei Vidic's helmet and go in the net?"

Fletcher huffs out a laugh. "I wasn't aiming at the goal. I was aiming at his fucking head."

The reporters clamber. "Was this a revenge play for the Orcas players throwing tampons? Did it get under your guys' skin?" a smarmy reporter asks.

I just laugh at him. "Are you kidding me? No one's offended by that. I almost went out there and picked them up myself. These things are expensive! I put them in my bag. They bought the nice ones too."

Fletcher smirks. "Guess the Orcas players should have spent less time shopping and more time practicing. They might have won."

Fletcher's worn out and happy, his dark hair plastered to his forehead as he escorts me through the throng back to the locker rooms and sits down at his berth.

The cameras are turned on us. It's weird having to pretend that they aren't there.

The rookies keep staring at them until Jonesy snaps his fingers in front of their faces.

Usually, the media don't want to be in the Rhode Islanders' locker room. The captain just gives a generic statement about losing and pucks in net and "we'll get 'em next time." Then the players rush to get out of the stadium and the stench of their loss as quickly as possible.

Now? We're the stars.

"Cookie! Cookie!" the players chant when he shyly comes into the room. Bramms and Carlsson hoist him up, almost banging his head on the ceiling.

"Are those Lunchables?" one reporter asks as I pop open the cooler.

"The players get an after-game snack," I explain.

"The pizza ones?" the rookies beg. "We won, so we get pizza Lunchables, right?"

"The after-game snack isn't about winning or losing," I remind them. "It's about how well you did at practice. And I warned you."

"But we fucking creamed them!"

"Do well at practice this week, you get the pizza Lunchables." I grab the juice box from Cookie before he can stick the straw in and fold up the top.

"What the hell," Fletcher says as he unwraps his own straw.

"You're wearing white uniforms. I'm not cleaning stains out of those," I warn, reaching for his juice box. "This is a preschool-teacher hack."

"I think I can manage." He stabs it with a straw. Red juice spurts out all over his shirt.

"Goddamn it."

"It's a fucking good juice box." Jovi leans back, downing the whole thing with no straw, just crushing it into his mouth, while I take a Tide pen to Fletcher's jersey.

"Oh man, I'm going to chill in the hot tub after this." Bramms pulls off his skates.

"Hot tubs? Room service? What kind of hockey players are you?" Granny Murray rages. "You just won your first NHL game. Go out and get lit and laid! I'm buying hookers, booze, and coke. I just made a half a million dollars betting on my granddaughter. We're all getting shit-faced tonight!"

"There's my winner!"

"The team did all the work, Mom!" I complain as my mom wraps me in a big hug.

"Crazy!"

"The most insane thing I've ever seen!" my cousins chatter excitedly.

"Yeah, that's right!" Uncle Bic drunkenly whoops at the passing Orcas fans. "We owned you out there!" He whips his jersey around his head, bare belly out.

"Didn't she do a good job, Nate?" My mom beams at my dad.

"That was…" He pats my shoulder. "Well, you guys got a few lucky shots off. You should have lost."

"But we didn't."

"Don't make a habit of letting Fletcher bounce pucks off people's heads," Dad warns. "The NHL is not going to like it if he makes a habit of it. Concussion protocols, you know."

I nod.

"Good news though," Dad adds. "With the team on the upswing, it will be easier for them to hire a real coach."

"She is a real coach, Nate." His sister socks him in the arm. "You were amazing out there, Ellie."

"And in the interviews."

"You know what I mean," my dad backtracks. "Like, a professional coach. Ellie, you saw how rabid the spectators were. I saw how the other players were treating your team. It's not fair for them to have to deal with that every game."

"Yeah, okay, Dad. I know."

"Don't listen to him. Go get laid! You earned it!" Granny Murray slaps me on the back.

"Not with a player," my dad begs.

Chapter 20

FLETCHER

I t takes a second for the crowd in the club near the stadium to recognize her, but with the pink suit, there's no mistaking it. She chews on her lip, looking around as the drunk patrons start pointing and snapping photos. She seems surprised when people want her autograph.

I watch her in the crowd, in that bright-pink suit. The coach responsible for one of the biggest upsets in hockey history.

She sees me in the corner and hesitates like she's not sure if she should come over. I jerk my head and follow the bright pink as she makes her way through the crowd toward me.

Most of the team is floating around the dance floor, where girls in Orcas jerseys are flirting with our players. And Zayne is actually controlling himself, only nursing a light beer while the younger players crowd around him, reliving the game while he laughs with them.

Ellie slides into the booth next to me.

"Didn't want to go barhopping with your grandmother?" I slide my scotch over to her.

She takes a sip and winces.

"What? Do you need a pink lemonade and vodka?" I tease, taking it back from her. Because I'm drunk on the beer and the win, she's actually, for once, not annoying. I try to get the attention of one of the servers.

"Don't. You don't need to," Ellie says in a rush. "I'm not staying."

"You're not going to celebrate your first win?" On the TV above the bar, they're replaying highlights of the game. Cookie floats through the air to score the overtime shot. Then there's a clip of Ellie taking a swig from a bottle of tequila. "You can't be that much of a lightweight." I nudge her.

"Um," Ellie says. She's fiddling with her headband. "Sorry," she says finally, "for, you know—" She nods up to the TV.

I tilt her chin up. "What?"

"You know, for the pink suit and the Barbie music and the, uh, feminine products all over the ice."

"Don't care." I lean in, rest my forehead against hers. "We won," I whisper. "I won my first NHL game ever in my life, and I scored and got an assist, and we won, Ellie. You can play the Barbie music after every game if we keep winning. I don't care."

"I won't," she promises, picking at the pink polish on her nails.

"No?" I tease her. "You don't want to petition Dana Holbrook to officially change the Islanders colors to hot pink and rose gold?"

"That is a superior color combination to the burgundy and gray." She sniffs.

I set my glass down and tense up when a group of Orcas players head into the club. "What the hell are they doing here?"

"You're probably in their hunting ground for picking up women," Ellie says with a forced laugh.

One of them, a defender, Kessler, who smashed me against the boards, sees the pink suit then sees me. Eyes narrowed, he heads in our direction. I stand up and shove away from the table as the guy approaches too fast, calling, "Hey, Barbie!"

I'm going to kill this motherfucker. "What did you just say to my coach?" Kessler takes a step back as I get up on him, the glass clutched in my hand like a weapon. *Wish I had my rifle.*

"Whoa, whoa there, big guy." He holds his hands up. I keep my body between him and Ellie. "Man, no wonder you're a menace on the ice, Sully," he says conversationally. "My mom and little sister really wanted to meet Ellie. They're big fans."

Ellie peeks around me. "Hi!" She waves as a smiling middle-aged woman drags a teenage girl over.

"I love your outfit!" the woman gushes as the Orcas player looks on, bemused.

"Can you sign my phone?" the girl begs, holding out an iPhone in a pink case.

"Oh, um—"

"Gold pen." The girl hands it to her.

Ellie writes her name with a flourish and a heart over the *i*.

"You were amazing out there." Kessler's mom sweeps Ellie into a hug. "Such an inspiration. Even if you did beat my son."

"Told you you were going to lose." The girl tosses her hair at her brother. He sticks his tongue out at her. "Gross!" she yelps.

"Thanks, man." He shakes my hand. "Good game."

Ellie slumps down in the seat as the server brings our drinks. "That was really strange."

"You're the hot ticket in the NHL now." I toast her. "You could get us all big endorsement deals."

She blows at some of the loose hair falling over her face. I tuck it back behind her ear.

"Maybe I'll get you a real coach," she mutters.

I grab her jaw, turn her toward me. "You kidding me right now, Ellie?"

"I mean—" She tries to wriggle away, but I cup her face.

"You are a real coach. You're the best goddamn coach in the NHL."

"You're just saying that because you're drunk."

"I'm saying that because it's true," I tell her sincerely. "You're probably the best coach I've ever had. You get on the ice with us, you seem to have a real plan, your plays aren't just scribbles." I release her. "You beat Seattle. Don't sell yourself short."

Her lip catches in her teeth. I want to bite it. "Seriously, you're the best thing that's ever happened to me, Ellie," I murmur. I want to tell her, make her understand, how she finally made the team matter, made me matter.

"Is it cliché to want to kiss your pretty, game-winning coach?"

"You can't kiss me." Her eyes are big in her head, almost black in the dark, pupils blown wide-open.

"I just beat the shit out of the greatest NHL team in the country. I think I can do whatever I want at this point," I murmur. "Don't think, just shoot, right?"

Over her shoulder, there's a well-dressed woman entering the club. A blond, well-dressed man next to her helping her with her coat as she chides him. She looks across the dark club, and her eyes lock with mine.

Dana Holbrook's eyebrow raises. I sit back. Ellie looks over her shoulder.

She plays hockey, I remind myself. *She's not some dumb puck bunny. She can read my body language like a book.*

"Why is Dana talking to Fitz Svensson?" Ellie says slowly. "He owns the Orcas."

Why? Because maybe Hudson is right and she is running some deal.

I snap a photo.

"What are you doing?" Ellie hisses at me as I roll the video.

"The hockey gods are on my side tonight."

"Are you recording Dana?"

"Nah. Your granny's doing shots off the Finn's naked chest."

"I don't see guys like you in the retirement home!" Granny Murray whoops.

"That's how she got kicked out for sucking dick in the lobby." Harlowe downs several shots.

"Ah, shoot, Gran," Ellie yells. "Gran! Stop licking my players!"

Chapter 21

ELLIE

"**D**o I get a thank-you or what?" Harlowe preens as we walk through the Costco toy aisle.

"Don't you think you should wait until we win a couple more games?"

"No, because what if you don't? We need to ink these deals while we still can. If Tangerine wants to design a pink purse in your honor, who are we to say no? Also," she adds, "Drew Barrymore wants you on the show."

"I feel bad you're taking on so many of my PR duties," I worry. "I should take them back."

"No way." Harlowe shoves me. "You know how much free swag people are sending me? I got the new limited-edition Mariah Carey vinyl. There's a kitchen set from Platinum Provisions—the pink one that they sent me to put in our PR—and Bath and Body Works is talking about hockey-themed candles. Ooh, we need to make one that smells like Fletcher."

"No one wants that," I say hastily. "I don't know how you could make a candle smell like sweaty male hockey player."

"Yeah, maybe that is gross."

"I mean, it's not supergross, just, like, musky, like truffles or something. Aren't those supposed to smell like that?" I ramble. "Like, sort of animalistic smelling. I mean, I'd take a candle that smelled like that. Do you think that Cookie will like stuffed animals?"

Harlowe opens her mouth then closes it. "Oh my god."

"Yeah, you're right. Probably should do some Legos." I scoop some smaller boxes into the cart.

"Friends are supposed to tell each other everything."

"I don't know what else there is to say… Do you mean about my dad?"

"Screw your dad. He's jelly of your success." Harlowe snatches the Marvel action figure out of my hand, throws it into the cart, and grabs my shoulders.

"You slept with him."

"Uh, no I didn't. Who? What? You roomed with me. I didn't bring anyone back to our room."

Harlowe scoffs. "I don't know, maybe you did it in the locker room."

"Who are you talking about?"

"Fletcher." She's on her phone. "I should have known by the way he was looking at you after the match."

"After the—you're delusional!"

Harlowe sticks her phone in my face.

"Besides, I told you he doesn't want me. He wants Dana."

"Dana's a goddess among men. She's not messing up her blowout for a man who doesn't even own his own car."

"I think he was just—" I think back to last night, the way Fletcher leaned in, his breath cool against my mouth, the silvery eyes almost blue in the pulsing light from the club. "He was drunk. He didn't want me."

"Girl, he absolutely would have had a celebratory fuck in the booth in front of everyone with you. Even in that pink suit."

"I'm burning that suit."

"You'll make Aunt Trina cry."

"I'm not—" I add a stack of vinyl hockey-themed stickers to the cart. "I'm not, like, hockey-girlfriend material."

"Well yeah, you haven't maxed out your credit card on boob implants."

"Also, why are we even having this conversation? I can't be lusting after one of my players. I promised my dad."

"Uh, I'm sorry." Harlowe rolls her eyes. "I know our entire family is like intermarried and extremely enmeshed, but your dad and you had a convo about you sleeping with the players?"

"He's very concerned. It could affect his job."

"If you getting your pussy slammed is going to get him fired, he needs to get a new job. It's the holidays. He could walk into the Christmas market and get a job." She smirks. "At least if your dad finds a new coach, you can freely fuck Fletcher to your pussy's content."

"Ew. Don't ever say those words."

"You have a discontented cunt."

I clap my hands over my ears. "Not listening! I'm not listening!"

Before we start practice, I rock slightly on my skates as I hold the oversized blue bag with glittered stars hot-glued on it. My mom and I spent all afternoon making it.

"I just want to give ourselves a big round of applause. Each and every one of you gets a sticker." I hold out the sheet. "Don't leave these on your shirts, because they get ruined in the washing machine. You can put them on your face."

"Can I have the net?" Jovi asks excitedly when I show him the sticker options.

"How come Cookie gets a prize?" one of the rookies whines.

"Anyone who scored can get a prize."

"Murph set up assists. Can he have a prize?"

"I'll defer my prize to the group." Zayne smiles indulgently at the players.

"You can have an extra sticker. How's that?" I offer.

He tilts his head down so I can stick it right on his chin.

"What about Ren? We would have lost without him," Carlsson says.

I wrap my arms around the goalie's neck and pat his helmet. "Seriously, Ren, fantastic goaltending. We wouldn't have won without you. Ren can get a prize, too, out of the surprise bag. And Ren"—I pull off a new sheet of stickers—"also gets a whole sheet to himself."

"As long as you keep me out of prison, darling," he says, accepting the stickers and pasting them on his helmet, "you're doing right by me."

"Carlsson, with an amazing goal in first period." I wave him up. The big man digs around in the bag and comes out with a stuffed rabbit wearing a Christmas hat.

"Heikkiläinen!" The blond man has a big grin on his face as he skates up. "Coming in with that beauty of a goal in second period!"

"Lego!" he announces, pulling out the small Santa's sleigh kit.

"What?" Carlsson complains. "I didn't know there were Legos in there. I want a do-over."

"No do-overs," Fletcher announces as Cookie skates up and practically sticks his whole body into the bag.

"Seriously?" Carlsson demands.

The Finn says something snarky in Scandinavian. Carlsson doesn't understand it, but he knows it's not very nice, and he lunges at Heikkiläinen.

"Boys! Carlsson, you can have a do-over."

"Legos!" Cookie surfaces with a Santa's workshop kit.

Jonesy raises his hand. "Do you have any hockey kits in there?"

"Why do you care? You're not getting anything out of the surprise bag," Bramms shoots at him.

"There's always next game." Ziggy sighs.

"Can I have your prize?" Jonesy asks Zayne.

"Fuck no," Ren says, skating up, stick in hand. "He turned over a puck in front of my net, and they almost scored. You need to have like the opposite of a surprise bag, Ellie. Like, you need a punishment bag that has roach traps and rat poison in it."

"You didn't want Legos?" Bramms asks Ren when he pulls out a demented-looking Santa toy.

"You can go again," I offer.

"You kidding me?" He sets his prize on the ice and pushes a button.

"You can't bring that thing back to the house," Fletcher complains as the Santa sings a filthy version of "Dashing Through the Snow" while dancing on his head.

Ren smirks. "This is what Christmas is all about. Hockey, cookies, fucking, and Santa Claus."

"Good practice," I call to the players as they skate toward the locker rooms.

"Will the surprise bag be here next game?" Cookie asks me anxiously.

"God yes, please." Fletcher skates past me.

"And you get a prize for every goal?" Cookie perks up.

"Oh yeah, no limits," I promise.

"Will there be Legos? Will there be hockey Lego sets?"

"Yes." Even if I have to fight a bunch of moms at the toy store for them, I will buy those toys to get goals out of Cookie.

"Okay!" Cookie says brightly.

"So does that mean you're playing next game?"

Cookie nods happily and looks down at his toy, pleased. The guys all whoop and pat him on the head and back as they head to the locker room singing "We Are the Champions."

"I like that second-to-last play we ran," Fletcher tells me, skating with me as I pick up the cones. He scoops up several of them easily, skating backward. "It gives Cookie a path to the net. I think we need more plays like that. You cracked the code on him."

"Bribe him with toys." I laugh.

"Hey. Men are simple creatures." He grins.

"Yeah, I should have just bought all Legos instead of so many stuffies."

"You buy these yourself?" Fletcher gives me an odd look.

"I mean, yeah? I always buy my kids prizes and stuff. I use my mom's Costco membership. You trying to exchange your prize?" I ask him. "You didn't get a Lego set."

"I actually don't want a surprise bag treat." He skates over to me.

"Oh," I squeak. He's so tall and huge in the oversized padding. "You played really well. You should get something."

He drops the cones he's carrying. They scatter at our feet.

"Maybe you want to select the walk-on music for the game? Maybe not Barbie, but dealer's choice."

He takes off the helmet. His black hair is plastered to his sweaty forehead. "I'll take that, but I scored two points, so I think I get two prizes."

"What do you want for your second prize?"

His rough glove comes up to cup the back of my head. "This."

The first touch of his mouth is sharp, like blades on fresh ice.

He completely envelops me as he tips my head back so he can kiss me deep, kiss me like he owns me. He kisses like he skates—powerful, sure, dominant. I drag my fingers through his wet hair as I cling to him, his tongue licking into my mouth like the soul-stealing cold of the first breath of winter air.

I want to crawl under all the padding, rake my nails over the washboard abs hidden by the jersey.

Then he pulls back, just a breath, still close enough that I can count the flecks of steel in his eyes.

"Shit." I gasp. "Maybe I should start sleeping with my players if it'll make them win games."

"Candy Cane, you let me fuck you, and I'll win you a Stanley Cup."

Chapter 22
FLETCHER

"**S**top trying to make Fletch happen—he's not gonna happen," Lawrence jokes.

"Ellie thinks I play good. She said I could pick the walkout song next game." I preen.

"What? Fletch is happening! Two NHL goals!" Lawrence crows.

"One of them barely counts," Jake argues. "It bounced off of Vidic's helmet."

I'd say I hate my family, but I'm still riding on the high of the win and the scoring and the kiss.

I kissed Ellie. My coach. *Fake coach, because you're a fake NHL player.* It doesn't feel fake, though.

"We need a progress report on Dana Holbrook." Hudson frowns.

"Screw Dana." Anderson crowds in. "What was it like being on the ice with Emil Maynard?"

"Who cares?" Talbot counters. "Zayne Murphy is so much better."

"Um, last season?" He and Talbot start squabbling.

"Damn, he looked sick out there!"

"What's his secret? Did he fix his diet?"

I glance up at Hudson. "Something like that."

"Looks like I do actually know what I'm talking about." Hudson smirks then grabs me by the collar of my jacket. "Our clients want an answer," he growls. "You owe me—don't forget." He tosses me back on the couch.

I jump up and brush past him.

"You going to finish the job?"

"No, I'm not. We're going Christmas-tree farming. It's a team-bonding activity."

I get there early. I want to kiss Ellie under the snowy trees, want her all to myself. Maybe convince her to let me eat her out in the back of my truck.

Too bad half the team's already there.

Cookie is clinging to Ellie. Ren is railing about the fact that he's not allowed to shoot any of the squirrels wandering around in the snow.

"You are on parole—you're not even supposed to have a gun," Ellie scolds.

"You give her a little power, and suddenly she's a damn yuppie," Granny Murray gripes as she passes out homemade snacks to the players standing around the trees.

"Can I have more hot chocolate?" Jovi's practically vibrating as Ellie parcels out more of what smells like extremely sweet peppermint hot chocolate.

Jonesy sprays canned whipped cream in his mouth.

"Hey! Other people have to use that." Bramms shoves him to the ground, and Cookie snatches up the can of whipped cream.

Ellie seems a little breathless when she sees me. "Hot chocolate?" Ellie offers. "Seasonal cookie?"

"There are sandwiches too," Carlsson says around a warm ham sandwich on a Hawaiian roll.

"It's manual labor, so you need a little treat," she says. Yeah, I want a fucking little treat, all right.

I eat the offered sandwich in two bites. The rest of them crowd around Harlowe as she doles out the sandwiches. "Save some for the rest of the team," she warns as Bramms tries to take a second one.

"They should have shown up on time."

"You're all early," I snarl, suddenly furious that I can't kiss Ellie.

"She brought more of the cheese straws too," Bramms says uncertainly.

"You liked those, Fletcher, didn't you?" Ellie bends down to rummage around in her enormous thermal bag. She hands me a little cellophane bag tied with a neat red ribbon.

"Why'd you bring all these snacks?" I settle for shoving Cookie out of the way so I can stand next to her.

"We're having a fun outing." She shoos me closer to Cookie, who holds up his half-eaten pastry as she holds up her phone. "Cookie, smile," Ellie coaxes.

I scowl at him. His mouth drops open in fear. Ellie snaps the photo and sighs. I shove Cookie toward Jovi.

Excitedly, she announces, "Everyone's going to have more fun if there's food involved."

"Should have brought alcohol..." Then I stop myself as Zayne walks up. Thankfully, sober.

I should be happy that I'm out here with my idol, with my team, my winning NHL team. But all I want to do is cup her face and kiss her mouth while her cheeks are pink from the cold.

The Finn stomps up next to me, looks between Ellie and me, and says something in Finnish.

"What the hell are you looking at?" I scowl at him.

He just grins and steals one of my cheese straws and lets out another string of gibberish. The only word I catch is, inexplicably, "raccoon."

"These are not for sharing," I say loudly and slowly. "Get your own. Ziggy, where's your Google Translate?"

Ellie claps her hands. Everyone shuts up and pays attention. "We need to find the perfect Christmas tree. Nothing scraggly. I want it nice and big. Sturdy. Thick."

I blink at her. She stammers and is saved by Cookie.

"Are we getting a Christmas tree for your house?" Cookie raises his hand.

"No, for your house—well, Zayne's. He's hosting the team Christmas party on Friday. Thank you, Zayne!" She beams at him. The veteran hockey player looks a little drunk even though I know there's only hot chocolate in his cup—I checked.

"We need some trees to liven it up. I'll come over before the party to help you all decorate. Make sure it's clean before I show up," she warns. "The place looks like a frat house."

"My frat house in Mississippi was real nice," Ren sniffs. "I don't know what you all do up here in New England." He says it like a curse. "Giving fraternity brothers a bad name."

We troop through the snow. The Finn is in his element. That fucker even brought snowshoes. Who the hell does he think he is?

He hefts a hand saw. "That doesn't look like it's going to cut through so much as a holly bush, let alone a whole-ass Christmas tree," I tell him.

The Finn responds in Scandinavian gibberish.

"I have a chain saw," I tell him.

"Ziggy." I point to his phone. "Tell him we're not cutting down anything with a hand ax. I don't want to be here all afternoon."

I heft the chain saw I stole from Hudson off my shoulder. "Ellie, which tree do you want?"

"Multiple trees. Zayne has a big house. This smaller one for the living room, this one for the piano room—"

"We have a piano room?" one of the rookies whispers to me.

"Anything's a piano room if you put an instrument in it. Well, I think Ren lives in it." Ellie flits between the snow-dusted trees. "And these two big ones for the foyer."

"Coming right up." Before I can swing the chain saw down, the Finn is kneeling at the base of one of the trees, attacking it with the hand ax.

Weirdo.

I rev the chain saw.

Wood chips fly from around the base of the Finn's tree, and it topples with a puff as Bramms and Zayne catch it then shake the snow off the branches.

He moves on to the next Christmas tree while the chainsaw chews through the base of my tree.

The Finnish giant proudly displays his trees to Ellie while she applauds. He smugly waves the hand saw in my direction and says something derisive.

"He says," Ziggy translates on his phone, "that a real man knows how to handle an ax."

"Fucker," I swear, picking up my tree.

"It's so nice having all these big, strong hockey players around." Harlowe giggles. "No trouble carrying out all these Christmas trees."

Bramms flexes his bicep at her. "Did you spike that hot chocolate with bourbon?"

"No, no spiking," Ellie squawks.

I let the team get a few paces ahead of us. "I'm a little insulted you didn't jump me in the locker room."

"Your ego's big enough."

"So you did want to?"

"I've seen your Christmas package." She swats my belt. "I'm not impressed."

"The lighting in that locker room is terrible, Candy Cane."

"Put in a complaint with maintenance."

Quick, like I'm faking out a defender, I pull her behind one of the oversized Christmas trees. I steal a kiss from Ellie, letting my hand rest briefly on the curve of her ass.

"You need to be careful."

I kiss her again, harder. Slide my hands up the curve of her thighs and ass. "I'm an NHL player—you pay me to take risks." I kiss the soft skin right under her ear.

She shivers but not from the cold. "If someone gets a photo of this, I'm blaming you."

"I hope they do," I murmur, not moving. "Make a nice Christmas card."

There's commotion up the path. I ignore it, settling my hands on her hips, grinding slowly against her.

"Coach!" There's more yelling. "Coach Ellie!"

She shoves away from me.

"He's touching it!" The rookies are freaking out as we walk up.

"Raccoon!" The Finn is amazed. He clutches the very large, very confused raccoon.

Ren has a gun pointed at it.

"That is not a pet," Ellie squawks.

Jovi sprays some whipped cream in the raccoon's mouth.

"Jovi, no. Drop it."

"But they're best friends. It's a Christmas miracle!"

The raccoon hisses at Ellie. I heft my chainsaw, and the raccoon trundles away through the snow, bag of snacks in his mouth.

"Ugh, shoo. Here." Ellie takes out her hand sanitizer. "Gross, guys, that wasn't safe."

Ren shakes his head, and the weapon disappears. "He's lucky he can play hockey, because that boy ain't right."

Dana's car is in the parking lot when we pull up outside of the stadium.

"That's not good." Ellie shrinks in her seat. "Dana never comes to the stadium."

I pick up the box of empty containers—the guys took every last crumb of leftovers. "You can tell her you're going to be in a very important meeting."

I follow Ellie into the building. Do I want to fuck her? Yeah. But more urgently, I need an excuse to go up to the offices and steal Dana's tablet.

Chapter 23

ELLIE

Kissing Fletcher? It was a mistake.

Actually, no. This morning was a mistake. At the Christmas tree farm? It was worse than a mistake. It was a betrayal. It was a betrayal of my father, of my ideals, of the sport of hockey, of the NHL.

"The *H* stands for 'hell,' which is where you're going," I whisper to myself.

My dad is going to be so disappointed, I think as I hurry to my office. Kissing a player? At least I didn't sleep with him, right?

Fletcher's boot catches the door before I can slam it shut. Eyes wide, I stare up at him.

"Can I come in, Coach Candy Cane?" The deep voice is a low purr.

He crowds me as he steps into the office, box of stuff in one arm. He quietly shuts the door.

I take a deep breath.

I'm the coach. I need to set the tone. I straighten up. "Fletcher—"

He's kissing my neck, his fingers trailing over the zipper on my vest.

"Fletcher, we can't—"

"We can't?" He hums, the vibrations sending tremors through my teeth. "What?"

"This." I try to push him away, but even without the protective hockey gear, he's solid granite.

"I'm your coach," I gasp. "It's against the rules."

"I don't give a fuck about the rules, Candy Cane."

I scuttle backward, away from him. My office is small. I hit the whiteboard on the wall.

His palms slam on either side of me.

"I can't sleep with a player. I can't be that girl."

"Guess what, Candy Cane," he whispers, the words harsh against my mouth. "You already are that girl. I bet your pussy is so fucking wet right now. Bet it was ever since I kissed you this morning. Swollen and hot and begging for a cock. I've seen you on the ice in those leggings. Ass like that deserves to get eaten."

"Don't tell me"—his hands are warm as they slide under my shirt—"that you got into hockey because you like the game. Or did you do it because you—"

I try to dart around him. He's right. I am a little horny.

He picks me up by the back of the vest easily, like I weigh nothing, and drops me in my chair. "Oof."

His large hands land on the back of my neck. "If I can't fuck you, then I at least want to see you come. You want me to win you another game?"

"You're so full of yourself. I have Zayne and the Finn."

"Fuck him." He kisses me roughly, possessively. "Fuck all of them."

He wrestles the vest off of me and unbuttons my plaid shirt. His mouth is hot on my tits. He sucks the nipple raw, teeth scraping it.

I should have worn pants with buttons, but it's the holidays, and his hand slips easy under the elastic waistband. Hockey player grip strength is unreal, and his fingers practically feel like a cock as they stroke me hard. His mouth swallows my cries.

Anyone who walks past can see my face, sweaty and red. Thank god everyone was fired.

"I'm not going to—" I gasp.

One big hand claps over my mouth then moves to my throat, the other between my legs, squeezing as his knuckle is hard against my clit.

"Come on, fuck yourself on my fingers." He's behind me now. "I feel how wet and hot your cunt is. Fuck, you're a little slut." I whine as my hips buck against the chair. "You'd let every fuckhead on the Rhode Islanders fuck your pussy right now, wouldn't you?" The hand squeezes harder on my throat.

"Guess what—you let any of them touch you, especially that fucking Finn, I'm gonna cut their fucking throat. Then I'm going to drag you into the locker room and fuck you till you can't walk."

Gosh, why does that sound like a fantastic way to spend the afternoon?

His index and middle finger slide into the tight opening of my cunt. I try to escape his fingers in my pussy, but my back presses against the hard back of the chair.

"We can't, we can't," I chant as his fingers pull out with a slick sound.

But I want it.

"No," he whispers harsh in my ear, "you just won't bend over the table, show me your wet, greedy little cunt, and let me fill you up."

It takes every ounce of willpower to say: "You're my player. We cannot have this."

The fingers plunge in my mouth, choking me on the taste of my own pussy. His other hand tangles in my hair, forcing me to lick his fingers clean. "Fine." He releases me with a shove. "You're the coach."

"Wait—" I mewl.

He turns at the door and gives me a long look—that predatory look, like he's about to do something crazy on the ice. "It's a shame. Pussy like that should get fucked by a nice big cock." The door slams.

I keel over. My head thunks the desk.

My pussy is throbbing. I can still feel his fingers as I try to readjust all my layers of clothing.

I should have just let him finish getting me off. Again. At least. Because as I try to rebutton my clothes, I'm seriously considering finishing it myself, almost let my fingers slip under the waistband of my pants—

Dana strides in. She's the picture of a refined business-woman with her blowout and those impossibly high So Kate heels. She immediately commands my office.

A perfect eyebrow raises as she takes in my disheveled appearance. "We had a team outing today," I squawk. "Christmas-tree farm."

"I don't care. How likely is the team to win the next game? I have people coming who are very interested in investing in the team, shall we say."

"Oh, um, well," I squeak, "we're looking good. Cookie's ready to go. Zayne is going to be in top form."

"Sober?"

"Er, yeah." I shrink.

"And Fletcher?"

"And Fletcher is very, um, motivated."

"Yes, men are simple savages. Put a mildly pretty girl in front of them, and suddenly they're able to actually complete a task."

"Right, yes." I clear my throat.

Dana stares down at me. "I need them to win tomorrow. Make it happen. I saw your grandmother putting up porn. If that's what did it, you can screencast it to the jumbotron—I don't care. Just make a win happen."

Chapter 24

FLETCHER

nod to Dana as I pass her office. She seems intrigued, pausing with her hand on the handle of her leather bag. She's the spider in her web—her massive leather furniture and mahogany desk very different from Ellie's pink-and-white office that doesn't look like any NHL or hockey coach's office I've ever seen. To be fair, Ellie has an ass and tits unlike any NHL coach I've ever seen.

I shouldn't have given in, should have stuck to the play, because now Dana's leaving and taking all her stuff with her. She gives me a piercing look as she passes me, perfectly balanced on her heels like a big cat, an apex predator.

I take the stairs down two at a time. Her car, a huge black Mercedes, sits gleaming in the sun, impeccably detailed—not a speck of salt stain on it. It's unlocked.

It's a trap! everything in me screams as I get in the car and sit in the plush leather seats. There's nothing in the glove

204 . Alina Jacobs

compartment or in the center console. I don't even know what I'm looking for.

"She charges her phone in here," I murmur. It's a stroke of genius. I fish in my pocket and find the dongle that will fit right in the car's charger port. She'll plug in her phone to charge, and this thing will, according to Lawrence, let him access it to steal the data right off her phone.

Done. So close to paying off my debt.

This better work. I have to have something to show Hudson. He's family and all, but that just means he doesn't feel guilty if he breaks my rib.

Crack!

"Fuck!" I jump as Ren's palm slams flat on the window.

"Should I tell Dana Holbrook you're about to jerk off all over her Mercedes?" He wrenches the car door open. The Southern accent is slippery as he leans into the car like a nasty little toad. Ren is wearing a cutoff Rhode Islanders T-shirt, and his armpit almost scrapes my nose as he crawls over me.

"It's not your business."

"You're trying to sleep with the owner of my team and the coach of my team, so sounds like I do have a stake in where you wet your weenie."

"Fuck you, I am not." I'm about to fight this motherfucker.

"Then what the hell are you doing, doodle? It's not like you can hot-wire a car," he snickers.

"Of course I can hot-wire a car," I scoff.

He crawls right over me, his knee digging into my thigh, and sits in the passenger seat. "All right, Yankee, let's see it."

Dana's coming out any minute—she never hangs around here long. If I was smart, I'd ditch the car and start running. But I can't. Now it's a matter of manhood.

My tongue flicks out. I lick my lower lip. "Fuck you, trailer trash," I mutter.

Ren just howls in laughter.

My multi-tool has pliers and a screwdriver on it. Modern cars have immobilizers on them that make them unstealable—unless you have a cousin who knows computers.

I make lots of noise as I duck down under the steering wheel and text Lawrence:

Fletcher: *Need in this car.*
Lawrence: *That Dana's?*
Fletcher: *Yes, hurry up.*
Lawrence: *Turn your phone's Bluetooth on.*

Ren snorts somewhere above me.

I hold my breath.

My phone chimes. Then the car roars to life.

"Well damn, son, you got a magic wand up your dick." Ren, for once, looks impressed with me. "Too bad you can't play hockey as good as you can steal a car."

"We should probably—" My hands are on the door handle.

"Goddamn pussy ass—"

I floor it. The car roars and the tires screech as we peel out of the parking lot.

"Whoo!" Ren whoops, opening the moonroof and sticking his head out like a gunner as the German engine roars down the street.

The goalie slaps the back of my head. "I didn't think you had the balls, fucking Yankee pussy-ass bitch."

I do donuts in the parking lot as Ren cranks the radio to rap music. I almost cream a Santa Claus–shaped trash can as the car's speakers crackle and Dana Holbrook's voice comes on: "Boys, bring my car back."

Dana doesn't seem to realize I left the data scraper in the small USB port of her car. I watch the black Mercedes peel out of the parking lot.

I'm too antsy to go back to Zayne Murphy's house, though I should. Maybe clean up all the empty protein shake bottles for the party he's supposed to be hosting. Between Ellie and the fact that I might be about to clear my debt after years of it hanging over my head, I don't want to go back to Zayne's house with all the rookies and the other hockey players and wait and stew. I'm wired. It's like my skin's too tight.

I make sure the liquor's still locked up tight at Zayne's before I bail. I want to win tomorrow, and he needs to be sober.

I walk through town, toward Main Street, hands deep in the pockets of my coat, boots crunching on salt-scattered sidewalks. The streets are strung with lights, the Christmas market glowing like a postcard. Ellie loves this time of year. I know—I heard her yap about it enough when she tried to make a PR video for social media.

I weave through the crowds. Couples press close, fingers laced. Kids squeal over caramel apples and wooden toys. A guy my age awkwardly buys a snow globe from a stall— must be for a girl he's trying to impress. Everyone's trying to hold on to something tonight.

I'm not.

I don't want all that happy holiday bullshit. I don't want to be a happy couple. I don't want to sit on a couch and watch Hallmark movies and argue about the tree topper.

I just want to see Ellie come. Over and over. I want to tear that neat little sweater off her, toss her clipboard across the room, and make her forget her goddamn name. I want to ruin her for every guy who comes after me, especially the one who eventually marries her.

The lights blur for a second. I clench my fists. The need to do something buzzes under my skin like static. Fight. Fuck. Play hockey. Break something. Steal something. Score something. Her.

It's dark now. The stalls are dressed in glowing pinpoints of light. It nags at me. Once upon a time, I used to like Christmas. Love it, even. I don't now—I love hockey. For a little bit. Until Hudson tells me they have the data they need. Then I guess it's over. My dream is done. No more Ellie.

Today in her office can't be the last time I see her.

I take out my phone—nothing from Lawrence.

It's easy, though, to find her address. Nathan Clarke is a midlevel hockey star, and his house is listed on one of those creepy fan websites. I'm not Lawrence, but I can work Google.

It's right around the corner, past the ancient library and the bakery that has the creepy gingerbread people that they'll customize like your family.

The sounds of town merriment filter behind me as I head away from Main Street—bells and cider and snowflakes and "Merry Christmases."

The Clarke house looks like a postcard. I circle it in the snow, searching. The oak tree is missing leaves, so it's easy to jump up and grab the lowest hanging branch and pull myself up until I'm at the level of the glowing window, holding my breath. I hope it's not her parents'.

Fuck.

I freeze in the dark, wishing I had my balaclava on. There's Nathan Clarke in the window. He's still got the NHL goalie reflexes. He catches the motion in his peripheral vision. He goes to the window.

Do I drop out of the tree and break my leg? Get caught sneaking around in the tree outside of his youngest daughter's bedroom?

His wife calls to him. I catch snatches of their conversation:

"... *need to be more supportive...*"
"... *don't understand...*"

Trina throws a pillow at her husband. He goes into the bathroom.

I scurry up the tree, very well aware that I'm a walking cliché, and if I had any honorable intentions with Ellie, I'd put on a clean shirt, comb my hair, for God's sake, shave, and introduce myself to her family.

But I don't have honorable intentions. I don't want to marry her or fall in love with her. Don't want to stroll through the Christmas market with her. I just want to fuck her into her mattress then fall asleep with my nose buried in her soft honey hair, drunk on the faint gingerbread scent.

I easily make the jump to the roof then curse because I'm pretty sure Nate will pick up the vibrations.

I wait. I don't hear him shouting or anyone cocking a gun.

There's a low roof in front of the other glowing window. I drop onto the slate tiles, lighter this time, absorbing the impact into my thighs.

Then I lose my breath as I stare into the window.

She's sprawled out on the bed, her legs hanging off the side, her tits rising and falling under the thin spaghetti-strap T-shirt. All I can think of is sucking her tits through the thin shirt fabric then fucking her into the mattress until she screams so loud her father comes running.

Chapter 25

ELLIE

"I literally can't," I groan as I pull up on the car-lined street.

"There she is! There's my favorite NHL coach!" my uncle booms drunkenly when Aunt Stacy throws the door open before I can get my keys out.

"Eggnog!" she yells. "Someone get this girl a drink!"

"No eggnog. Water. She needs to hydrate." My dad's cousin shoos her away.

"Can you"—my cousin waves a sports drink with a home-printed label on it in my face—"make the team drink this?"

"All sponsorships have to go through me!" Harlowe hollers.

"Protein! She needs protein!" someone exclaims.

"She's not playing," another uncle argues.

"She's got to let the players run a train on her," Dakota says drunkenly. "Isn't that how you won the last time?"

"Which one has the biggest dick?" My cousin Bella giggles.

"Fletcher's pretty hung." Her mom cackles.

"Ooh, but Ren has all those tattoos."

"Ren's missing most of his teeth."

"Oh my," Mom cries, "I forgot about his poor teeth. I made candy canes for the boys for the game tomorrow."

"Trina, they can't eat candy."

"It's just one little candy cane."

"Are you serious? These things"—Aunt Babs holds up one of the biggest candy canes I've ever seen—"look like elephant cocks."

"Oh, do you think Ren's hung like that?"

"Fletcher for sure is."

My cousins all collapse in laughter while my face burns as I try not to think about how close I came to his, er, candy cane in my office.

"You need to stop chasing after men with a prison record! That's why you're thirty-four and not even married yet!" my aunt screams, chasing her daughter around the crowded living room.

Nate chokes on his merry meatballs—my mom's specialty.

"She's just joking." My aunt slaps my dad on the back. "You got your panties stuffed so far up your ass, bro."

"You're not sleeping with them, are you?" Nate asks as my uncle hands him another beer. "I assured everyone at the NHL that it was just the press giving you a hard time—that you promised me."

"No way, Dad," I squeak, pretending to be very interested in the buffet spread of Christmas-themed appetizers and nibbles.

"She needs to be sleeping with one of the players!" Granny Murray demands, walking through the house with a band saw.

"Granny, what are you—"

"I had to pawn the band saw that was in the equipment closet at the stadium, and I know how sensitive my son-in-law is about his tools—which is rich, because I ain't never seen him use one before. I need this to trim the sticks for the game tomorrow." She hefts it.

"Is that what happened to the freezer?" Harlowe scrunches her nose.

"Just move those turkeys your mom bought out of the way and put the game-day pucks in the deep freezer," my sister Angie tells her.

"You can use my makeup fridge," my sister Maxie offers, "to take them to the rink."

"That's not—" Dad hisses out a breath. "That's not regulation."

"She knows how to keep pucks cold!" one of my mom's cousins starts yelling at Dad.

He looks unimpressed. "It could affect the game if they aren't the right temperature."

"Um, my makeup fridge gets cold, thank you very much," Maxie says.

Nate smiles wanly at me. "How was practice? Ready for your game tomorrow?"

"It was, you know, fine. They're very excited about the surprise bag."

"Genius idea." My uncles pat me on the back.

My dad frowns. "Now, don't be too down on yourself if you all don't win. Sometimes good teams lose games—it doesn't mean the Rhode Islanders are suddenly playoff contenders."

"Boo!" Granny Murray waves the band saw at him threateningly. "You're gonna win, Ellie. You got those guys on their knees eating—"

"Mom," Trina begs, "can you help me in the kitchen?"

I busy myself with loading my plate up with my favorites: stocking-stuffer mushrooms, frosty flatbreads, Santa sliders.

It would be easier to obey this one simple rule of, like, not thinking about your players in a sexually gratifying way if Fletcher hadn't left me hanging on a knife's edge.

I need to get it together. We have a game tomorrow—a game Dana says we have to win.

It's late by the time the last of my huge family leaves.

"Fine!" Granny Murray screams at my dad. "I will go buy a freezer even though this team can't afford it because you all clearly don't care about Ellie. You're lucky I won all that money on the Orcas game." The front door slams.

I pull off my shirt and my bra and flop down on my bed in my shared bedroom, breathing a sigh of relief now that the underwire is on the floor. I'm in my chemise and panties.

If Granny Murray is out, I have like half an hour. That's enough time.

I'm feeling a little dizzy—for someone who's supposed to convince twenty-five grown men to play their hearts out and win against a top-ranked team in our conference, I really overdid it on the wine.

I roll over on the bed, and a giant candy cane digs into my hip. I clamp down a giggle as I wonder: *Is Fletcher that hard?*

No. We will not go there, brain.

I roll back over on my back. It doesn't help, because all I can think about is him crawling on the bed to straddle me, pushing me back into the pillows and the Christmas-themed comforter.

My fingers aren't enough. The candy cane seems like a stupidly good idea. It's hard and thick in my pussy as I rub it in my swollen cunt. Feels so good. My hips jerk as I think about Fletcher there, spreading me, asking me if I think I can take his cock.

"No, no, no," I try to tell myself. Think about literally anyone else—think about Chris Evans or Henry Cavill—but all I can think about is Fletcher, the scar on his pec, the huge ass and meaty thighs, the rough hands, the iron grip of his fingers as they curl in my pussy.

I jump as my phone buzzes.

Fletcher: *I know you're up there thinking about me in your cunt.*

Ellie: *Go practice your puck handling.*

Fletcher: *I'd rather see you stick handle.*

Ellie: *I'm reviewing game tape, not doing… that.*

Fletcher: *You're so full of it.*

Fletcher: *I know what you're doing.*

Fletcher: *Close your eyes. I want to watch you touch yourself.*

Wait, watch me?

Shit. I scramble upright. The window rattles. I stifle a scream. The last thing I need is for my dad to come running up here and see one of my players—that I just got done promising I wasn't going to sleep with—in my bedroom window.

Go away, I mouth.

Fletcher ignores me, jimmying the window open and leaping inside more gracefully than a man his size should. His skin glows in the soft light of my Rudolph bedside lamp.

"Get out! You can't be here! What if my dad sees you? Did anyone see you? Did you sneak into my house?"

"You didn't lock your window."

"I was thinking about the game tomorrow—"

One of those huge hands materializes between my tits, shoving me back on the bed, and I realize I'm not going to be able to concentrate until I know what he looks like when he comes.

"Oh my gosh, I told you," I croak, wriggling under him, which only makes his nostrils flare and his eyes go dark. "I'm not sleeping with a player."

He takes in the disheveled state of my clothes and the slickness on my fingers then grabs my hands, eyes still locked with mine, and twists my fingers in his mouth, closing his eyes while he licks them clean.

"You were thinking about me." The soft, thin fabric of the chemise slides up easily over the mounds of my tits.

"No I wasn't. I was thinking about Alexei Vidic."

Wrong thing to say.

His mouth crushes to mine. "Fuck"—he bites my lower lip—"you." One huge hand slaps my ass then tangles in the panties. The lace scrapes against my thighs as he pulls them down. "You aren't going to be fucking him. I don't want you bending over for him or even thinking about him."

I shudder as his mouth moves down to my tits, teeth catching the soft underside of my breast as his fingers meanly push my legs apart. They brush the candy cane, slick with my pussy juices. The corner of his mouth twitches. "Dirty little slut."

"I'm not! I don't know how that got there!"

But Fletcher claps a hand over my mouth. "I knew you were a little cock slut. Candy Cane."

He takes it out of my hand and lets it hang by the bow on the crook of his finger. He unwraps the cellophane with his teeth.

"You can't—" I moan as he rubs it along the length of my slit, the peppermint tingling.

I grab at his hands. "That, uh—"

"I thought you wanted me to eat your pussy. You don't want to make it nice and sweet for me?" The end of the candy cane teases the opening of my cunt. "You're so fucking horny you'd fuck this instead of me."

He twists his body, flipping over onto his back and bringing me with him. Hands dig into my hips and haul me up so I'm hovering over his face. "I've seen you on the ice. I know you have good core strength. Ride my face," he orders.

I still have a child's bedroom, and there's no headboard to grip onto. He's right—I spend a lot of time on the rink, and it's nothing to sink down on his face.

I feel his mouth, his tongue, his lips. His fingers trail up to grip my tits as I ride his face. Then the candy cane is back. Sticky streaks of bright red are all over my chemise.

I suck on it as his tongue works in my pussy, licking up the sticky sugar until I'm coming hard, rocking against his rough jaw, riding the orgasm out.

He grabs my hips, rotates me quickly, and brings me back down as I squeal, slapping my ass when I make too much noise. Then his tongue is all over my pussy, dipping in my opening where I want his cock then up to flick at my asshole.

"Shit!" I try to scrabble away.

As I balance on the rock-hard plane of his abs, he has one leg propped up on the bed. If I had any wherewithal, I'd move—but it's all I can do not to moan and freak out my parents as he eats my ass.

I bite down hard on the candy cane as his tongue plunges inside me, the crunch reverberating through my jaw. His thumb rubs my clit and pussy raw until he has me coming on his face again.

"Fuck me," I whimper as the chills of pleasure leave me. "I need—"

"You need a cock," he whispers, his mouth back, hot, on my pussy.

I fumble at the zipper of his ripped black jeans.

"You better suck on that candy cane."

I moan as he shoves me off of him.

"Your pussy still wants it, doesn't it?" His eyes are heavy lidded in the dim light. He looks at me—sugar spread all over my face, on my hands and knees on my bed. He leans in and kisses me, licking the sticky red off my mouth.

"You want me to fuck you like this with your daddy downstairs?"

"Uh-huh."

Two fingers press on my swollen clit, rub fast like he handles the puck. Then I'm coming, knees trembling, while his teeth sink into my tender nipple.

"Fuck me. Stop teasing," I slur.

"Spread your legs."

I feel his fingers spread me. All I want is that cock.

He picks up the candy cane off the bed next to me. The candy cane plunges in my pussy. I groan as it slides in me.

"You really do want a cock, don't you?"

He sucks my tits through the stained chemise as his fingers work in my pussy, my cunt clenching on the thick candy cane. He uses the curve of it to work inside of me, his other hand between my legs making me come again, my hips jerking against him. He pulls out the candy cane and licks it off.

"You taste"—he gives me one long lick—"like Christmas." Then he kisses me, the sweet spice on his tongue making its way into my mouth, his fingers sticky in my hair.

"I should come all over your face, make you extra festive."

"Yes, please," I pant.

He slaps my ass. "Wear a skirt tomorrow. I'm gonna win this thing then fuck you."

A loud knock thuds on the door. Fletcher kisses me then slips like a shadow out the window while I scramble under the covers.

"Ellie, are you alright? I thought I heard—" My dad's eyes narrow. I know he picks up on the current of cold air Fletcher left in the room.

"Heard what?" I hope my face doesn't look too red and sweaty, and I have to clench my hands to keep from reaching up to feel my hair to see if there's candy stuck in it.

"Nothing. Just, uh… good luck at the game tomorrow, kiddo."

Chapter 26

FLETCHER

The locker room's buzzing as I pull on my gear. The rookies are antsy like the dogs we'd use in the military that just wanted to go loping over the bombed-out desert landscape for hours on patrol.

I lace up my skates tight. I'm itching to get on the ice, itching to skate, to win.

"We gonna win, you think?" Jovi is twitchy next to me. Now that we've all had a taste of victory, no one wants to go back.

"We better." Bramms wraps clear tape around his shin guards.

"You're all winners to me!" Ellie's mom bustles into the locker room.

"Trina, goddamn it, don't listen to her!" Granny Murray rails. "I have money riding on you all."

"I thought team employees weren't supposed to place bets."

"Goddamn little snitch." Granny Murray waves the stick she's carrying threateningly at Cookie. "They don't pay me enough to keep me from gambling my social security check. I earned that check."

"Are you all decent?" Ellie pokes her head in.

I can't keep my eyes off of her as she runs through the plays.

Everyone's locked in. Zayne hasn't had a drink in days—I know because I slept on a mattress at the foot of his bed and made sure of it—and he looks like he's twenty-five again, about to dominate the hockey world. I can taste the win.

"And remember"—Ellie claps her hands—"anyone who scores or gets an assist chooses a prize out of the prize bag."

Jovi raises his hand.

"Yes, Jovi, everyone will get a sticker for participating."

"No, um, that's not what I was going to ask. Can I ask my question?"

"Yes."

"Are we getting pizza Lunchables for snack?"

"Yes!" Ellie claps her hands.

"Fuck yeah!" Bramms and Carlsson whoop.

"Pizza Lunchable." I manage to pick out the words from the Scandinavian licorice mouth of the Finn.

"It's the reason we saved your asses in World War II."

He scowls at me and slams his helmet on his head.

"You better—"

"Don't worry, Elvis." I smirk at Ren. "You might wanna bring a book because no pucks are coming to your net tonight."

I catch Ellie as she trots into the equipment room. She's wearing a skirt.

I slide my gloved hand under it. "I wish I'd fucked you last night," I whisper in her ear, making her shiver.

She's not wearing a pink suit. This one is white with a plunging neckline. The skirt's flouncy and short. She twists away. I grab her arm, pulling the fabric to revealing a crescent of red lace.

She yelps when I grab the back of her neck.

"What are you wearing?"

"Just in case you need some extra motivation." She blinks up at me and fusses with her neckline.

My nostrils flare. I can practically taste her. "I don't need the promise of your pussy to win." I slap my helmet on. "I'm going to do that anyway."

My team is vibrating by the time we line up in the tunnel. Helmets on. Visors down. The roar of the crowd echoes down the tunnel.

Zayne's the captain. He stands at the end of the line, slapping each of the players on the thigh with his stick as they pass.

I take my spot as alternate captain, second to last in the lineup.

"You ever figure out your song choice, Fletch?" he grins, the music still pounding through our chests.

"Fuck yeah, I've been knowing what I'm playing," I holler to him as we head down the tunnel. I feel like I'm about to jump out of a C-130 airplane into the pitch-dark.

We're electric. The crowd is deafening. And then I hear it.

My song.

Ever since I was a kid, I daydreamed of this being my walk-off song when I played in the NHL.

The bass drops. The plexiglass almost shatters as the first of our team steps onto the ice, powerful, invincible. I bribed Ellie's cousin who works the sound system to turn the bass way the fuck up, and the beat of the rap song makes the jumbotrons shake.

I can feel it pumping in time to my heart. Can't even make out the words to the song—it's just that unrelenting beat.

It's even better than I imagined when I was in high school, daydreaming about this moment.

And when the announcer goes, "Your alternate captain, Fletcher Sullivan," and my name and picture flash on the shaking jumbotron, the crowd goes fucking wild.

I light up the ice, making a powerful lap around to the screams of the crowd, all in my team's colors.

"Fuck yeah. We play for the fucking NHL!" Bramms screams at me over the eardrum-bursting music.

Ellie's laughing, her hand clapped to her chest, watching me. I wink at her and line up for the national anthem.

Then we slaughter the other team. We're all locked in together. It's the best we ever played. The second the buzzer sounds, we're all over the puck. The energy is unreal.

Ellie's plays flow off our sticks effortlessly.

The Finn sinks a nasty goal before the other team even knows where the puck is. Jovi executes a no-look backhand pass to Zayne, and he makes one of those impossible shots that's going to make the highlight reel. The other team tries to rally, but Bramms checks a guy so hard the crowd audibly groans.

And me?

I dominate the boards, I wreck their top scorer, and when I score in the second period—my second goal of the night—I don't even celly. I just point my stick at Ellie. I'm getting laid tonight, if I don't die of adrenaline rush first.

Cookie is the ringer. He waits like a bird dog for Ellie's signal, then he zips onto the ice, knifing through guys, taking the quick-release puck Zayne shoots in a pocket for him, then goal!

Ellie got the little fucker to go in every period and score. He even went in twice in the third period, which earns him a hug and a kiss on his helmet from Ellie while the crowd chants, "Let him cook!"

It's a shutout. We win six to nothing and pile onto Ren at the end of the match while the home-game crowd roars their approval.

"Fuck, I love hockey!"

"Goddamn it, Yankee, I do believe you might be able to play the game of your Northern people after all." Ren grins his gummy smile at me.

"Cookie! Cookie!" The crowd throws hats on the ice, and we gather them up, piling them on the kid's head.

"So proud of you." Zayne cups his face, giving him a rough shake.

"Let's go eat some fucking pizza Lunchables!" Jonesy whoops, jumping on my shoulders as we troop victorious down the tunnel to the locker room.

"You won!" Ellie's ecstatic. "Beautiful goal, Fletcher." She praises all the players. "Zayne, of course, setting up plays like a master, and Cookie, who got on the ice four times today."

"It's gotta be some sort of record," I say. "I mean, total, he was on the ice what, two minutes, and scored four goals?"

"Insanity."

"We won! We won!" we chant as Ellie passes out the little plastic squares of processed bread, meat, and cheese.

Cookie intently measures out his sauce, cheese, and cold pepperoni on the little round flatbreads.

The Finn looks absolutely revolted and refuses to touch it.

"Can I have yours?" The rookies pester him.

"Ziggy, tell him he's insulting our culture." I grin around my own pizza Lunchable. I toss the little candy bar that comes with it to Cookie.

Ren glops the sauce on two of the soft crackers, adds cheese, and mashes them together. "Shit, I bet we get a wild-card spot, at least in the playoffs." He chews noisily.

"We keep playing like that, we're going to the Eastern Conference final," Zayne crows, leaning back so he can stretch his hamstring.

"The press wants you, Fletcher!" Harlowe calls to me.

I yank my jersey over my head, still soaked in sweat and adrenaline. My heart's pounding like the bass from the intro music, and I feel ten feet tall. "Tell them I died," I call back to Harlowe, squeezing the ice-cold juice box into my mouth. The sugar hits my brain.

Fuck, that's good.

"Nope," she says, smirking as she sticks her head into the locker room. "You scored twice and body-checked that guy into 1996. The cameras want your pretty face. Shirt on, please. They want you and Ellie."

"No, shirt off!" Granny Murray boos.

I grab my stick and thud down the hall to stand next to Ellie like a knight. She gives me a brilliant smile.

"Coach," I drawl.

"Do you get something out of the surprise bag?" one of the reporters demands.

"I got two goals, so I'm entitled."

The reporters titter.

"I hear the Legos are popular items."

"What it really needs are alcohol and condoms."

Ellie gets very serious. "I have condoms in my tote bag. And I will give them away free to anyone who asks. We are not getting anyone pregnant—no baby-mama drama, please!"

"Are you in a relationship with one of the rink rats?" one reporter snickers to me.

"I actually prefer my fuck buddies to be hockey players."

Chapter 27

ELLIE

"Hey guys... you're here." I grimace as my aggressively large family crowds in the vestibule in front of the locker rooms.

"They wanted to see some hot NHL ass." Granny Murray jerks her thumb. "I said I'd hook 'em up."

My cousins all smile gleefully when they see Fletcher step away from the media scrum and head to the locker room. His silvery eyes narrow when he approaches.

"Fletch, you're so hot!" my female family members catcall.

My dad is shoved to the front of the group.

Suddenly, my father, who always called me his baby girl, is face-to-chest-plate with the guy who snuck into my childhood bedroom and had his face between my legs.

I cross them.

Fletcher looks down at me from that impossible height, and his mouth twitches into a smirk.

"Uh, Dad, this is…" *The guy who had his candy cane where the sun don't shine.* "This is our centerman."

I can blame the flush of my cheeks on the media lights, right?

My dad doesn't seem impressed. "Nice shot on goal," he says to Fletcher flatly.

Fletcher tips his head down to look at me briefly then back up to my dad. "I have a good coach."

His stick shifts in his hands, then the flat of it presses briefly but definitely on purpose right on my backside. I jump and grab my skirt.

"Well, Fletcher needs to go, uh, get changed…"

My cousins are drunk, and their normally minimal filter has turned into no verbal filter whatsoever. "We won't keep you from fucking in the locker room."

I kick Violet in the shins.

Fletcher raises a dark eyebrow under his visor. My dad gives him a suspicious look.

"Don't wait for me," I babble as I give Fletcher a shove toward the locker rooms. "I'll get a ride back."

"Ellie!" my family calls.

"See you later! Thanks for coming to the game." I practically sprint away from my family. I can't take it. I'm sure my dad knows something's up.

The players are all in various states of undress in the locker room, so I scurry away into the back to my windowless office.

Shut the door.

Lean against it.

Try not to think about Fletcher.

Is he going to show up at my bedroom? My mom is hosting a postgame party for the whole family.

I could just surprise him in the locker room shower…

No, that's a bad idea. We'd get caught. I need to stop obsessing over him. He's my player.

I don't even like him. It's the fact that he's a forbidden hockey fruit bat—that's the problem.

I pull a makeup wipe out of my bag and blot at my face with it. Try to get myself together.

Watching him on the ice, the way he moved, the raw power of him… "Bet he fucks like he plays," the part of me that's the bad daughter, the bad coach, singsongs.

I unbutton my suit jacket and fan myself. It doesn't help. I've been half gone since he snuck into my room last night, like he had every right to be there.

I mean, who does that? It's the same kind of cocky that lets a man just walk onto a NHL team from the minors and score goals.

The door handle rattles.

"Just a minute," I choke out as I fumble with the buttons in the dark. "I'm coming, I just—"

The door opens. Fletcher stands there in the doorway, a huge, dark shadow. He's still in his skates, balanced on the knife-edge of the blades inside their guards.

"You didn't want to get showered?" I croak.

Full disclosure here, everyone: you can't be a straight female with NHL-adjacent family members and not at one point in your life wonder what it's like to get absolutely railed by an NHL player decked out in his full gear.

The way Fletcher's looking at me… the sweaty dark curl of his hair peeking out from under the helmet…

"I think," the deep voice rumbles, "I told you I wasn't going to fuck you until after I won you that game."

My mouth opens, ready to argue—but then his fingers are at the lapels of my white jacket, pulling it off in one fluid move. The pads underneath his burgundy-and-gray jersey shift, exposing the sweat-slicked skin at the base of his throat.

I stare.

"You think I'm doing all this because I'm confused?" he asks. "You think I bust my ass on that ice for the sticker or the prize bag?"

He moves toward me slowly, deliberately. I back into the desk. His skate guards click faintly on the floor like a warning.

"You should leave," I whisper.

"Tell me to. Order me to." His teeth graze my neck.

My lips part. But no sound comes out.

"You're the coach. You own me. So tell me not to bend you over and fuck you." Fletcher leans in, one hand braced on the desk beside me, the other cupping the back of my neck like he did earlier—possessive. "I'm going to kiss you now," he says, voice low. "Unless you order me not to."

I don't. I can't.

And when his mouth crushes mine, hot and hungry and devastating, I realize I'm already gone.

"What drill do you want to run, Coach? Hmm?" His head dips down, helmet bumping my jaw as he pulls my tits out of the lacy red bra.

He pulls his plastic mouthguard out, tosses it on my desk, then attacks my tits, working the nipples with his teeth, his tongue sucking them raw as the heavy gloves force my legs apart.

I pant as the raised logo slides against my clit—the best kind of friction.

The red lingerie has a secret surprise that makes for precarious sitting. Wearing the fabric of the gloves, it takes him a minute. He stares down at the wetness on his gloves.

"It's a good thing you won." I look up at him, chest heaving.

"You got your cunt all nice and pretty for me, didn't you, Candy Cane?"

"I just wanted a win."

"Nah, you wanted to get fucked."

"No." I grab the chin strap of his helmet. "If you lost, I would have made you sit there and sweat and watch me get myself off."

He growls low in his throat. "I won, so your pussy is mine." He gives me another bruising kiss. "You ever been fucked by an NHL star?"

"No," I whimper.

"No, your daddy didn't let you fuck any of his NHL buddies. You didn't spread your pussy for any of them?"

"I'm not a virgin," I choke out.

He uses the handle of his hockey stick to tease my pussy. The taped handle nudges at my opening. I groan as it slides in.

His rough glove is on my neck. He pushes up the short white skirt and falls to his knees, the heavy padding clicking and shifting under the jersey as he goes down on me.

I clutch at the smooth helmet, the clear visor bumping against my hip as his tongue forces its way between my pussy lips, lapping at me as my cunt soaks the thin scraps of my crotchless lace panties.

"Does the NHL know how much of a puck-bunny cum slut their newest coach is?"

I moan as his tongue twists on my clit. Then I screech as he stands up abruptly, my head almost crashing into the ceiling tiles.

He thuds me against the whiteboard; the markers clatter to the floor. "You're hell on my knees."

"We'll have to do more leg strength training. I have some drills." I breathe then moan as he gives me a punishing lick. I know what he can do. I've seen him on the ice.

I wrap my legs around his neck and ride his tongue, ride the fingers until I'm coming all over his face and helmet.

"You gonna actually score, or you just going to play around on the ice?" I pant then groan as he continues to lick my pussy clean.

He pulls me off of him. Drops me to the floor in front of him. His gloved hands briefly squeeze my tits then moves up to cup my jaw.

I can't read his eyes in the shadow from the helmet as he says, "Coaches are supposed to take care of their hockey players, so I need you to get my dick nice and hard for you."

You'd think his cock would look small against all the thick padding, but it's not. It's fucking huge. I can barely take it in my mouth.

One glove grabs the back of my head, forcing me to him, so I take the whole length down my throat. My eyes sting as he makes me take all of it. He's powerful, forceful, but he never loses control—just glides that thick cock into my mouth as I pant through my nose around the length, sets it there for a split second, then slides it out.

I grab his powerful legs as he fucks my face.

"I told you you're a good coach, Candy Cane, taking care of your players."

My nails scrabble against the thin fabric of the burgundy pants over the thick padding. But it's not all padding. I'm wet again, pussy throbbing as I think about those huge thighs, slabs of granite ramming this thick cock in my pussy.

He pulls out of my mouth with a wet noise. "Damn, you'd look good with my cum all over your face and tits."

His mouth twitches into a smirk. Then he grabs the back of my neck and slams me over the desk, sending my little cup of paper clips all over the floor.

He runs rough gloves down the expanse of my body. I arch my hips into his hands.

His tongue licks a stripe along my dripping-wet pussy. Then up to my ass.

"You only get to come in my ass if you score a hat trick," I manage, barely keeping the upper hand.

Fletcher hisses. His gloved hand comes down hard on my bare ass, making me squeal.

"Fine. I'll destroy your pussy." He cups my jaw, pulling my head back so I arch against his cock, rock-hard against my swollen pussy. His hands in the huge gloves are rough. The gloved fingers push in my mouth. I taste the leather and sweat.

His glove comes off, and he stuffs it in my mouth. "I don't want an audience while I fuck you," he whispers in my ear as I hear a condom packet rip.

He doesn't give me a minute to adjust to the fact that I'm about to do it—I'm about to let one of my players turn me into a puck bunny.

But he's forcing my legs apart. I feel a slight cool breeze on my pussy, then he rams that huge, thick length in me while I curse around the glove in my mouth, my fingers scrabbling for purchase on the laminate desktop.

"Take it, Ellie, take it. That's my little cum slut. Damn, I want to fill you up. Take my cock." The filthy language flows from his mouth as he drags me backward onto his cock, making me take every thick inch of him until he's seated deep inside of me.

"You like that, don't you?" He shifts my hips up and snaps his hips, somehow seating his cock even deeper in my cunt. "Your cunt is so fucking tight on me. I think this is the nicest pussy I ever fucked. You feel even better than your mouth."

He does that little microthrust again, rolling his hips so that I feel that thick cock deep inside me. He leans over me, forcing my back to arch up with his cock so he can run his hand, warm and rough, over my tits, squeezing them, rubbing my raw nipples as I whimper, my legs split so he can wedge his huge body, bigger in the padding, between my legs.

"You take a cock like a winner, Candy Cane." He slides out then slams into me again. "Fuck." He lets out a low growl. Then he's bucking against me, burying that huge cock in me over and over again. The pace is brutal.

"You haven't been fucked until you've been fucked by a pro athlete."

And he's right. On the ice, Fletcher's all raw power, brutal grace. He fucks like he plays—raw power.

"I love fucking after a win. I wanted to fuck you after that Orcas win." He says it like we're just having normal pillow talk, like he's not pounding in me like he's defending against the boards, jackhammering into me with blindingly powerful, inhumanly quick thrusts, destroying my pussy in the best way as I moan and whine and beg wordlessly against the glove, which muffles the porn sounds I make as he takes me until I'm shuddering on his cock.

He gives two more powerful thrusts, then I feel him explode in the condom as he rolls his hips into me, using my throbbing pussy to wring out the cum.

I spit the glove out as I collapse on the table. He turns me over, and I just lie there in a puddle on the desk, my tits out, the red lace of the teddy in sweaty tatters.

He runs his hands all over my perspiring, tremoring skin. Like I'm better than any hockey trophy he's ever won.

He hooks one of my legs around his neck. His helmet is cool on the inside of my thighs as he licks me with long, slow, powerful strokes from his tongue. His fingers, glove-less, slide into my throbbing pussy, stroking in me not as deeply as his cock but still enough that he's wringing another orgasm out of me before I can catch my breath from the last one.

Then he's between my thighs again, his cock pressed against my raw pussy as he slowly grinds against me. Inexplicably, I feel him grow hard against me.

"I can't," I gasp.

"You won't get a prize from the surprise bag," the deep voice taunts.

"You don't even have another condom," I whimper.

"Yeah, because I'm going to come all over your pussy." He wraps my legs around him, grinding against my pussy, teasing my clit with his hard cock.

I arch my back off the table and groan when I feel the head of his cock at my ass. "You didn't get a hat trick."

"Just a little motivation for next game." I feel the slight burn of him pressing against my ass, then it leaves, and that thick cock is sliding bare in my pussy. "Your cunt can take it." He hooks his fingers into the panties, the thin straps digging into my skin as he slides that impossibly long length into my abused pussy until I feel his balls, huge, against my cunt.

He bends over, smothering the begging and pleading and moaning with his mouth. The helmet falls off, and I wring my fingers in the sweaty dark waves of his hair as he fucks me with a smooth, unrelenting pace.

"I'm gonna ruin your fucking pussy," he grunts, hiking up my hips so he can drive his cock deep into me. "You're never going to spread your legs for anyone but me, are you?"

I pull at his jersey. "I'm gonna—are you gonna—" I gasp. Part of me wants it, wants to feel what it's like for him to empty all that cum in my pussy.

"Shit!" He pulls out, the sensation making me finally come.

He strokes himself twice as he watches me in front of him, legs splayed, pussy bare for him, then I feel it—the hot thick cum spray all over my tits, my stomach, coating my pussy and my thighs in white to drip down my desk.

He takes my hand, slides it into my messy pussy, mesmerized as he uses my fingers to tease my clit.

"I can't, I'm—" I pant.

He moves my hand, coated with his cum and my pussy juices, forcing my fingers in my mouth. I suck my finger as he works his own hand in my pussy, stroking me roughly until my hips betray me, rolling erratic and lazy against his hand until another orgasm twists out of me, my legs clutching his wrist until the last of the tremors pass.

"I've done some shit, but this is a new low point." I breathe hard as Fletcher adjusts the padding. He's sweaty and messy from the hockey match and fucking me. Me? I shouldn't look like I just got fucked in an alleyway.

"It's not completely low. You didn't let me come up your ass." He kisses me hard, possessive, as he slides his gloves back on.

Chapter 28

FLETCHER

"We play the Montreal Vortex tomorrow," Ellie announces the next morning at practice.

I wanted to crawl into bed with her last night, fuck her, ride her, make her scream and moan my name, fill her with my cum. I even jogged in the cold and sleet to her parents' house, but it was packed with her family celebrating the Rhode Islanders' win.

"Everyone did great. You all earn a sticker," she says as she passes out the prizes.

"Can I have my surprise later?" I murmur so only she can hear me when I step up to the bag.

I can't keep my eyes off her during practice, can't stop thinking about how good it felt to be buried inside of her.

I'm going to fuck her again soon. Hopefully, tonight after the holiday party.

We're supposed to be doing a passing drill, but I can't concentrate from watching Ellie. She's balanced on the toe of her skates, legs spread wide, knees bent. *The same position she'd be in to ride a cock.*

No, *my* cock.

She rises and falls slowly as she demonstrates a puck recovery move to Ren she wants him to try.

I'm not the only one watching her.

"Damn, you think if we win at least the Eastern Conference, she'll sleep with the guy who scores the game-winning goal?" Eddie snickers. "Might rethink my stance on female coaches if I get some pussy on my—oof!"

Eddie doubles over, choking on the words as I break my stick into his gut.

"Ooh," the guys near me all groan as I bring the stick down on Eddie's back.

"Fuck you, Sullivan." He spits blood at me.

"*Fuck* you, Eddie. You say one more goddamn thing about our coach, and I'm going to gut you."

"You don't have the balls. You're her fucking lapdog," he sneers at me.

I grab him by the collar of his jersey and lift him up so his skates dangle above the ice.

"Hey!" Ellie yells, skating over. "Fletcher, put him down."

I ignore her.

"You have been misinformed if you think I'm some lapdog. While you were drinking and playing video games and losing hockey games at Boston University, I was in combat. So no, I have no problem gutting you right here on the ice," I snarl into his ear before I drop him in a heap on the ice. "Fucking try me."

Eddie scrambles up. "Wait, combat?" He narrows his eyes at me like he's going to say something, like he's going to tell everyone that I'm not who I said I was.

I lock eyes with him, channel Hudson when he's at his coldest.

Fortunately for me, Eddie's a little shit. He storms off the ice.

"Fletcher…" I stare down at Ellie until she gulps. "I will handle my team as I see fit." Her voice doesn't tremble.

Jovi is nervy. Cookie hides behind Bramms as I skate slowly to the blue line.

I can't tell what Zayne's thinking. And honestly, I don't care. No one speaks about my coach like that.

I look them each in the eye.

"Line up for the next drill."

"What are you doing?" Ellie demands, stopping me in the hallway before I can follow the rest of the team into the locker room.

"Going to shower. You want to join me?"

"No, I mean with Eddie," she demands.

My teeth grind. So she heard him.

"People are going to say mean things about me. Sticks and stones, you know. You can't just jump in and defend me every time. That's crazy."

"I'm not Ren, but I'm not sane either. And no one is going to say shit about you when I'm around," I tell her sharply.

"It's bad for the team."

"Fuck the team," I growl.

"We can't let this"—she gestures between us—"come in the way of winning."

I make a frustrated grunt. I want to kiss her, want to take her to a secluded place, want to fuck her to remind her she's mine.

"This isn't going to work if you're more focused on me than playing. Oh my god," she groans. "My dad—"

"I don't give a shit about what your dad thinks, Candy Cane."

She gives me a hurt look.

I run a hand through my sweaty hair. "Is Dana Holbrook going to be at the holiday party?"

"Dana Holbrook?" Ellie looks distressed.

"Trying to change the subject since we will have to agree to disagree that you deserve to be treated with at least a bare minimum of respect."

Zayne's house is warm and loud and chaotic, exactly the kind of place a normal person would love to be in for the holiday—teammates yelling over each other, Christmas lights flickering out of sync, holiday music blaring over the speakers.

But my jaw is tight, and the weight of what I'm about to do hums low in my chest like a warning. "I don't know why you're bothering to decorate this place," I mutter to Ellie as I pass, eyeing the tangled garland and precarious string of lights someone duct-taped to the mantel.

"You should've seen it before we cleaned, Coach," Bramms chirps.

"Did you clean it?" Harlowe deadpans, pulling a sock from behind the couch.

"I told you to move the couch!" Carlsson yells at the rookies, who all suddenly find the floor fascinating.

Zayne's wearing a Santa hat, happily humming to the Christmas carols blaring from the speakers. Jovi's setting up, trying to get the bass just right.

Eddie hasn't come back to the house since the blowup on the rink. I'd say good riddance, but technically, we do need him at the next match.

I glance around then steal a kiss from Ellie behind the tree, just a quick one, hot, needy.

Bramms is already eating the snacks. Carlsson complains loudly.

Ellie jumps away from me, guilty, as he comes over.

"I'm just trying to convince her to trade Eddie," I say to the Finn, who watches us, eyes narrowed.

"Can we eat? Can we?" Jovi bounces around. He's been crushing Christmas treats since practice.

The doorbell rings and rings.

"It's not a party without girls!" Granny Murray bursts in with a ton of young twentysomething women.

"Dayum. Eddie's gonna be sad he missed this." Jonesy whoops.

"Merry Christmas, boys!"

"Hey!" Ellie stomps over to them. "This is a private team party."

"Yeah, Violet," Harlowe sighs, recognizing the leader of the cousin crew.

Ellie turns to Zayne, her mouth twisting as she introduces her family. "Sorry. Cousins. Second cousins. Sisters. One of them might actually be an aunt."

"The invite said 'and family,'" one of the girls says, snapping her gum. "We're family."

"We brought liquor!" another one cheers.

"Don't drink too much!" Ellie shouts after them as they flood the room like glittery locusts.

Zayne looks out happily over the crowd—sober, but still happy.

"This," he says, taking a sip of mineral water, "this is what it's all about."

"What?" I ask, distracted. My eyes are on Dana Holbrook, who just stepped through the front door, a big fur coat wrapped around her white winter pantsuit. I'm barely listening because Ellie is greeting none other than Dana herself.

"Life, Fletch. This is what life's about," he says, a little wistful.

"Right."

"Gonna go say hey to the boss," I mutter and drift toward Dana. Ellie's watching me; I can feel it. But I can't stop. I have a mission.

"We can't party too late," Ellie warns. "We have practice tomorrow. This was supposed to be a low-key holiday gathering."

"Is she always such a buzzkill?" Dana saunters over to the wet bar.

"Damn, I didn't know a pantsuit could be that sexy," Carlsson whispers.

"I'd be her house husband," Ren drawls.

I elbow Ren. "You'd need to get teeth first."

The music changes. Ellie's cousins scream, dragging players into the middle of the living room. "I love this song!"

"Shots!" Granny Murray hollers.

"Do you still have that purse full of pills?" Ziggy jokes.

"There's a game tomorrow," Ellie rushes around reminding people.

I sidle up to Dana. "Didn't think you'd want to mess up your nice shoes in a place like this."

Dana snorts as I dance next to her. "You should have seen me in college."

"Yeah, were you a party girl?" I ask, trailing my fingers on her pantsuit, hoping I feel her phone and can snag it.

Zayne is giving me that *I'm going to fuck you up* look that he gets before he creams someone on the ice.

I can't care, can't feel the weight of his disappointment. Or of Ellie's.

Sure, that might be Ellie looking jealous, but I have a mission. And it's not "fall in love with my hockey coach," no matter how cute she is.

Dana catches me looking at Ellie. She's too good of a businesswoman to let me get a read on what she's thinking.

"Boss lady," Ren drawls in that molasses accent. "I believe they're playing our song."

A country pop song blares from the speakers as Ren practically tosses Dana up onto the coffee table to cheers. I bleed back into the shadows, watching as the players dance with Ellie's pretty cousins and sisters.

The music pulses. Jovi's taken over DJing duties.

I drift into a side room. Dana's purse is among the pile of coats in what Carlsson calls the "smoking room," but really, it's where Ren has moved onto the couch.

I don't hesitate. Anyone can come in, but I just pray that there's enough of a window.

Out comes her iPad. I have the decoy tablet in my jacket for easy access, and I swap them out.

Just in time. Dana saunters in.

"Can I help you, boss?"

She raises an eyebrow. She's a little drunk.

I need to stall, need her not to wonder why I'm in here, not at the party, and what that iPad-shaped thing in my coat is.

"Uh-oh." A smirk plays around her mouth. "Did you make my coach mad? Did she put you in time-out?"

"Someone jealous?" I slowly roll out the words. I don't need to worry anymore. I have acquired my target. Once Lawrence hacks into this iPad—hopefully, all the evidence Hudson's client requires will be on it—my job will be done, debt repaid.

"Not me."

"Hmm. Too bad. Because I still want to know what it's like to fuck a billion dollars." I wink at her and head back into the party. I need to duck out, get the iPad to my cousins.

The party is full chaos. Granny Murray is showing Cookie and her granddaughters how to play strip poker. Jonesy's passed out on the couch. Bramms is slow dancing with an inflatable reindeer. Harlowe is trying to fish someone's underwear out of the punch bowl.

Ellie stands alone by the tree, a red-and-white Solo cup decorated like Rudolph in her hand, her eyes tracking me with a frown that's half suspicion, half something softer.

I walk straight over to her, my pulse still hammering from the risk, the deception. Hopefully, the win. "You're not dancing."

"Trying to manage the party." She seems a little frazzled.

I get a text from my eldest cousin:

Hudson: *Talbot's down the street. Stand by. He'll find you.*

"Going to hit the head." I lean in to kiss her.

But she moves her head at the last minute. "Okay, I should probably refresh the snacks."

I grab her chin. We're in front of everyone. But that's not what it is. She's lying. I can see it. But I don't have the bandwidth to weasel it out of her. After tomorrow, I'll probably never see her again anyway.

The sudden realization is like taking a puck to the teeth.

I look at her—really look at her—and I almost cave. I want to wrap her up in my arms. I want to kiss her like this party isn't happening. Like she's mine.

I turn away before I can wrap her in my arms and tell her I love her. *There was always a time limit on this*, I remind myself. And I'm out of time.

I look around at my teammates, at my dream.

This was never meant to be mine.

Chapter 29

ELLIE

"I heard him," I hiss to Harlowe as we scurry into the stadium for the early-morning practice—way too early.

"He said to Dana Holbrook, 'I want to know what it's like to fuck a billion dollars.'" I blink back tears.

"After you guys had hot, sweaty, nasty postgame sex in your office."

"Yeah, guess that didn't mean anything to him." I stare down at the ice.

"He's a hockey player—they're fuckboys," Harlowe tells me gently. "You can't get attached to them. Did he say he loved you, or was he talking about relationships or anything?"

"No." I sniffle. "And it's not like we could even..." I make a helpless gesture. "I told him I can't sleep with players. I told him it was affecting his game," I admit.

Harlowe waits a bit. "Yikes."

"Yeah." I sigh. "You think I blew it?"

"Well, now we know why he was chatting up Dana. He was trying to make you jealous."

"I don't know."

Harlowe snorts. "Have you seen all the puck bunnies hanging around the stadium ever since we started winning? He could have a new one every night. But he's flirting with Dana because she's unobtainable."

"Or he just hates me." I feel miserable, even though Fletcher moving on is the best possible outcome.

"Be an adult and talk to Fletcher," Harlowe coaxes me. "Tell him you want to be exclusive."

"I can't be in a public relationship with him. I mean, my dad would have a fit."

"Your dad's not the one with the ticking biological clock and overbearing grandbaby-hungry mother."

"I can't think about relationships. My life is already screwed up enough." I wipe my eyes and fan my face. "I need to keep it together—we have a big game tonight. It's against the Montreal Vortex. They're a good team. Not as good as the Direwolves, but good."

"I think the Rhode Islanders can take them."

I'm not so sure. The team seems off at practice. I made everyone clear out of the party early, but maybe I shouldn't have thrown it at all, I worry. It's just that Zayne had scheduled it before we were contenders, and it seemed like punishment to cancel it.

It seems like maybe it wasn't just the party, though. Something shifted in the team's cohesiveness.

They're a step behind on the drills. Fletcher snaps at everyone. Zayne seems out of it. Eddie straight up didn't even show up. Cookie misses the net on a drill, which triggers a panic attack, and I was only able to calm him down enough for Zayne to bundle him off home.

Fletcher doesn't try to sneak a kiss or anything after practice—just stomps to the locker room and throws on his clothes. He doesn't even look like he showered when he heads past me, barely acknowledging me.

Probably going to see Dana.

Harlowe's wrong. Why wouldn't Fletcher want to be with the team's owner instead of the temporary coach who can't manage to keep any sort of winning streak going?

I notice that his eyes do drift to the puck bunny who managed to sneak past the lackluster stadium security. I feel sick. None of those girls has a hockey-player body.

"Back, back!" Granny Murray rushes out with a broom. "Fifty bucks to touch our star centerman! No free lookie-loos!"

I'm not confident about the game. It's probably better that Fletcher doesn't get handsy in my office. I need to focus on how we're going to beat the Montreal Vortex.

Practice was horrible. "It's because they're all hungover," I lie to myself as I suck down my lukewarm coffee in my office. "Nothing's wrong with the team."

I have a pounding headache myself, after all, that has nothing to do with my heartbreak over Fletcher.

Heartbreak? Who's heartbroken? I'm young—I can have a hookup without getting emotionally attached.

I shake my head. My mom has a hangover cure recipe. I need to go shopping. I'll make a list of the ingredients.

Someone raps on the door.

"Fletcher?" I flinch as my dad opens the door.

He seems a little taken aback at my reaction. "Ellie? I, uh, well, I wanted to talk to you."

"Sure, Dad, yeah, have a seat." I gesture to the seat that is right next to the trash can that has a freaking condom in it. Ugh, why did they fire the janitorial staff? Frick. I try very hard not to look at the trash can, not to draw any sort of attention to it, as I slowly sneak my foot out from under the desk, all while I lock eye contact with my father.

"I..." he stammers. "Well, I've been asking around, and I think we found someone who wants to take over the coaching job here. With the way the team performed the last couple of games, seems like there's some renewed interest."

"Great, so Ellie pulls the team from the brink of disaster, and some idiot with a small penis and a bald head gets to come in and steal all her credit?" Granny Murray says as she slams the door open.

My dad cringes.

"I knew you were up to no good, Nathan!" Granny Murray hollers at him. "I knew as soon as I saw you walk in the building—that's a shiftless male if I ever saw one."

"I'm trying to look out for her!" my dad cries. "Ellie, people think you're sleeping with the players. You should see all the horrible things people are writing about you online. Your mom's so upset she cries every night."

"Lies!" Granny Murray thunders. "Trina is fighting the good fight online—this yellow-bellied turncoat is the one weeping in his pillow! Fucking pussy, man the hell up!"

"Mom's arguing with people in the comments?" I groan. My headache is getting worse.

My dad grabs my hand. "This is why I didn't want this for you, Ellie!"

"You tell whatever coach you scraped up that Ellie is going down with the ship!" Granny Murray rails.

"I don't know, Gran. Maybe I should leave." It's going to be awkward with Fletcher. It already is awkward. And now the team is broken—I'm not sure why. Maybe they're getting horrible comments online too. They had tampons thrown at them in Seattle, after all. "Maybe it can't hurt to see what a real coach could do."

"Exactly! It doesn't hurt to just explore other options." My dad raises his hand as Granny Murray hefts the hockey stick I keep in the corner of the office. "I'll tell the NHL you're open to stepping down."

"Traitor!" Granny Murray hollers, berating my dad as he leaves.

"I'm just trying to help—"

The door slams. I sit there in silence, ears ringing, for a moment.

Give up coaching? It's not like it was my life's calling.

Besides, clearly, I'm not very good at it. I failed the test of not sleeping with a player. Also, isn't that illegal? Probably would get me fired anyway, so maybe it's better if I resign before I, too, am hauled away in handcuffs.

Or maybe I'm just a wuss. I don't want to coach the rest of the season and watch Fletcher make bedroom eyes at Dana Holbrook or start sleeping with Dana Holbrook (if he hasn't already—*Shut up, brain!*), or dating Dana Holbrook, or—*Gulp*—falling in love with her.

I will fresh hot coffee to appear in my mug as I grab my skates. Maybe shooting some pucks will help clear my head. I can test out some of the moves, too, for next practice. When I head down the dark hallway, I almost run into someone.

Cookie is standing outside the locker room, tears in his big brown eyes.

"Cookie! I thought Zayne took you home."

"I forgot my hat." His lower lip trembles.

"Oh, we'll find it—let's check the lost and found, okay?"

He shakes his head.

"What's the matter?"

"You're leaving us?"

Chapter 30
FLETCHER

A fan whirs in the field office as Lawrence and the rest of my cousins comb through the data copied from Dana's iPad.

"Does she know her iPad is missing?" I ask.

"She's been pinging it from her phone." Lawrence looks over. "I've blocked it."

I shift on my feet. "I can just take it back to the stadium, stick it in the lost and found."

"We need it to unencrypt some of these files."

"Oh, here we go!" Talbot whoops. "The mother lode. Look at that."

"Shit." I read over his shoulder. "That looks intense."

"Yeah, this is tax-loss harvesting."

"She's just running the team into the ground to offset her tax burden for this year." Anderson whistles.

"Damn." It's a gut punch.

"We tried so hard." I sit down slowly on a folding chair. "This team… It's people's entire lives, and it means nothing to her. It's just numbers."

My cousins don't seem that emotional about it.

Jake shrugs. "Them's the breaks of dealing with billionaires."

"Just business as usual," Talbot adds.

"They all do squirrely stuff around this time of year, with it being the tax deadline and all." Lawrence shrugs.

"Why I hate Christmas." Hudson glowers.

"Bah humbug, Hudson," Anderson chirps. Hudson kicks his brother's chair.

"If we didn't have to package all of this for the Svenssons, we'd come see your last-ever game at the NHL." Elsa is cheery.

"The team's not dead yet," I grumble.

"Your debt is repaid," Hudson informs me. "You're free to go after this game. *After*, you understand? Don't want to tip anyone off until the Svenssons are ready to move."

"I'll write you a receipt." Elsa waves me over and prints out something I don't read.

Hudson signs it, then he burns it.

Lawrence makes a papal cross in the air with his energy drink.

"You coming to Christmas?" Elsa calls after me.

"Nah, he's gonna go travel, finally live life as a free man after the military and Hudson." Jake snickers.

"He should be grateful—if it weren't for me, he'd be in jail," Hudson says.

The door to the nondescript field office slams shut behind me. I'm alone in the alley. The winter wind rushes in my ears as I zip up my jacket.

My last NHL game. Ever. In my entire life.

And the last night I'm going to spend with Ellie.

I don't know what the Svenssons are planning, but it sounds like it might end with the team folding and her out of a job.

Once I quit the team, Ellie will know that I was a fraud. She won't want to be with me anyway.

Ellie's on the ice. I watch her skate for a moment—sharp, focused, relentless. Every movement is clean. Controlled. Beautiful. Her quick release sends puck after puck at Ren in the net, and I can't help but admire her form even as something curdles in my gut.

I trudge into the locker room and start pulling on my gear. If this is my last night in the NHL, I'm spending every second of it on the ice.

Zayne's sitting on the bench, hunched over, looking like he needs a drink. He probably already had one. Eddie shoots me an angry glare when I walk in. Cookie's sobbing on the floor, his helmet still on, his gloved hands covering his face. The sound rips through the room like a gut punch.

"What happened?" I demand.

"Guess you didn't hear the good news," Bramms mutters bitterly.

"What?"

Bramms says, "She's leaving."

My gut clenches. "Who?"

Bramms stares at me, dead-eyed. "Ellie. They're hiring a new coach. She's leaving us."

Jonesy sighs. "Does that mean no more snacks?"

"Shit," Ziggy says soberly. "No more winning."

A black hole opens up inside my chest. This is not how I'm going out.

"Put your gear on. Now," I snap at the players, trying to dig deep and remember whatever that self-important colonel preached in that leadership seminar they all forced us to take one rainy day on base. "I don't fucking care if Ellie's about to… leave." I almost choke on the word. Almost. "We're in the NHL. We're here to play hockey, and we're here to win."

I look around, meeting every eye. "If we don't want her to leave, then we give her a reason to stay."

I don't know if I'm getting through. I'm not a captain. I'm not an inspiration. I'm not Zayne. Especially not sober Zayne.

My hero looks shaky as he puts on his skates. He thinks I don't see when he takes a swig from a bottle that's not water.

The walk-off song makes me want to vomit, the vibrations rattling my ears when we step on the ice, circling to the roar of the crowd.

She's leaving.

Leaving.

The words loop in my head like a curse.

Ellie is leaving.

The crowd's too loud. Everything feels like it's cranked up a dial too far.

The captain reeks of alcohol as he takes his position for the face-off.

He loses the face-off.

The Montreal Vortex take the puck, and I already know—we're done. My head's not in the game. My legs feel slow.

All I can think is: this is it. The last time I'll play in the NHL. I can't enjoy it, can't go out in a blaze of glory—instead, it's the agonizing death of my dream.

"What the hell is wrong with you, Yankee?" Ren hollers at me, slamming his stick on the net. "You forget how to play?"

"Ellie's leaving."

"She what?" He chokes on his water—it leaks out through his missing teeth onto his jersey.

"They're hiring a new coach," I say desperately. The lights are too bright here on the ice. I squint at the players.

"Fuck." He lets in a goal then rallies, but it's too late.

The team—my team—implodes on the ice. We can't keep possession of the puck. Ren is a hair too slow. The fans are disappointed. Our last two wins were a fluke. The scoreboard lights mock us, goal after goal, and by the time the final buzzer sounds, the stands are half empty—fans filtering out before the traffic hits.

The buzzer sounds, and mercifully, the game is over.

Back in the locker room, we're wrecked. Silent. Beaten.

"Well, I know that's not how we wanted this game to go," Ellie tells us when we're nursing our wounds in the locker room.

I can't even look at her.

Is it her decision to leave? Really? Or is it my fault?

It's good I'm leaving. I don't deserve to be here.

Dana probably caught wind of what Hudson and the Svenssons are digging up. She's trying to get ahead of it. Cut her losses. Fire Ellie, sweep the damage under the rug.

"This was it." I feel delirious. "My big shot, and it's over."

I look to Zayne for something—comfort, wisdom—but he's slumped on the floor, drunk as shit. So I stare down at the bright-yellow Lunchables package in my hand. "Jovi," I call, raising it to toss to him.

Before he can catch it—

BANG. The locker room door slams open. Lights flicker overhead.

"You fucking piece of shit."

Dana Holbrook descends into the locker room. She's one of those ancient Greek goddesses—vengeful, divine, terrifying. The kind I used to read about in battered mythology books on stained casino carpets while my mom gambled away her sister's disability check.

"You think I didn't know it was you the whole time?" Dana rages at me.

Shit. I look to the exit, but it's blocked by shocked hockey players.

"Guess I shouldn't have come back to play after all," I mutter.

"No." Dana's voice becomes poisonously sweet. "You should have run far, far away, because you can ask anyone on the Eastern Seaboard—no one fucks with me and gets away with it."

"Oh my God, you *were* sleeping with him?" Ellie screams.

The rookies gasp. Dana's mouth twists in derision as she turns back to a teary Ellie. "That's what you think this is about, Ellie? *Sex?* Grow up." Dana turns back to me. "You stole something from me, Sullivan. Or should I say, Wynter?"

"That's, uh, my mom's maiden name. And I, um, my cousin actually has your tablet." My voice cracks worse than when I went through puberty, and my balls are shrinking under Dana's wrath.

"Look," Ellie, who's a head shorter than Dana in her high heels, cuts in. "I don't know what happened, but Fletcher is my—"

"Fletcher Sullivan isn't a hockey player," Dana spits out. "He barely graduated high school. He didn't play in Switzerland—he enlisted in the Marines to escape prison. He is certainly not NHL material. His cousin bribed someone to let him into the minors then bribed our former GM to get him put on this team, all so he could spy on me."

My teammates are shocked.

Jovi looks betrayed. "But I saw the stats," he says in a small voice. "On Hockey Match, you had all those seasons on that Swiss team."

"I played hockey when I was a high schooler, and it's actually really easy to doctor a website"—I stare down at the rubber floor—"when your cousin is a computer guy."

Watery ice puddles at my feet, melting off the skates.

"Wait, Fletcher—" Ellie's voice breaks. "But you can skate—you're good. What do you mean you're not an NHL player?"

"He's as much a player as you are a coach," Dana says snidely.

"No wonder you're cutting and running," Eddie snarls.

"Did you know about Fletcher?" Bramms demands.

"What? No!" Ellie cries.

"Did you bribe someone to be on the team?" Eddie yells.

I jump to her defense. "Leave her the fuck alone," I snarl at the team as Cookie sobs into the Finn's shoulder. "She's not the problem. Dana—"

Her blue eyes flash at me. I steel my spine. If I'm going down, she's going down too.

"Dana's defrauding the team," I yell over the chaos. "She's using it for tax harvesting, purposefully running the team into the ground. Bet you're going to sell it for parts in the new year, huh, Dana?"

"You can't—" Ellie gasps, tears welling up. "Dana, that's horrible."

"Are we getting paid?" Carlsson demands.

"Oh my God, I didn't get paid this week!" Jovi freaks out.

"We get paid every other week, so next Friday," Jonesy says out of the side of his mouth.

"Should have stayed in the minors." Bramms shakes his head.

"Shit, I should have stayed in Germany," Carlsson snaps.

"Dana, everyone here worked so hard." Ellie clutches her arms around herself. "I can't believe you'd do this to all the players, the fans. That's not what hockey is about."

"Oh, fuck off, Ellie," Dana sneers. "Considering you're fucking one of my players, you don't get to have the moral high ground."

The room explodes.

"I fucking knew it!" Eddie snarls. "That's how you got the A, Sullivan! You're her little fucktoy. Or is she your little puck slut?"

My fist hits his nose with a crunch. Blood spurts. He goes down hard.

Bramms moves, but I growl—and he freezes.

The Finn gives me a look I can't read.

"So she gets to play house with some fake-ass player and then peace out? Nah." Eddie coughs blood. "No thanks."

I knee him in the jaw. "Fucker."

"I'm…" Ellie is teary. "I'm really sorry. I'm so sorry. And I didn't have any intention of quitting. The NHL just thought that you all deserve a real coach, especially since you all started winning games."

Dana has a sour look on her face.

"We wanted you," Cookie says in a small voice.

"I didn't," Eddie mutters.

I kick him.

"Stop hurting my player," Ellie snaps. Eyes flashing, she turns on me. "Fuck you, Fletcher. You're a liar. You took a spot from someone more deserving. There are people who work their entire lives to make it to the NHL."

"I could say the same thing about you," I roar at her. "You're not a real coach—you're a preschool teacher playing grown-up."

"I never lied about my qualifications," she screams at me.

"No, but you made us all believe in you. If you're not going to fight for your job, then why should anyone believe you're going to fight for us?"

"Stop making this about me," Ellie screeches. "You snuck in here and pretended to be part of this team, pretended to care."

"I do care."

"Liar. You're just here to steal from Dana and get your dick wet. You were planning on leaving after this game, weren't you?"

The room stills.

"Weren't you?" Her eyes flash. "You were going to leave us all high and dry."

"What does it matter?" I'm up in her face. "You just said I didn't deserve to be here, that I was stealing someone's spot, so what does it matter if now I'm about to leave? You just said I wasn't important to the team. Or…" I circle her. "Are you mad I fucked you and lied about it?"

"I don't need whatever the fuck is happening here," Dana cuts in. "You can have your little girlfriend-boyfriend spat—not on my property. And the NHL doesn't get to tell me what I do with my team, Ellie. I don't care what your father thinks," she sneers then turns to sweep her gaze over the team. "Ellie will be at practice, and so will all of you, if you want to get paid," Dana warns.

"But you." She points at me. "You need to clean out your locker. You're done."

Chapter 31

ELLIE

"I never should have taken that coaching job," I sob to Harlowe. "My dad was right—I'm not an NHL coach."

"You are technically, and you're the only person who made that team win. And hey, who cares if you slept with Fletcher? You have to use all the tools available to you." Harlowe pets my hair.

"I was so dumb. Fletcher was just sleeping with me so he could get close to Dana and expose her lies."

"'Lies' feels like a strong word. I think she's just doing capitalism with great hair."

"She ruined the sanctity of an NHL team."

"Okay, Ms. Sleeping With Her Own Players."

"Ugh, not so loud." My stuff clatters out of my hands onto the porch. I'm not ready to go in and face the disappointment of my parents yet.

"So what if your dad finds out?" Harlowe helps me pick up the sticks. "Look on the bright side—now that Fletcher's not on the team, your dad can't get mad at you for sleeping with a player."

I call Fletcher again. He's not answering his phone. I don't even know why I'm calling him. Instead of his voicemail, now the phone screams that this number has been disconnected.

Someone pulls back the curtains from the living room. I hear excited cries of "There she is! She's here! She's back! Did she bring her boyfriend?"

On the street, cars are parking with more family members summoned by my life imploding.

"Ellie!" my aunt cries as she totters up the icy sidewalk on high heels. "Your mom says you're moving to San Francisco!"

"I'm what?"

The front door flies open. My dad is furious. "It's completely off the rails!"

"Now, Nate, come sit down. I made you some herbal tea," my mom says soothingly.

"A disaster!" he hollers as his brothers haul him to the couch.

"This will be a good thing." His sister pats his hand.

On the TV, a blond man with gray eyes and a very expensive suit is giving a press conference.

Fitzgerald Svensson. Obviously.

"As the owner of the Orcas team, I'm appalled that the NHL let this go on so long. It's devaluing the brand. Dana Holbrook should be in jail. The Rhode Islanders team should be moved to San Francisco immediately. And I believe the majority of the team owners will support me in this motion.

I'm open to any and all questions," he says smugly. "I'll give my unasked-for hot-take opinions free of charge."

"Ellie's not moving anywhere," Nate tells my aunt. "We're looking at a new coach."

"Damn it, Nate, you can't replace Ellie. She's won two of her three games!" My uncle waves his beer bottle around.

"I lost the last game," I remind them sadly.

"That wasn't on you—those players are lazy."

"Bag skates! You can't be so soft on them, Ellie," Uncle Bic slurs.

I'm so over the NHL, so over hockey. "Who are you looking at for the coaching position?" I blink back tears.

"Gordy McRae," my cousin says acerbically.

All my male family members complain loudly.

"Terrible choice!"

"He's a braggart!"

One of them throws his peppermint-bark popcorn at Dad.

"He's a good coach," Nate protests.

"Gordy?" my great-uncle booms. "You saw what he did with the Whalers—he just collected a paycheck and ran that team into the ground."

"You're stupid if you let the team hire Gordy," another uncle tells Harlowe.

"She's not in charge of hiring, Dad," his daughter tells him as she videotapes the carnage.

"Who's in charge of hiring? I need to speak with the manager." My drunk cousin waves her wineglass around.

"Well, it's not Nate." His brothers snicker.

"Seriously, Dad, you want Gordy to be the coach?" I cross my arms. "I thought you were going to look at someone like Buzz Hanley on the Arctic Avengers minor-league team, or maybe Doug Rourke—he coaches at Boston University. He has a gentler coaching style. Cookie's freaked out, and you can't have someone force him onto the ice because he gets overwhelmed, not to mention he's just too damn good for most of the team to play with him. Bramms is the most offensive defenseman ever, but you have to have a strong D down low so you can take advantage of him, and none of these coaches are going to know that, and the team's going to keep losing."

My dad looks at me strangely.

"And Fletcher… he's…" My throat tightens. "Fletcher, he's my centerman and… and…"

"I knew you were sleeping with that player!" Violet screeches as she and her sisters fly into the room.

"You did what?" Nate bellows, jumping up.

Granny Murray raises a hand. "I didn't snitch!"

"Of course not—it's all over the gossip sites." Bella grabs the remote and turns the channel to the entertainment news. There's my official Rhode Islanders corporate picture, where I look like I'm in a hostage situation, and Fletcher's, who looks like a model posing for a mug shot, wearing his predatory *I want to fuck you* gaze with the slightly parted mouth.

"… in a relationship," the entertainment host is saying.

I cover my eyes, peeking through my fingers at the horror on the screen.

"This news comes to us directly from Edward Lasky, one of the Rhode Islanders players. Eddie, could you tell us what happened?"

"Yeah, Fletcher was just some guy she brought in off the street. He lied about his stats, and that's how he's on the team. I should have been a starter, and she gave him preferential treatment."

"He did score a lot of points," one of the hosts says.

Eddie looks furious. "Because she was sleeping with him!"

"All I see is a queen motivating her knights." Violet snaps her fingers.

My dad groans.

"Wait, Eddie's been traded!" My eyes scan the headline crawling across the bottom of the screen.

"For a first-round draft pick." My uncle whistles.

"How? Eddie's not worth that." I scrunch my nose.

"Well, it's to Boston, so what do you expect?" one of my uncles says derisively.

"Now we're down a player."

"Call up Jack Malloy from the minors," someone suggests.

"No!"

My cousins clamor around me. "No, call up—"

"We'll call up Walt Stratton. I've been watching his tapes. I think he'd fit well with—I was going to say Fletcher, but he quit."

"He quit?" My uncles are shocked.

"I have money on this game! You lost the last one—you need Fletcher!" Granny Murray hollers.

"You heard them," I cry. "He lied!"

"So? He's good, ain't he?" a male family member says.

"Big fucker too," a male cousin adds.

"Let's turn it back to normal hockey TV before Nate strokes out," a great-aunt says as she pulls out a Tupperware container to steal food.

My dad is laying ashen-faced on the floor, moaning, while his sister screams at him to "Get up, Nate! You're

272 . Alina Jacobs

such a little bitch—you always make everything about you, and now you're making your daughter's sex life about you!"

"Honestly, you should be happy. I know Trina was worried she'd live at home for the rest of her life," his second cousin adds.

"I want my baby girl to stay here—ow!" my dad yelps when his sister kicks him.

"If you want to win that game, you better suck that man's dick to make him come back," Granny Murray states. "Francine, get your mitts off that alcohol—that is not a party favor."

Fletcher. I need to find Fletcher. But how?

Chapter 32

FLETCHER

don't know what I'm doing back at the rink.

The security guard gives me a weird look then decides that it's not his business.

I push through the heavy doors and breathe in the familiar smell of the ice mixed with sweaty hockey gear—that sharp, clean cold cuts through with the musk of a thousand practices and games. It's a smell that's been burned into my memory since I was seven years old, wearing skates that were two sizes too big because that's what we could afford.

I lace up slowly, each eyelet a small ritual, a meditation I've performed thousands of times before. Now for the last time.

I don't put on my gear—just drift into the center of the ice, look up at the rafters of the brand-new stadium where, for a brief moment in time, I thought I might have my flag up there.

I've watched those videos a hundred times—NHL players hoisting the Stanley Cup, tears streaming down their faces, pure joy radiating from every pore. And in every single one of those videos, there's someone next to them. A wife, a girlfriend, someone who matters more than the trophy itself. Someone to share the moment that makes all the pain worth it.

I can't imagine doing any of that without Ellie. She must hate me. No, scratch that—she does hate me. I basically told her she didn't deserve to be here, which is the furthest thing from the truth. She deserves to be here in the NHL, more than anyone. More than me, certainly.

"What are you still doing here?" Hudson's voice booms across the ice.

"Just can't quit hockey," I say, not bothering to skate over. My voice carries in the empty arena.

"You don't have a job."

"I know."

Hudson studies me for a long moment. "You're passable at this one, though. Not great but passable. I always need workers who understand how to infiltrate, how to get information." He jerks his chin at me. "I need to send someone to the Midwest—pays good, if you're interested."

"I can't leave my team," I say, though even as the words leave my mouth, they sound hollow.

Hudson laughs, but there's no humor in it. "The team's not going to be there after Christmas, so whatever. Suit yourself."

My blood turns to ice water. "What?"

"Rumor has it Dana's selling the team. They're moving to the West Coast."

The words hit harder than taking a shoulder to the head.

"They can't do that—Dana can't do that." I shake my head. "Ellie worked so hard for this. Poured everything she had into making this team work, into proving herself. You should have seen the shit they said about her." My fists clench. "And they're just going to yank it away from her."

I didn't even get to tell her I love her.

"While I find your white-knighting for your coach revolting, I actually think it's probably more because Eddie told the news she was having an affair with one of her players."

"That *motherfucker*."

"I thought you knew. Figured you were here because you want a crack at Eddie." He clocks the confusion on my face. "He went to the Boston Harbor Hawks."

"I'm sure he's shit-talking her to them," I glower. "He did it to hurt Ellie. Fuck, I should have just stayed here and beat the shit out of him when I had the chance."

I want Hudson to fight me, want to unleash the anger.

Hudson just smirks. "That's why you're good at this job—you're aggressive, want to win at all costs."

"I'm going to fucking kill him!" I roar, the words echoing around the empty stadium.

"There it is. I'm putting money on your game."

Chapter 33

ELLIE

"Aren't you supposed to be getting ready? You have the game in a few hours." My dad knocks on my open door.

"I thought you were hiring a new coach," I say from where I'm lying on my bed, eating the last of the Blitzen bites, looking through the au pair website to see which family looking for cheap live-in nannying seems least likely to lock me in a cellar in the middle of the Austrian Alps.

"Well, it's not like the NHL can just usurp the team owner and hire a coach for him. Her," he corrects as he gingerly sits on the edge of my bed. "Besides, none of the coaches we looked at are as good as you."

"I suck as a coach," I say miserably. "I lost my last game, one of my D-men defected, my star player can't manage to stay sober, all the rookies are neurotic, and I slept with a centerman."

My dad pats my leg under the covers. "You know, my first NHL game as a goalie—they called me up from the minors at the last minute. I was young—I was your age. I was so freaked out I puked as soon as I stepped on the ice. They had to delay the whole game to clean it up. We lost awfully. I thought the D-men were going to knife me in the parking lot." Nate grimaces at the memory. "They had to call an ambulance for the coach because he was so furious they thought he was stroking out when he was screaming at me."

He huffs a laugh.

"I told the GM I was sorry but clearly I wasn't cut out for hockey and would see myself out. He just laughed at me and told me I take this game way too seriously, that this night was going to be a funny story I tell after a long and successful career." He rubs my arm.

"Probably should have taken that advice to heart. It's hockey—it's not life or death. I need to remind myself of that. It's not more important than your family, your kids, than you." He puts an arm around my shoulders. "And this is going to be a funny story that you'll tell people after your team wins a Stanley Cup. So get up. I think your mom made pregame snacks for everyone."

I stare miserably at my computer. "I can't show my face."

"I didn't raise a quitter. I raised a hockey player and NHL coach, apparently," my dad says wryly.

"Well, the team is being moved to the West Coast," I remind him. "So I'm not a coach for much longer."

"If the team is leaving, then you should finish it out."

"No way. I can't go back—it's humiliating." I pull a pillow over my head. "My players hate me. They think I gave Fletcher preferential treatment."

"I'm not so sure," Nate adds wryly. "I don't know if I mentioned it, but the NHL has been getting a number of angry emails from your players." He smirks. "Zayne Murphy sent a very heartfelt message about how you embody the working-class spirit of hockey. The chairman apparently got weepy when he read it. There are a number of emails with poor grammar about how you're the best coach ever, and someone named Stonewall Renwick left a message on the answering machine threatening to blow up the NHL headquarters if you get replaced."

He shows me an email on his phone. "Also, Google Translate says this is a death threat, but it's all in Finnish, so who knows." He tucks the phone back in his pocket. "Come on, Ellie, get up. Your team needs you. Up. Up!" He drags me upright then gives me a big hug.

"I can't."

"You can. You have." My dad pulls back to cup my face and look at me, eyes wet. "I'm so proud of you. And I'm sorry I wasn't more supportive. That's not the kind of father I wanted to be. And I'm going to be cheering you on from the stands."

"Don't waste your time—we're going to lose."

"Don't bet against hockey."

"Please don't bet any money," I beg.

"Too late—already got my retirement check on the game." He grins at me.

"Well," I tell him, "at the very least, I broke up with Fletcher. So that's one less thing you have to worry about."

"Your mom's going to be upset to hear that—she's already started sewing baby gear. Besides"—Nate smiles at me—"you might want to rethink that. I think you're going to want him on the team."

"He won't respond to me—he disconnected his phone number."

"The way he played hockey? He loves the sport. I've been in the NHL—trust me, he's not done with hockey." My dad pauses in the doorway. "And I saw the way he looked at you. He's not done with you either. He'll be back."

Chapter 34

FLETCHER

"Well, well, well. Look what the Zamboni dragged in," Zayne rasps, swirling a bottle in his hand.

I drop my bag on the floor and climb up to sit in the stands next to him. "We have a game tonight. Where else would I be?"

Zayne picks up the bottle, doesn't drink it, just looks at it—the bright high bay lights reflecting off the bronze liquid inside. "Why'd you come back?"

I shrug. "It's the NHL. It's hockey. This is my team."

"Huh. So not for Ellie?"

The name punches through my chest. "No," I snap.

I think about Eddie on the TV. Eddie who we're going to play tonight. I'm going to break Eddie's face. And I'm not losing another hockey game.

"Ah, hockey."

"Hockey is everything," I remind him. "It's all I have. I want to be like you." I sigh. "Always did—play in the NHL, get paid to play, to dedicate my life to being the best. Your whole life is just pure hockey, and it's perfect. Winning cups, the endorsements, everyone worships you." I wrap my arms around my knees. "If the team is moving, this is it. This is all the hockey I have left."

"You know," Zayne says after a moment, "I was engaged once. A long time ago. Was supposed to get married, have a family."

"Oh yeah?" I squint. "I vaguely remember that. It was a while ago, right?"

"She wanted to get married immediately. I kept putting it off. There was another Stanley Cup to chase, the Olympics, Worlds. She waited and waited. I kept promising her I'd retire. We'd start a family when I retired—that's what I said." He takes another swig from the bottle. "But every year, I thought, what's one more season? I'll quit when I win four cups, when I win a second gold medal, just one more playoff." He trails off.

"I wasn't ready to quit. And now it's all I have." He swirls the bottle. "She finally left me. I didn't even realize it for a week." He laughs bitterly. "Now she's with another guy. Pregnant with their second child. They go to Disney for family vacations. Cute kids. Throw big holiday parties... You don't want to be like me, Fletch. I promise." He lifts the bottle to his lips. "Don't sacrifice your life for hockey. Hockey doesn't keep you warm at night."

"Maybe you should take your own advice." I reach out gently and take the bottle from him.

I throw it. It lands in the trash can. Nothing but net.

"You have to find happiness where you can get it, when you can get it." Zayne slaps me on the shoulder.

I think of Ellie. Think of the team, how this is it—not just the end but the epilogue. "I'm not sure I can get it anywhere. Might have blown it," I admit.

Zayne gives me a knowing smile. "When you're young, you think love just shows up when it's convenient. But then you wake up, and you're old. Don't just give it up when you find it."

"You're not old. You're not even forty," I remind him.

"I'm an eldritch terror in hockey years."

I sling my arm around his shoulders and haul him up. He's surprisingly steady. "Come on, let's find the boys."

The locker room doesn't seem as depressed as I thought it would be.

"One pretzel," Ellie is saying. "Take one pretzel. Make sure everyone else gets one first before you have seconds, Jovi."

I just stare at her, can't believe she's there—that there's not some bald-headed, beer-gutted coach coming in with bluster and incompetence.

I want to kiss her in front of everyone. Not sure how that's going to go over. Instead, I settle for standing in the doorway, drinking in the sight of her.

"Fletcher!"

"Aw, I wanted his pretzel."

"Fletch!" Bramms jumps on me as the rest of the team crowds around, slapping my back, ruffling my hair.

"The prodigal son has returned," Ren drawls. "It better not be to eat up all the food."

I snatch the pretzel out of his mouth and take a bite. Then I sit under my name, still painted on the bench.

Ellie clasps her hands behind her back then crosses them. "What are you doing here?"

"Yes, what are you doing here, Fletch?" Carlsson demands.

"You're my team," I tell them simply as Zayne sits down next to me. "We're about to play hockey in the NHL. Where else would I be?"

"Hell yeah!" they whoop.

"Fletcher Sullivan." The rookies huddle behind Ren in his bulky goalie gear as Dana, in impossibly high heels and a skinny pencil skirt, saunters into the locker room like she owns it—which she does, although not for long.

"Fletcher's playing," Ellie tells her defiantly, stepping in front of me. "We need him to win."

"Fine," Dana says after a moment, staring down at Ellie. "But I'm not paying you to be here, Sullivan."

"That's fine. I'd lose with these guys for free."

Dana's perfectly arched eyebrows slant. "You better not be losing. Those idiotic Svensson brothers think they can back me into a corner, think they can make me look weak."

"Ma'am"—Ren takes off his goalie helmet—"I don't believe any man of average intelligence would ever make that mistake."

"Well, I think they might make it, but they'd only make it once," I say.

Dana smirks. "I'm not going down without a fight. But I'm not spending money to do it," she warns. "Yes, I was going to take the massive tax write-off on this team. But you can obviously play, so I'm willing to pivot if it makes me a profit. But you have to win. I want results in this game. Win, or else I'm selling this team tonight."

Her phone rings. "Belle, you better tell your husband to tell his brother to fuck off," we hear her snap as the door slams behind her.

I look at the team. My team.

"We play the Eastern Conference champs from last year," Carlsson says quietly.

"We're going to get slaughtered," Bramms adds.

"No, we won't," I say automatically.

The rookies don't seem convinced. Cookie looks like he's about to hurl.

I pick up my stick and throw it against a wall, making it crack. Bramms jumps. Several rookies yelp. The Finn swears in Scandinavian.

"The fuck we are," I snarl at them. "We beat last year's Stanley Cup champs. That means we're the best goddamn hockey team in the league. We came from nothing, and we blew through the Orcas, the Mammoths, and now we're going to slaughter the Boston Harbor Hawks. And I'm sending Eddie to the hospital while I'm at it." My eyes lock with Ellie's wide ones. "The stadium is packed full of people waiting for a miracle, and we're going to give them one. Cookie," I address him, "I need you to play tonight."

"The whole game?" he squawks.

"More than five minutes of it, yeah."

"Um, okay?"

"All of you need to play." I survey them. "We're a team. We've done a lot of losing together. Now we're going to do a lot of winning. I don't care what it takes. Who's ready to give the crowd a show?"

Carlsson blows out a breath. "Hell yeah. Let's do it."

"You damn better." Ren slams his palms on his goalie pads, stands up, and points his stick threateningly at the players. "'Cause I'll tell you one thing, as I live and breathe—I ain't moving to California."

"You better listen to him. He has a gun in the trunk of his car." I smirk at the players.

"Someone get this man a jersey," Bramms calls.

Granny Murray comes in with the burgundy-and-gray jersey with my name on the front and the number 25 on the back. She holds it up, grinning.

"What's that?" I point to the C on the chest. "You're the captain," I tell Zayne, frowning.

He claps me on the shoulder. "No, son, you are. You got this. I'm proud of you."

"Yeah, you do it right as we're losing." I sigh.

"You all are complete morons." I can't figure out who said that until the Finnish giant stands up and crosses his arms. "Ellie, could you please give us a rundown of the plays for this game? Some of us are actually here to win and not waste time." He says this in perfect English with a British accent.

"You speak English?" Jovi hollers.

"My mum's British," Heikkiläinen says simply.

"Why weren't you speaking with us? We had to use Google Translate," I demand.

"Because you all are brain-damaged idiots and I wanted you to leave me alone."

"Well, I'll be damned." Ren throws down his glove. "Shiftless Europeans. Ain't that just the way."

Chapter 35

ELLIE

I can't read Fletcher's expression as the guys line up, rolling their shoulders, flexing in their skates as they wait to head out onto the ice.

Fletcher is quietly arguing with Zayne about who's going out last.

"You have the C on your shirt," Zayne insists.

"I didn't put it there. You're Murphy's Law—you go last."

"I went last the last time, and we lost."

Fletcher huffs.

"You can't argue with the logic of superstition," I tease. I smile at him then quickly look away. He's back, yeah, but that doesn't mean I know where we stand.

The crowd roars. The game's about to start.

"The announcer yells, 'And here are your Rhode Island Hockey Club!'"

The bass of the rap song drops. I brush the sleeve of Fletcher's jersey.

"Any last-minute tips, Coach Candy Cane?" He pauses before stepping on the ice.

"Just…" I shrug helplessly. "Thanks for coming back."

He looks like he's about to say something, but I yelp, interrupting him in panic as I recognize the music of the Barbie song. "Why are they playing this? They can't play this song!"

Fletcher just smirks. "It's the Nicki Minaj version. A little of you, a little of me." He winks at me. "Let's go win a game, Barbie."

The crowd sings along as the announcer yells, "Your new captain, Fletcher Sullivan! Give it up!" He speeds around the ice. It's not lost on me that there are more than a few women who lift up their Rhode Islanders jerseys to show pink lace bras as he zooms by, flying through the crossover.

And some of them I'm related to.

Great.

"Yeah, here's your motivation, boys!" Granny Murray whoops behind me.

"Gran, put your shirt on."

"People are ruining the sport of hockey, turning it into a Disney movie! This is a working-class sport!" She shakes her fist.

I have to clutch my clipboard to keep from chewing on my nails in anxiety.

"Good thing you wore the pink suit," Granny Murray tells me as she nudges me with a bottle of tequila. "You won the last time when you wore the pink suit. This is going to be a tough match. We need all the luck we can get. Shoot, I even brought some tampons to throw at them. They need it," she tells an irate Harlowe loudly. "You should have seen them at practice. Between you and me and the betting market, I don't have high hopes."

Fletcher lines up at the red line for the face-off. Austin, the Boston captain, is across from him with Eddie directly behind.

Fletcher's locked in.

The puck drops. Fletcher smashes it to Jovi, then the two teams go at each other, each trying to gain and keep possession of the puck. The crowd groans or roars when the puck heads toward their net or ours.

I cringe. We can't get it out of the neutral zone. Neither team scores, and during the breaks between periods, the guys all chew on their mouthguards and suck down Gatorade while I go over offensive plays.

It doesn't help. The Boston Harbor Hawks are known for their defense, and they dig in.

I keep switching out the lines. Cookie is chewing on his mouthguard. He didn't score the last time he was on the ice, and I can see him getting shaken.

"Cookie, let's go!"

Cookie jumps onto the ice over the boards. He's on with Zayne and Fletcher and the Finn.

The line is probably too stacked with talent, but we need a win. We have to put everything on the ice, or the Rhode Islanders are toast.

They break through the defenders. The Finn and Fletcher going breakneck down the ice, clearing a path. Fletcher passes the puck back. Zayne collects it and defends it. The Boston defenders chase him around the net as he ducks and weaves.

"You didn't give Zayne anything, did you?" I ask Granny Murray suspiciously. "He looks like he's twenty-five again."

Zayne makes a quick release pass to Cookie. Cookie takes an incredible backhand shot and—

"GOAL!" I scream as the horns blare. It's one to nothing, our favor.

The players jump on Cookie, patting his helmet. He plops down on the bench.

"You got us a goal!" I pat his head.

"Yeah," he pants happily.

I let him have some Goldfish crackers and Gatorade.

"I won." He holds up the bottle cap. "I get Direwolves tickets."

On the ice, the Harbor Hawks are pissed. My guys are chirping them, telling them they're about to lose to a girl.

"I'm gonna mail you a box of tampons," Carlsson hollers at Eddie. "Fucking traitor!"

I look up at the clock and cringe. "We have another seven minutes until the game is over. That's a lot of time. Anything could happen. Boston could easily score another goal." I chew worriedly on my lip.

Fletcher jumps the boards, grabs me around the waist, and sets me on top of the bench. "Nah," he says, leaning back to rest against my legs. "We're going to win. And if we don't, Ren has a gun in the trunk of his car, so one way or the other, this is over."

Ryan West, another hockey superstar, *thanks for coming*, calmly calls out line changes for the Harbor Hawks. His son Mason is new, a rookie, but he's going to be as good as his father.

The first line isn't out on the ice, and Mason's locked in. Ren readies himself in the net as Mason flies down the ice, dangles the puck, then—

"Goal!"

I cringe. "Dammit, we're tied."

"I'm going to get another goal," Cookie says happily, handing me the bottle cap for safekeeping.

"Please do."

Cookie's magic as he flies around the Boston players, the puck glued to his stick. He sends it to the Finn, and then, tic-tac-toe, it's a—

"Goal!"

"Yes! Surprise bag is mine!" Heikkiläinen whoops, skating past on one leg, pretending to play his stick like a guitar while Cookie dances to the Barbie song and my players throw tampons that Granny Murray has provided into the air like money in a rap video.

The ref blows his whistle at us.

"Sorry," I tell him.

Eddie glares at me as he skates by to get a drink of water from his bench during the commercial break. He seems furious as his team digs in for the face-off.

Fletcher wins the face-off, and the puck flies to Cookie. One of the bigger forwards sprints at Cookie. He dodges him but loses the puck. Zayne is there, knocking the guy off-balance and collecting the puck.

Cookie already put himself in position. Fletcher's keeping pace with him but gets tangled up with Boston's centerman.

The Finn makes a break to the net, passes to Zayne, then back to Cookie. He's about to score.

Mason cuts him off. Cookie quick-whips the puck to Fletcher and sprints toward the net. It's a play we've practiced. If Fletcher gets him the puck, he's going to score, and we're going to win.

"We're going to make it," I breathe.

I can barely watch as Cookie hurtles down the ice. Then Eddie clips Cookie. The kid's skating so fast that he goes flying, smashes into the boards, and lands in a heap to yells from the crowd.

"Cookie!" I cry.

Fletcher doesn't even hesitate. He leaves the puck he was chasing and turns on Eddie.

Technically, the rules state that fighting is allowed, but it's supposed to be a fair fight—drop the gloves, no weapons.

That's not how the Marines trained Fletcher to fight, apparently, because he goes after Eddie with his stick, smashing it over him, kicking him, and trying to slash his throat with his skate.

"Fletcher, stop it! You're going to kill him!"

"He's going to get a massive fine and be banned for the rest of the year." Harlowe sucks in a breath.

Zayne grabs Fletcher around the arm, trying to get him off of Eddie as Eddie's new teammates jump Fletcher. He uses his hockey stick to slash at them.

Ren is screaming obscenities from the net.

Finally, the Finn wades through the carnage and grabs Fletcher around the waist, hauls him away, and dumps him on the ice.

Fletcher bounces back up, ignoring the blood streaming down his face. "You!" He muscles through the Boston players, not even registering when they hit him. He gets up in Eddie's face. "You touch any of my teammates or say a goddamn thing about my fucking girlfriend again, and I will kill you. Because guess what?" He gives a mean, bloody smile. "You're right. I'm not an NHL player. I'm a goddamn Marine."

"Hey!" Harlowe nudges me. "You're not single anymore! And you thought he didn't care."

The ref shoves Fletcher, bleeding and bruised but unapologetic, into the penalty box. Cookie is helped to the bench. He plops down next to Braxton, who is playing his video game.

Granny Murray starts measuring out vodka for Cookie.

"Gran, he can't have that. He's a child."

"He's eighteen. He's a grown man."

Cookie slugs it back then immediately throws up.

There are two minutes left on the clock. The game is tied.

The Boston team is on the power play.

With Fletcher out and Cookie out, we're down a man because of the penalty. I swap out to more defensive players, but it's not enough. The Harbor Hawks use the advantage to knife through our line and score on a furious Ren.

The game is tied again.

"We can take them in overtime. Maybe." I can't put Cookie back in, though. I'm worried about his leg.

In the penalty box, Fletcher is breathing hard, furious eyes locked on the play, breathing fog and flecks of blood against the glass.

Forty-five seconds to go.

"Go," I tell Zayne. He jumps over, swapping out with Bramms.

Fletcher readies for the penalty minutes to countdown, up on the balls of his feet, stick raised.

As soon as the ref opens the door, he shoots down the ice.

Zayne already has the shot set up, and the puck hits Fletcher's stick. He quick-releases it, textbook, through the defenders into the corner of the net.

"Goal!"

"We win! We won!" I scream.

"We're staying!" Cookie cries.

I hug him.

The players in the box jump over the boards. The Finn politely helps me over to join the crush of players in the middle of the ice as we cheer, throwing gloves and sticks and mouthguards in the air.

"We're staying!"

"We survived!"

I jump into the fray, breathless, laughing, hugging any player I can get my hands on. "Rhode Islanders for life!" Jonesy hollers. We celebrate like we just won Game 7 of the Stanley Cup Finals, screaming and rolling around on the ice while everyone looks on like we're insane.

Then suddenly—he's there.

Fletcher. Standing in front of me in the center of the ice, breathing hard, bloody from the fight. And the stadium, the noise, the chaos—all of it falls away.

"You won," I whisper, a little breathless, trying not to cry.

He doesn't even look at the crowd. His eyes are locked on mine, soft now in a way I've never seen on the ice. "You won," he says simply.

The cameras broadcasting the game circle us, but he has eyes only for me. Then he leans down, wraps me in his arms, and kisses me in front of the whole stadium and my family and all the cameras.

"You can't do—"

He kisses me again.

"If you want me to quit," he says, "because you refuse to date a player—I will. I'll walk away right now. I don't need hockey. I need you. I love you. You got me further than I ever thought I'd go. I can quit. And I'll be happy."

I stare up at him, heart slamming against my ribs, throat tight.

I rise onto the tops of his skates so I can kiss him again, wrapping my arms around his neck. "I can't have you quit and be happy," I murmur against his mouth, "because at least one of us wants to win a Stanley Cup. I might be the one having to quit my job, though."

Fletcher smirks. "I wouldn't count on it. Though the NHL is a big, soulless organization, they have nothing on Dana, who will happily sacrifice her morals for profit."

The press is waiting when Fletcher grabs my arm to lift me over the lip that leads off the ice.

He is unapologetic when the press demands, "Are you with your coach?"

"I don't get paid shit," he says, "so I'm going to sleep with my coach because I'm in love with her."

"When they're together, we win," Jovi says simply when the press hounds him. "You can't mess with superstition." He knocks on the side wall.

Ziggy snickers. "It's like Mom and Dad. She brings the snacks, and he'll beat you if you step out of line."

"He gets her pregnant, we're going for the Stanley Cup," Carlsson jokes, slapping Fletcher on the back.

"Grandbabies!" my mom squeals from the stands, making me choke on my spit.

The press clamors for quotes. "Are you going to spend Christmas together? What are you getting her for Christmas?"

"An engagement ring, hopefully," my mom interjects.

"No! Get a hot tub." My drunk female family members whoop.

"Do not bring a hot tub to my house," I warn them.

"You live at home, Ellie."

"Fuck." I groan.

Fletcher snickers.

"Are you moving into her parents' house?" Bramms asks him, confused.

"No." My dad muscles through. "They're going to date, then they're going to get married, then they can move in next door to me."

Fletcher's eyes narrow.

My dad stares back.

"You, me, Ellie—we're all gonna be roommates!" Granny Murray throws her arms around me and Fletcher.

"Can I move in with you?" Cookie begs.

"No," Fletcher barks. Then he kisses me again in front of all the cameras.

"Don't act so offended," he tells the press, leveling that cold gray gaze on them. "I'm the captain of the Rhode Islanders. And Dana Holbrook didn't hire me for my good behavior."

And in that moment, I got everything I didn't know I wanted for Christmas.

My team.

My dream.

And him.

Chapter 36
FLETCHER

Everyone's families crash the locker room when we finally detangle from the press.

Cookie's mom bursts in first, trailed by what I can only assume are his siblings. She points a sharp finger at one of them. "Don't touch that. I swear if you break anything, I'll make you scrub floors for a year to pay it off. Ah, Ellie!" She smiles broadly. "I can't believe you managed to get him back on the ice after all that—I said don't fucking touch that," she yells at one kid. She drags a toddler off the skate sharpener. "Whatever you said to him worked. It's a Christmas miracle! We got to see our boy skate in his first NHL game."

"I like to make learning fun. We believe in positive reinforcement," Ellie replies with a smile. "And Goldfish crackers."

"My little goal scorer," his mom says as Cookie protests while she plants kisses on his forehead. "You need a haircut, sweetie."

The Finn's father—tall, Viking-esque, and blond—shakes Ellie's hand in both of his. He says something long and dramatic in Scandinavian while his son stands beside him nodding proudly. Ellie just smiles and says "Thank you" like she totally understood all of it.

Then Dana struts in like the ghost of Christmas capitalism. She poses in the doorway, arms crossed. I stand up straighter as she surveys us.

"Looks like you're not a losing investment after all. Since you beat the Harbor Hawks against all the odds—thank you very much, I won a new yacht betting on you—you're staying," she announces. "The team isn't moving to San Francisco."

The room explodes in cheers. Someone throws a jock-strap in the air like confetti. Carlsson catches it and throws it back in disgust.

"I'm dumping a ton of money into this franchise," Dana continues. "Everyone gets a raise. *Next* season." The guys groan. "Provided you all play like this again," she adds, waving her perfectly manicured hand. "I expect more wins from you." Her lip curls. "You're lucky you're not actually in the Direwolves division. I had to fuck some guy to make that happen."

The room goes dead silent.

Ellie's mother gasps.

Then her sisters cheer. "Goals!"

"She's so perfect."

"That boss-bitch energy."

Dana smirks. "So don't ever let them tell you that it's wrong to use sex to get what you want. It's a very powerful weapon women have in their arsenal. Men don't want us to use it."

Granny Murray raises her tequila bottle in approval.

Dana's gaze swivels to me. "Fletcher Sullivan."

Ellie appears at my side, slipping her hand into mine.

Dana purses her mouth. "I'm sure your brother has some sort of *job* lined up for you." Her nose wrinkles on the word.

"You're leaving?" Jovi gasps, horror-stricken. "But we won!"

"Of course he's not leaving." Dana tosses her hair. "You're getting a real NHL contract, not this two-way nonsense. And you can tell Hudson I said to go fuck himself."

"Whoo!"

"Party at my house!" Granny Murray whoops.

"You mean my house." Ellie's father sighs.

Ellie's childhood home is like something out of a set where the perfect family lives.

String lights twinkle everywhere. There's hot cider, cookies shaped like hockey sticks, and the soft hum of Bing Crosby. It's a holiday movie.

Of course, I'm sure Walt Disney probably didn't mean for the perfect family to have an elderly woman hawking condoms and Jell-O shots.

"Oh, Ellie doesn't need one of those," one of Ellie's multitude of aunts says, waving Granny Murray away from me.

"I can't believe you're spending all that time playing hockey," her aunt chides her. "Poor Ellie will snatch defeat from the jaws of victory and won't manage to seal the deal

300 . Alina Jacobs

until your eggs are all dried up. Now," the aunt tells Ellie, "I told your dad to stay out of your room if you and that Fletcher want to celebrate the win."

Ellie drains her glass then takes two Jell-O shots for good measure. "Thanks, Aunt Babs."

I make the rounds through Ellie's loudly curious family. They clap me on the shoulder and offer advice.

"Get those endorsement deals early," one uncle slurs, poking two fingers in my chest as he talks.

"Being captain's a big deal, son."

"Are you in a captain's group chat?"

"I think maybe you should give it back to Zayne."

"No, he's not giving that up." An elderly man muscles in. "Make them give you a signing bonus!"

"My daughter has a PR company." A young woman—Violet, I think?—shoves a card in my hand.

"She does! She represents Ryder O'Connell," the woman yells at someone who is, I'm assuming, her sister.

"Where is Ellie? You like this or this?" someone asks.

"What?" Ellie shouts from across the noisy, crowded room.

"For your new uniforms! You cannot do this burgundy—it clashes with his skin. He's a winter, not an autumn."

Ellie makes a helpless gesture. "Call Dana."

"I'm not calling Dana. You have her number! Call her! Tell her we want a meeting."

I duck around several small elderly women who are carting a huge roast turkey through the living room, trailed by several boys who whine, "I thought you were going to fry it! Why can't we have fried turkey? Is there gravy?"

"Gravy!" Jovi says happily as the rest of the team pours into the house.

"Come on." One of Ellie's aunts cups his face. "I'll make you some gravy."

"Get him some ice! Ice! Get them ice!" A cooler is passed around.

I accept the ice that's slapped on my wrists and knees then make my way to a far corner of the room by the stairs. Zayne leans against the wall, alone, sipping his punch, watching the chaos with a dopey, happy smile on his face.

"This is just peak Christmas—like pure holiday magic." He ruffles my hair. "You're lucky, Fletch, you know that?"

"Yeah." I watch Ellie arguing with her sister while she dishes up protein-heavy plates for the players and coaxes the Finn to "just try the Jell-O salad."

"It has marshmallows in it!" he roars.

"And mayonnaise." Bramms smirks.

I nudge Zayne. "You know," I tell him, "it's not too late for you."

"Eh." Zayne sips the holiday fruit punch. "I don't know. Probably. But I'll be happy with what I have."

"I think Ellie has some single aunts." One of them with huge red hair looks over and winks at him. "There's always Dana," I snicker. "Can't say I don't recommend dating the boss."

"I think Ren's got that covered." He jerks his chin to where Ren, in his wifebeater, is chatting up Dana.

"I don't date children." Dana sniffs. "Also, you're missing half of your teeth. I couldn't take you anywhere."

"That's part of my charm."

"Dana, I found Ellie a boyfriend! I can do the same for you too!" One of Ellie's mom's sisters calls from the crush of Ellie's family.

"You didn't find him! I was the one who told her to get with him," Granny Murray hollers.

"Mom!" Ellie's sisters are horrified. "You can't just find her a boyfriend! You don't know anyone her caliber."

"We are so sorry," they simper to Dana. "She's so crass."

"She doesn't understand your greatness."

"Of course I do." Trina swats her daughters with a tea towel then envelops a stunned Dana in a big hug. "I just think she's doing a great job. You should have someone special to share Christmas with."

"Don't let the boys get you down, sister!" Granny Murray thumps her fist on her chest.

"Please excuse our family," Ellie's sister begs Dana. "How about some wine?"

Later in the evening, once the noise of the party has mellowed into background laughter and the scent of gingerbread hangs thick in the air, I slip into the kitchen to grab a drink and take a breath. Try to make the ringing in my ears subside. Ellie's family is worse than a full stadium.

That's when Nate steps into the doorway and blocks my exit. He's wiry, built like a goalie—tall. I'm broader than he is, though.

Not that it matters.

I've done the meet-the-father thing before. I know what he's gearing up for.

This is probably the first time that I actually cared, though.

"Fletcher," he says, folding his arms.

"Sir." I nod, putting the rum-laced cider down. My mouth's suddenly dry.

He eyes me, assessing. "I'm not gonna pretend I like this," he says. "My daughter dating one of her players."

"Fair," I mutter.

"But," he continues, sighing heavily like this is physically painful for him, "you make her happy. And you play like hell for her."

"I'd do anything for her," I say quietly.

Nate squints at me then slowly nods. "Just don't move in with her yet."

"Also fair," I say, trying not to smile.

"And if you hurt her—"

"I won't," I interrupt.

He holds my gaze. "You better not. She's my little girl."

"Dad!" Ellie rushes in, face flushed.

"I'm not threatening," Nate mutters. "I'm just stating facts about consequences."

Ellie sighs. "Be nice."

"Oh, come on," Aunt Stacey yells from the living room, where she's got a mimosa in one hand and a Christmas cookie in the other. "Let the man be in love! Fletcher's a star player now!"

"He scored the game winner!" Harlowe shouts.

"He bleeds for this team!" one of Ellie's younger cousins says from under the kitchen table, where he's got a plate of Christmas cookies.

"I like him!" Granny Murray adds as she pours more rum into the holiday punch. "He's hot! And you should see him in the locker room getting undressed. Lawd! Gather 'round, children, for an early Christmas present! I've got nude photos!"

"Gran, you didn't!" Harlowe protests. "You're supposed to keep her from taking photos, Ellie! Delete that right now!"

Nate groans and mutters something about needing a stronger cider. Ellie's cousin grabs the phone as Ellie scrambles to try to hide it.

Her female family members shriek as Ellie chases them around.

"Oh my god, Ellie! No wonder you took a pay cut to get on the Rhode Islanders."

"Damn, he's hung."

"Sorry." Nate winces. "You are kind of family now."

He waits a beat then adds, "You should have seen what Trina's sisters did to me when they found out I snuck into her bedroom one night after her parents were in bed."

I blink then turn to look at him. He's just fucking with me, right?

The corner of his mouth twitches. "You're not the only one who has ever been young and horny and in the NHL, son."

"Motherf—"

Ellie trots up, phone in hand. "Sorry! I'm deleting these right now."

I pull her to me, kiss the top of her head, then kiss her mouth. "Don't. Send them to yourself."

Ellie wraps her arms around my waist and leans into me.

"Damn right!" Granny Murray hollers. "You're going to be glad I took those photos when you're old and wrinkly. You can remember what you looked like in your prime!"

"You'll leave me for one of your younger players long before then," I murmur into her neck.

"No, I won't!" She shoves me. I pull her closer.

She looks up at me, big brown eyes serious. "I love you. I want to spend every Christmas with you."

I can't stop the grin splitting my face. "Yeah?"

"Yeah."

I kiss her. "Too bad that'll never happen."

She jerks back. I swing her around. "We're both in the NHL, and we play hockey games on Christmas, Coach Candy Cane."

"Hell yeah!" her family cheers.

Chapter 37

ELLIE

"I can't believe you guys still have energy to play," my dad complains as the handful of Rhode Islanders players who couldn't make a trip home for Christmas zoom around the ice. "You played an NHL game last night and had practice this morning."

"I always have energy for hockey!" Fletcher fights with my brother Adam for the puck.

"Our game is better!" my cousins yell from the sidelines, where they're dancing to the holiday music that blares from the sound system in the community ice rink. "We have cocktails!"

"If Fletcher Sullivan is your cousin, how come you're not a better player?" my uncles demand as Hudson loses the puck to the Finn.

Heikkiläinen just casually lifts the puck and flicks it toward Ren in net. In the net, Ren doesn't stop crushing a can of beer, just holds up his glove and snatches the puck out of midair.

Zayne skates by and casually tosses a pass toward me. Fletcher, naturally, is gunning for it, but I cut in front of him and snag it.

"Rude," he huffs, grinning. "I thought you loved me."

"I do. That's why I'm not going easy on you."

One of my sisters is actively trying to climb onto Carlsson's shoulders from the back while my aunts keep cat-calling Zayne Murphy and asking if he wants to let Mommy kiss Santa Claus.

"I am so sorry," I tell him as I pass him, heading to the net.

"Hey, I have to go to work tomorrow," my uncle complains as Fletcher shoves him out of the way to try to snipe the puck from me.

"It was bad enough with Ryder O'Connell, but all of you? This is unfair." Another uncle breathes hard as he tries to chase down the puck.

Ryder snipes the puck from me. As I curse him, he's off to the net, dodging around guys until he sends the puck spinning toward Ren. Ren knocks it away with his stick and throws his empty beer can at Ryder.

"Damn, you're hard to shoot on," Ryder says cheerfully as he turns sharply around the back of the net.

A shriek sounds from across the ice as Granny Murray wobbles out of the warming hut holding a tray of shot glasses and a bottle of peppermint schnapps. "If you're playing, you're drinking!" she hollers.

"Granny, no," I protest, but she's already pouring.

"Shots or penalties!" she bellows.

Fifteen minutes later, I'm lining up for a face-off, tipsy and warm in my puffy jacket and favorite pink toque. The ice is full of players, family, and chaos.

"Now it's fair!" My uncle says as the bottle is passed around for another round for the NHL players, minus Zayne.

"I don't know," I say. "I'm pretty sure they can still play drunk."

"Hey, boys!" My dad yells at my brothers. "No! You are underage! Trina, get your mom—she's getting the boys drunk."

Ryder grabs the bottle away from Adam and Jace.

"They need some hair on their chests! I saw them balk at a fight at the game the other night." Granny Murray boos. "Don't back down from a fight. Bringing shame to the fam like that. Your sister cussed out that ref yesterday."

"Maybe she needs to back down," Fletcher mutters. "You almost got thrown out of the game, Ellie."

"The ref's biased," I say with an eye roll.

Fletcher accelerates and lays a hit on his cousin. Hudson goes flying then pops up and jumps Fletcher.

"That's my player!" I squawk.

"Gracie, come get your man," Harlowe yells.

"Little fucker." Hudson punches Fletcher. "I have an actual job I have to go to tomorrow," he growls.

"Damn, I need to make sure I stay far away from you." Ryder whistles as Fletcher shakes himself off, glaring at Hudson.

Adam skates around. "He came out of nowhere," he says, nodding toward Fletcher. "Didn't even play juniors."

"Yeah," my other brother says, skating behind Ryder. "I heard he was in the Marines. That's gotta be it. Hockey's a mental sport."

"Everything's mental if you're not in shape," Uncle Bic gasps from the bench, where his wife fans him and tries to get him to drink water.

Just to be a dick, Fletcher does a stutter step as he comes at Hudson, sending him tripping over his own stick. The puck zips past, and Fletcher barrels toward the net, glancing over his shoulder with a wink.

Hudson curses Fletcher as he races to goal then fires a shot on my dad. My dad braces himself in goal. Fletcher fakes left, fakes right, then fires—and absolutely roofs it over my dad's shoulder.

"Goddamn it," my father mutters as the puck hits the back of the net.

Fletcher skates back, triumphant and grinning, slapping hands with the Finn and my cousins as they whoop and holler.

"Not bad for a guy who got here on a forged stat sheet," I say, smirking.

Fletcher loops around, snow spraying up as he stops short beside me. "What can I say? I play better when I'm trying to impress my girlfriend's family."

"Is this traditional in your country? A Christmas barbecue?" the Finn asks, genuinely concerned as he watches one of my uncles try to light a pile of wood with a homemade holiday candle an aunt gave away as a stocking stuffer and the confidence of a man who's definitely been hitting the spiked punch hard.

"Oh, this isn't a barbecue," I tell him, grinning. "You'll have to come back for the Fourth of July."

"Yeah," Harlowe adds, already halfway through a spiked hot chocolate. "Fireworks, red meat, and a good ol' game of 'find uncle Art's fingers.'"

The Finn blinks, horrified. He points at the huge metal pot balanced precariously over a propane burner. "But... you are cooking something."

"That?" I shrug. "We're just deep-frying a turkey. Thanksgiving extras. They were on sale."

The Finn actually gags. I'm not even sure if it's exaggerated for effect.

I help one of my cousins dig two rock-solid turkeys out of the snowbank beside the garage. "Don't make that face, Ren," I say as I pass one to him. "I know you deep-fry turkeys in Mississippi."

"Yeah, but we thaw 'em first," he mutters. "And we sure as hell don't bury 'em."

"It's fine," I insist. "The snow keeps them cold. Nature's freezer."

"It's not right," the Finn mutters.

"You literally bury your food outside in Finland." Fletcher smirks at Heikkiläinen.

"Not... an entire bird carcass," the Finn replies flatly.

"Turkey! Turkey! Turkey!" my brothers chant, parading the birds toward the fire like a triumphant offering to the gods of poor decision-making.

Ren hurries over to where my uncles are poking at the fire under the bubbling oil with broom handles. "That oil ain't hot enough!"

"Do you need a thermometer?" I offer.

"I'll know it's hot enough—I can feel it." Ren passes his palm over the tops of the bubbling vats of oil then adds more wood to the fire until the flames lick the rim of the pots.

Then, without so much as a countdown, he drops a bird in.

For one single second, everything is silent.

And then—

FOOOOOOM!

A flaming tower of oil erupts into the air. Everyone screams and runs. It's total chaos.

Fletcher and Hudson move in like they're storming a bunker, grabbing fire extinguishers from the porch and grimly aiming them at the turkeys.

"Don't ruin the food!" Ren rails, jumping in front of them while behind him, the last few leaves left on the dormant oak tree catch fire.

"Call the fire department! None of these damn NHL players have taken off their shirts. I want a man for Christmas!" Granny Murray shouts as Zayne grabs the hose and sprays the storage shed that is smoking.

"I thought you knew how to cook a turkey." Fletcher scowls.

"Y'all were the ones who froze it!" Ren complains, shoving Fletcher away. "You always overreact. It ain't that serious—just getting a little bit of char. That's where the flavor is." He kicks at one of the pots then scurries back, goalie reflexes the only thing saving his feet.

More flames shoot out. "Welp, there go our chances." Harlowe hands me a fresh glass of eggnog that smells like it's mostly rum.

Ren drops the other turkey into the bubbling oil, hollering obscenities as the oil spatters.

Fletcher waits, scowling, for the fireball.

I down my eggnog and hiccup. "Yum, deep-fried turkey."

He looks down at me. "Is Christmas with your family always this…"

"Exciting?"

"Unhinged." He leans down to kiss me.

"I love you," I whisper against his mouth.

I feel him smile before he says, "No, I love you." He drops the fire extinguisher so he can kiss me properly. "Do me a favor, though."

"Yes, I can sneak you into my bedroom tonight. Granny Murray said she'll leave the room free."

"No, that wasn't—well, obviously, I'll be there, Candy Cane. But I need"—he murmurs against my mouth—"you to make sure that we make it to the Eastern conference finals, at least. I need that pay raise from Dana. I'm buying you a house."

"We can host the holiday party there!" I clap my hands to his cheeks and kiss him drunkenly.

"No, that's not what I meant…"

Granny Murray comes over and wraps an arm around Fletcher's shoulders. "Little elf just told me you all need a roommate, and it sounds like I might be getting evicted. Gigi's a real estate agent—she'll hook you up. Imma be needing a separate in-law suite for me!" She heads off.

I grimace. "Merry Christmas?"

Fletcher leans down to kiss me, long and slow. "Sure, Candy Cane, move your crazy granny in. As long as I can sleep with you in an adult-sized bed."

A Short Holiday Romantic Comedy

DECK the HALLS and DROP the GLOVES

Chapter 1

ELLIE

"All right team, I need you to dig." I clap my gloved hands together and try to summon whatever remains of my coach voice after two grueling NHL matches in packed stadiums. "They're a tough opponent, but we can kick their butts. This is the most important game of your holiday season."

Twelve little faces stare back at me from beneath crooked helmets and oversized pads, most of them beneath Christmas-themed jerseys decorated to look like Santa's elf costumes.

One tiny hand shoots up. "Coach Ellie!" says Maya, the team's most enthusiastic skater—and definitely the one least in control of her limbs. "Coach Ellie, I have to use the bathroom!"

I sigh. "I told everyone to go to the bathroom before they got their gear on."

"But I didn't have to then."

"Go," I say, already waving her toward the tunnel before the rest of the girls suddenly decide that they, too, actually need to use the bathroom even though they were reminded repeatedly earlier.

She slips and slides away like a baby deer on a frozen pond, arms flailing, helmet slightly askew. A couple of the NHL players pause to watch her with mild concern.

The other little girls bounce on their skates, excited to be in the Rhode Islanders stadium. The jumbotron is playing "Frosty the Snowman" while I try to get the team organized.

It's the Elves vs. Santas hockey game for my U6 girls. Their opponents? The NHL Rhode Islanders team, all wearing Santa hats.

I straighten up and turn to my other team—the one that requires far more supervision.

It's a fun PR event. The media's here, ready to eat up every frame of towering hockey players "accidentally" losing to tiny kids. Parents are in the stands, kids from local schools are cheering, and I am about five minutes away from stress-eating an entire sleeve of candy canes because while I love kid stuff, I do have a big NHL game at night that we need to prep for...

"When are we getting snacks?" Jovi raises his hand as next to him, Carlsson ping-pongs a hockey puck on his stick.

Off on the sidelines, Harlowe is waiting with covered trays of freshly baked treats.

"It's only two fifteen-minute periods. We will survive. Somehow."

Fletcher, smirking beneath his crooked Santa hat, skates over to me. "You doing okay, Coach?" he asks, glancing behind me at my squad of glittery little demons spinning around in circles or looking excitedly in the crowd for their parents or asking when, in fact, is snack time.

"Just trying to keep them facing the same direction."

He grins. "Good thing you've had us working on evasive maneuvers."

"Hey!" I call to my team. "Elves! Get ready! It's almost game time!"

"Should we go easy on them?" one of the girls stage-whispers to me. "They're old."

"Sure," I say. "But only a little."

And with that, the buzzer sounds, the ref—one of the NHL refs, grinning because everyone likes this event—drops the puck, the crowd roars, and the sparkly little girls charge the ice like it's Christmas Eve and someone just opened the doors to the North Pole candy vault.

Game on.

Fletcher is gentle with the little girls. He lets them win the face-off and lets them whiz around the huge men, taking the puck to goal.

The girls start off focused, but after about ten minutes, it devolves into them wanting to be swung around by the huge NHL players or race them over the ice or pass pucks back and forth.

"Girls, focus!" I blow the whistle, but I'm ignored. Ziggy is letting one of the girls tie tinsel around his elbow pads, while Bramms teaches two more how to dangle pucks. A few girls doggedly keep playing. Ren, in goal, is trying to figure out how to guard the net without stepping on anyone.

I look over at Fletcher, who's flopped on the ice while several girls crawl over him, giggling as they try to move him.

He's so good with children. I sigh as I watch Fletcher play with the mini hockey players. I need to do something nice for him for Christmas.

"You know your mom made you that new dress," Harlowe bounces on her feet.

"I know, but I need to shave my legs, and I'm in the middle of hockey season."

"Or there's that lingerie you got last Christmas that you haven't worn. You could spice things up, give him an extra-special Christmas present. Maybe a spa day, clean up those nails, maybe a wax…"

"Thankfully," I tell her, "it's winter, and I can wear gloves."

Harlowe sighs loudly.

"Look," I protest, "I haven't been the greatest friend, but I'm just really busy with all this NHL stuff, and I had to hire a strength trainer—"

"Look, I'm going to be real with you here because you're really not getting this, are you? Your boy there is proposing tomorrow."

"But tomorrow is Christmas Eve!"

"Yes, so you have less than twenty-four hours to make yourself look Instagram presentable or forever be shamed at family gatherings and held up as a cautionary tale of how not to prepare for your engagement," she says flatly.

"I'm getting proposed to!" I shriek.

Harlowe claps a hand over my mouth. "Shhh! It's a secret. It's supposed to be a surprise, so you have to act surprised, but friends don't let friends look like homeless people when a man is giving them a really expensive diamond ring. So tomorrow morning, I have you booked for all the waxing, all the nail treatments, and you're going to wash your hair, for God's sake. Just because these NHL guys have questionable cleanliness habits doesn't mean you need to as well."

I can't contain my happiness through the rest of the event. I, Ellie Clarke, am going to be Mrs. Fletcher Sullivan. I practically float as I drift around greeting parents, telling the girls what a great job they did, and handing out the little snack bags my mom and I made.

All the while, I'm dreaming of my wedding—not just the wedding; it's going to be a whole year: engagement party, bridal shower. They're going to be nicer than my cousin Jenny's wedding events, because I got a pay raise as a coach and I can buy the nice plastic plates with the little flowery designs stamped on them.

It is the ultimate crafting experience—what a girl trains for! Ooh, I bet I could get custom monogrammed plates. I might need to get a new Cricut. I hum.

I'll need to bring hockey into it, making it a tasteful nod. Definitely the invitations and the cake—can I work it into the flower arrangement?

Fletcher's the last one in the locker room. He stayed late to pose for photos and sign autographs with all the fans.

I'm carefully taking down the cards and drawings the girls made for the guys, wishing them good luck on their next game, so that the cleaning crew can come through in a few hours and get the locker room ready for tonight's game.

"Candy Cane." The deep voice echoes around the empty locker room. The voice of my future husband.

I can't help it. I jump him.

Wrapping my legs around his waist so I can kiss him, I peel off the layers of protective gear. "I'm so in love with you," I whisper as I kiss his face, his neck, his collarbone. "Super in love."

"God, Ellie," he growls against my mouth, his hands gripping my waist possessively as he spins us around to press my back against the cool metal of his locker. The contrast of the cold metal against my heated skin makes me gasp. "You're incredible."

I can feel the raw energy still pulsing through him from the event, that dangerous electricity that always makes him so intense after being on the ice. His Santa hat has fallen somewhere on the floor, and his dark hair is disheveled from where I've been fisting my hands in it, pulling him closer.

"You were so good with them today," I murmur breathlessly, nipping at his jaw before soothing it with my tongue. "Maya's never going to stop talking about how Fletcher Sullivan let her score three goals."

He chuckles and pulls back, the sound vibrating through his chest and straight through me. "She's got a wicked slap shot for a six-year-old. Reminds me of you... all that fire." He smiles. "I want a little you."

My heart soars. He wants kids too!

"We could make one right now," he says with a grin. His hands slide up my sides, deliberate and claiming, thumbs brushing just under the curve of my breasts through my team jacket. The touch is light, but it sets me on fire.

"Maybe a wedding first," I tease, grinding against him just enough to feel how hard he already is. His eyes go dark, pupils blown wide, and there's that predatory look—the one that makes me feel like I'm about to be devoured.

"Maybe." His voice drops to that gravelly tone that goes straight to my core. "You're going to be such an incredible mom someday... but right now, I need you to be mine."

The words hit me like a body check, especially knowing what I know about tomorrow. About the ring. About how this man is going to be mine forever. The thought makes me bold, reckless.

"Fletcher…" I breathe out, but he's already moving, his hands spanning my waist as he lifts me effortlessly, pressing me harder against the lockers. I wrap my legs around him, feeling the solid muscle of his thighs, the way he fits perfectly between my legs.

"I know we've got the game tonight," he says, his voice rough with want as he carries me toward the training room, his mouth never leaving my throat. "But I need you right now. Need to be inside you."

"The cleaning crew—"

"Won't be here for hours." He kicks the door shut behind us, the sound echoing in the empty space. His mouth crashes against mine, all teeth and tongue and desperate need. "You drive me crazy, you know that? Watching you today, being so perfect…"

I should protest. But then his hands are under my jacket, palming my breasts through my bra, and I'm arching into his touch like I'm starving for it.

"I love you," I gasp as he sets me on the edge of the massage table, his body pressing between my thighs. "I love you so much it makes me want to do reckless things."

He pulls back to look at me, his eyes burning. "Like what?"

"Like let you fuck me right here where anyone could walk in." The words tumble out, bold and shameless, and I watch his control snap.

"Christ, Ellie," he groans, his hands fisting in my hair as he captures my mouth in a kiss that's all-consuming. "You can't say things like that to me."

"Why not?" I challenge, reaching for the hem of his practice jersey, desperate to feel his skin. "Because you might lose control?"

"Because I already have." His voice is strained as he helps me pull the jersey over his head, revealing the hard planes of his chest and the tattoo that curves along his ribs. "God, look at you. So fucking beautiful."

His hands are everywhere—sliding my jacket off my shoulders, working at the buttons of my shirt with an urgency that makes my pulse race. When the cool air hits my skin, I shiver, but then his mouth is there, trailing hot kisses down my throat, across my collarbone.

"Fletcher, please," I whisper, my fingers digging into the muscles of his shoulders.

"Please what?" He looks up at me, his eyes dark with desire and something else—love so intense it takes my breath away. "Tell me what you want."

"You," I breathe. "All of you. Right here, right now."

Something shifts in his expression, becomes almost reverent as he reaches up to cup my face.

If only he knew I already know. If only he knew I'm already planning our entire life together, dreaming of the moment he gets down on one knee. But for now, I lose myself in the heat of his touch, the way he makes me feel like I'm the center of his universe.

His mouth is hot on my breast. My hips jerk up, and I strain into his touch.

For a brief moment, I think, shit, I really should have taken Harlowe up on that spa offer sooner. But Fletcher doesn't seem to care as he tugs my leggings off, strokes my clit, curls his fingers in my pussy until I'm coming, gushing all over the table.

He tugs my hips down. Starbursts in my eyes.

I pant as I hear a condom rip, then he's thrusting that huge length in my throbbing pussy, silencing my moans with his mouth.

His hair is a little longer, and I tangle my fingers in it as he fucks me.

I can't wait to do this on our wedding day.

Thankfully, I don't say that and let it slip that I know about the big proposal! Because he slides out then whips me on my front so he can fuck my pussy hard from behind, my teeth clacking from the force of those inhumanly large thighs pumping that rock-hard cock up my cunt, his huge hands spreading my legs out so his balls smack against them with every thrust. I arch up into the force of him every time his cock takes me, buries into my pussy, until finally I feel him speed up and his hand tangle in my hair, pulling my head back while giving me three deep thrusts, and then he explodes in the condom, and I'm coming around him while he bites my shoulder, his hand cupping my tit, squeezing, pinching the nipple as he wrings the orgasm out of me.

"Damn, Candy Cane. I'd say you should take on a new career as a puck bunny, except I'd kill any other hockey player who comes near you."

"Win tonight," I manage to gasp, my nails raking down his back.

He grins that cocky smile. "Don't I always?"

"I don't know. That was a real shameful loss to the Ice Bears last week."

He snorts and slaps my ass.

The game that night is intense. We're playing the Calgary Stormriders, and those fans are nuts. They bused down to our stadium, and it's a sea of blue in the crowd.

They boo their star player when he loses the puck to Zayne. He's checked by the team's big, burly Latvian defenseman, and the crowd cheers.

They fight for the puck, Bramms trying to get it to Zayne, Cookie zigzagging across the ice.

Speaking of ice… should we have an ice rink at the wedding? Is it tacky to have an ice rink? Maybe an ice sculpture, or is that overdone?

No, stop thinking about the wedding, watch the game. Be a professional, Ellie. Gosh, you're giving female coaches a bad name.

"Ellie, watch out!" Harlowe shouts.

"What?" I focus back on the game just in time to see a black flying saucer hurtling right toward me.

Chapter 2
FLETCHER

I'm good, I'm good!" Ellie yells as Granny Murray helps her up. Harlowe has a wet towel pressed to her face. "Everything is good."

The ref blows the whistle to stop the play of the game.

"Just keep going." Ellie's words sound like she's talking through a mouthful of jelly.

I need to do something.

The Calgary player who hit the puck looks ashen-faced. "Sorry, sorry, man!" he stammers as I round on him.

The ref grabs the back of my jersey.

I'm the captain. I shouldn't throw gloves over an honest mistake.

The other player looks like he's going to puke. "It's my first game," the kid squeaks. "I got called up from the minors…"

"Carry on," Ellie mumbles.

"They can't just play. They need a coach!" Harlowe hisses to her as Ellie half collapses on her friend.

"There's half a period left." Her mom presses a bloody towel to her face.

"I'll coach the team!" Granny Murray announces. "Boys, I want four fights in the next inning or you're all on the next bus to Vietnam. Who wants shots?" She holds up a bottle of liquor.

"Ellie needs some, Gran. I'll just take that." Harlowe takes the bottle of vodka and sighs. "Do we have nonflavored vodka?"

Granny Murray rummages in the cooler. "I got you." She hands her a bottle of pills. "Probably want to do these as a chaser."

"I think these are her teeth?" Cookie looks queasy as he holds up a glove full of bloody white squares.

"We'll just glue those back in." Harlowe grabs them and pops them back in Ellie's mouth.

"Play on, boys! War doesn't stop because someone got shot. Suck in your balls and move!" Granny Murray hollers.

Fortunately, we are up by two goals.

Not for long, though. The opposing team scores another.

Our defense is worthless, and offense can't keep their heads up. It's chaos, especially since Granny Murray is mixing up the lines and keeps shouting directions that don't make any sense.

I am part of the problem—I fully own up to that. I'm not concentrating either. I'm too worried about Ellie.

I almost miss a pass from the Finn. He roars at me in Scandinavian, and I curse, hustling down the ice trying to correct the mistake.

We're on our back foot the rest of the match. It doesn't help my foul mood.

We win but barely, and no one feels like celebrating.

I'm itching to go see Ellie in the locker room, and I'm terse with the press. All they want to talk about is her injury. And if she's going to have to be out the rest of the season to recover. And did I think a male coach would have handled it better?

"How about I hit a puck going eighty miles an hour into your face and see how well you're able to do your job that you're overpaid for," I snarl at one reporter. Bramms and Jovi have to haul me back and shove me down the hall.

Ellie's not in the locker room when I storm in to see everyone milling around.

"They took her to urgent care." Zayne wraps an arm briefly around my shoulders.

I try not to let Ellie and me being in a relationship affect how I act in the locker room or on the ice. I don't want it to turn into a thing with the team. And so far, it's worked.

But not today.

I don't even shower, just throw on my clothes. I need to see Ellie, make sure she's okay.

No one is answering their phone.

I have a car now, thanks to the NHL paycheck. Nothing flashy, and I definitely don't drive it like Ellie does. I tensely grip the wheel as I head to her parents' house.

There are cars parked up and down the street in front of her parents' house, where she still lives, where I have to go visit her and suffer the awkward interactions with her dad because he was in the NHL and he knows why I'm visiting his daughter. In her bedroom. And it's not to trade hockey cards.

"Um… hi! Hi, Fletch. Fletcher." The door swings open to reveal Harlowe. "So, Ellie's resting."

"I need to see her," I growl.

Harlowe blocks me. "She's pretty loopy. Why don't you just give her the night, go out with the boys, check in tomorrow." She rocks on her feet.

It's not a suggestion. I'm not going to be allowed inside.

I turn back and step off the porch into the snow.

Does Ellie not want to see me? I thought we were in love.

"Maybe she wants you to get a haircut."

"You do need a haircut."

"Hockey players have long hair. It's like the Canadian Viking aesthetic."

"He doesn't look like a Viking. He looks crazy."

My brothers pepper the warm Christmas-spice air with their unasked for commentary.

"I am crazy." I pace around Hudson's living room. His wife, Gracie, has piles of wrapped presents under the tree.

Christmas Eve is tomorrow. Ellie's favorite.

The day I was going to ask her to be mine, be my wife.

"And we spent all this energy warning you that you cannot lose any teeth or get hit in the face," Gracie jokes.

On the screen above the fireplace, a recap of the nation's various hockey games plays, and "one coach got more than she bargained for," the announcers say. I feel sick as I watch Ellie get hit in the mouth in slow motion.

"How many teeth did she lose?" Talbot asks.

I shrug unhappily, watching the replay.

"You don't know?"

"They won't talk to me about it." I glower.

"I'll go over there," Gracie assures me, "and see what's going on."

"It's snowing. You're going by yourself?" Hudson stands up.

Gracie shoos him away. "I need to pick up Dakota and Ryder from the train station anyway."

"Sounds like she's not going to get to eat Christmas dinner this year," the sports announcers joke.

"That looks really bad," my cousin says.

"Thanks for that really perceptive observation," I snarl.

"I'm just saying, your big proposal plan might need to be rethought." He winces.

"Maybe he should not propose to her." Talbot grimaces.

"Yeah, no girl wants to get proposed to after losing all her teeth." My brother nods.

"I want to propose to her. I don't care how many teeth she's missing." I will make her my wife.

"She probably cares," Anderson says pointedly. "She wants the nice photos to put on social media."

"Well, postponing it will give you a chance to do something about your hair."

"Postpone till New Year's?" I scowl.

Elsa grimaces. "She lost a lot of teeth. Is her jaw broken? Could be a few months."

"Months?"

"Then it will get into playoffs, so maybe you can propose in the summer."

"I don't want to wait till the summer." My hand clenches into a fist. Hudson will gut me if I punch one of his walls, though. "She wants a Christmas wedding, so it pushes everything back."

"What are you rushing toward?"

"My future. Being with her all the time. Knowing that she's really mine—all that's left is the formality of the wedding, signing a paper."

"If it's *twoo wuv*, then it can wait." Elsa bats her eyes at me.

"Fuck off, Elsa."

The worst thing about holidays is your family. And fuck all of them.

I'm not waiting.

Chapter 3

ELLIE

"Let's see the new smile!" my dad calls when Harlowe helps me inside.

His face quickly shifts into a mask of horror. "Oh god." He turns green and leans over the sink.

"You look fine, Ellie. Don't worry about him. Nate, be nice. Come sit down. Aunt Gigi made you some soup."

My tongue is flopping around in my mouth. The emergency dentist had to yank a couple out, but I was given the happy juice, and I can't feel a thing. In fact, this is going to be the best Christmas ever. I'm getting proposed to, and Santa's coming. I'm going to get that Polly Pocket, too, and a unicorn that shoots glitter out of its horn.

"Oh no, she's listing. Harlowe, grab her!"

"Get her up there." Granny Murray hoists me back in the chair. "You need some vodka to help take the edge off."

"They gave her Vicodin."

"Trade ya."

My siblings crowd around.

"Ooh!" Adam's eyes are wide. "You lost a lot of teeth, Ellie."

"Fortunately, she doesn't have a broken jaw," Harlowe says.

"Yeah, your teeth took all the impact." Jace snickers.

Our dad bats him on the back of the head. "Go help your uncles with setting up the heat lamps outside. And don't let your cousins throw anything other than wood onto the bonfire," he yells after them.

"Ellie, do you want to go lie down? I'll bring you up some soup," my mom says anxiously, bustling around the kitchen. I just drool at her.

"Oh no." She hugs me to her chest. "It's like when you were a baby. I'm going to feed you and bathe you."

"She'll feel better after she sleeps off the drugs." My sister pats my head.

The front door bursts open as I'm helped to the stairs. "Ellie! Let me see your new face!"

"Oh my god."

Everyone's come by to see the disaster.

"Ooh, no."

My family members crowd around me.

"I'm so glad I made the trip up for this." My second cousin snaps pictures. "I haven't seen anything this bad, and you know my Jayden was hit in the face with a puck."

"No, Ma, he was riding his lawnmower drunk to the gas station. He wasn't playing hockey."

"He was."

They bicker.

"Has Fletcher seen this?" My cousin Violet raises an eyebrow.

"I saw him outside," another aunt says, jerking her thumb. "Guess we're about to find out."

Fletcher's here? Except it comes out "Mhhhm muhhh," a mumble around the cotton in my mouth.

"He can't see her like this," Harlowe directs. "Granny Murray, take her upstairs."

I want to see him. Mumble, mumble, drool.

"Don't worry," Harlowe assures me. "I'll keep him away."

My eyes start rolling back, and two aunts sling my arms around their shoulders and drag me up to my bedroom as I hear Fletcher's deep voice from the doorway.

"They gave you the good stuff." Granny Murray chats as she takes off my shoes. She tips the bottle of vodka up to my lips. "A little for you, a little for me."

Then she bustles into the bathroom. "Sponge bath time."

"Granny, let's just let her rest." Harlowe sighs as she comes into the room.

My mom tucks a blanket around me, almost chokes me with some soup, then wipes my face with a warm wet washcloth. "There you go, my drooly little baby girl."

"Hey, Aunt Trina." Gracie comes into the room unwinding her scarf and pauses, taking in my face. "Oh dear."

They go back out to the hallway while I stare up at the ceiling. *I should put up some glow-in-the-dark stars. Would that be weird?* I giggle to myself. Glow-in-the-dark stars while I'm getting dicked by my boyfriend.

I freeze when my brain makes out what my cousins are talking about.

334 • Alina Jacobs

"… can't propose to her."

"I mean, he doesn't even want to look at her."

"It's a disaster."

"Her pictures are going to suck."

"We can't put that up on social media."

"I don't think that Ellie's getting proposed to," Gracie is saying.

Not getting proposed to? No.

I drag myself upright. I will have that ring.

I roll over and slowly swing my legs over the side of the bed and immediately half slide to the floor.

There's a timeline. I can't push the wedding—then it pushes pregnancy, and I have to wait for another good time in the season.

I feel sick, not just from the painkillers and the vodka and that pounding noise from outside. He's not going to propose.

Maybe this is just the excuse Fletcher needs to dump me. He realizes I'm a mess. He regrets everything.

At the big Christmas Eve dinner tomorrow, he's not going to show up, and I'm going to have to eat a ham-and-mashed-potato smoothie and wonder how I screwed up my life.

"Oh no!" Harlowe and Gracie rush back into the room and dump me back on the bed. "Let's get you some ice."

"She needs a little more of this." A vodka bottle sloshes.

"Gran…"

"It's an antiseptic. And don't worry, Ellie," Gran tells me, "I'm going to go bunk at Gracie's until you're feeling better."

Gracie makes a pained expression.

Harlowe turns out the light. "Get some rest. It's Christmas Eve tomorrow!"

"No, I have to see Fletcher," I try to mumble around the cotton. "My ring, my engagement."

They don't hear any of it.

"… awkward Christmas."

"… have to rethink the holiday plans," I hear Gracie say as they shut the door.

Rethinking plans? Fletcher really is done with me.

Chapter 4
FLETCHER

"You can do a nice proposal in a few months." Hudson claps a hand on my shoulder.

"Maybe Valentine's Day?" Gracie offers as we head over to Ellie's parents' house on Christmas Eve.

"She doesn't like Valentine's Day." I'm surly.

"Every girl likes Valentine's."

"No, she likes the day after Valentine's because everything is fifty to eighty percent off," I rattle, "and she likes to read all the Valentine's Day horror stories on her tablet while she eats her discounted candy and desserts."

"Well, you haven't seen her face. She's really not going to want a proposal," Gracie tells me as Hudson knocks on the front door.

My cousin turns to me, serious. "Don't say 'eww' or scream or make an off-color joke."

"I, too, was in a war zone. I know how to act around an injured person," I snap at him. "However, I am also a hockey player, and so is Ellie, and she might appreciate an off-color joke."

"Hmm." Gracie purses her mouth.

The front door opens. "Hey, you made it." Zayne stands there with Finn.

"I thought you were going back to Winterfell," I snap at him, mad that Ellie seems to have let them around her but not me—her fiancé. Not fiancé. Not yet. Maybe not ever? Definitely not today.

"Harlowe didn't think you were coming. I don't know if she really wants to see you..." Zayne trails off.

I push past him inside. There's a crush of Ellie's and Gracie's family inside.

"She's not presentable yet," Granny Murray says when she sees me. "But don't worry. The ole vag is still working. Those pain pills can make you horny. You should have seen me after my hysterectomy."

"Gran." Gracie sighs.

"We have to get her face on." One of Ellie's aunts hands me a drink.

"It's rough. Prepare yourself." One of her cousins—Violet, I think—giggles. "You might want to think about finding a new coach to sleep with."

"Fletcher's a man of integrity," Granny Murray cuts in. "He also likes to get his dick sucked, and let me tell you, with the hole in her pearly whites, the getting's good is all I'm saying."

From the doorway of the kitchen, her father looks on, horrified.

Hudson knocks back his drink.

"I just want to make sure she's okay."

"She's not," her aunt says, then they all split over, laughing drunkenly.

"All the men are outside." Nate ushers me out.

Ryder is there grilling half chickens. He gives me a sympathetic look. "Don't worry. There's a good dentist in Manhattan. I've already called him. He fixed Philly's teeth. Ellie will be back to her old self eventually."

"I haven't actually seen her."

Ryder cocks his head. "Probably for the best."

"Jesus, how bad was she hurt?" I'm antsy.

Seems like the party must have started at seven a.m., because there are already people dancing drunk on the tables, and it's barely lunchtime.

I look around. "'Scuse me... excuse me." I try to catch the attention of one of her aunts. I haven't even seen Ellie's mother. The ring is burning a hole in my pocket.

"All I Want for Christmas Is My Two Front Teeth" starts blaring on the speaker system.

"Here she comes." Her brother doubles over, snickering as Trina helps Ellie outside onto the porch.

Ryder glares at them, and they shut up. Good.

I stand up to go over to her. Her family has their phone cameras out, hoping to catch some carnage.

"Heyyyy, Fletchhhh." Ellie grimaces, revealing all of her front teeth missing. A few on the bottom are cracked.

"They saved as much as they could," Harlowe tells me.

"I have your old teeth. We can put them under the pillow for the tooth fairy." Trina helps Ellie to a chair and spreads a blanket over her daughter.

"Well, you can talk now. That's something."

Ellie's bottom lip is split.

"Here's a Christmas cocktail." Granny Murray shoves a holiday-themed glass in her hand.

"Gran, that's not the cocktail I made. That's just vodka." Gracie sighs.

"Gotta keep her mouth clean."

I bend down gingerly, cup her bruised face. "I'm going to kill Sanders."

"Hey, Fletch, it was an accident." Zayne's there, concern on his face as he grabs my upper arm. "Sanders wrote me a really long email about how bad he feels, wanting to know if you're angry at him."

"Tell him I am," I snap. "Ellie, how are you feeling?"

"Terrible."

She's sick. I should have been there with her. I want to cut my heart out. I can't have her away from me.

"And they won't let me stay here."

I have to make her mine. I have to. Then she'll never be away from me again.

I kneel down in front of her to gasps from her family and pull out the ring box.

"Oh my god," Gracie groans.

"Ellie," I say, the words spilling out as I completely forget the proposal that I'd been rehearsing for weeks. "I've been waiting to do this since last Christmas. I can't stand being away from you. I want to make you my wife and take care of you and give you every Christmas you deserve. This being away from you while you're hurt is killing me. I can't go through it any longer. I'm sorry, but you're going to have to marry me—preferably today, but I am prepared to wait."

"NO! Fletch, what are you doing?" one of my teammates hollers.

Ellie starts sobbing.

I cringe. Shit. Gracie and Hudson were right. I should have just waited.

"Uh…"

The Finn is staring at me and slowly shaking his head.

"And he proposes, against everyone's better judgment." Harlowe throws a roll of paper napkins at me.

"Okay, maybe this wasn't such a good idea," I mumble.

"Sorry, Ellie." I stand up quickly. "I take it back."

"Noooo!" Ellie wails. "You can't take it back! I love you, and I wanted you to propose to me today. Harlowe said you were, and I've been looking forward to it."

"You have?" I laugh in relief. "I love you, Ellie."

"I love you, too, and I really want to be your wife, but I was afraid you wouldn't want to propose anymore, and you didn't want me. Gracie said…"

"Dammit, Gracie," Hudson says.

She punches him in the side.

"It's going to be a minute before you can get teeth put in, so you'll have to wait on the wedding." Harlowe sighs.

"You don't have to wait on grandbabies," Trina gushes.

"Oh my gosh." Ellie chokes back more tears. "I thought you wanted to dump me."

"Never." I take her hands. "I want you in sickness and in health." I kiss the top of her head.

"It's more like in facial disfigurement and health," her brother says.

"Smile for your engagement photo!" Her sister holds up a camera.

Ellie stares up at me, a huge gapped smile on her face. "You're beautiful," I tell her honestly and kiss her on the nose because her mouth looks like it hurts.

"No, kiss me for real. I played pill roulette this morning with Granny Murray, and I got good luck. I can't feel a thing."

I press my mouth to hers gently, gingerly.

"Whoa, there she goes." The kiss lasts only a second before I move to catch Ellie as she starts to list to the side.

I pick her up and cradle her in my arms, and someone yells, "Say 'hockey'!"

Harlowe hands me a Polaroid picture after inspecting it. "Well, only one of you looks like a real hockey player."

Merry Christmas!

Acknowledgements

A big thank you to Red Adept Editing for editing and proofreading.

And finally a big thank you to all the readers! I had a great time writing this hilarious book! Please try not to choke on your wine while reading!!!

About the Author

If you like steamy romantic comedy novels with a creative streak, then I'm your girl!

Architect by day, writer by night, I love matcha green tea, chocolate, and books! So many books...

Sign up for my mailing list to get special bonus content, free books, giveaways, and more!

http://alinajacobs.com/mailinglist.html